Praise for TOXIC HEART

"[A] long-awaited urban dystopian adventure . . . Aria and Shannon are very different, yet both are strong, well-developed female characters."   —*VOYA*

"Recommended for dystopian fans."   —*School Library Journal*

"Original, action-packed, and a delicious mix of genres, this novel is a romantic thriller that anyone will love, whether you are a fan of dystopia or new to the genre."   —*Next Page Reviews*

"Theo has managed to keep you guessing right to the last page."
—*Much Loved Books*

"Full of intense action and betrayal but also loyalty and magic. . . . An excellent follow-up to *Mystic City*. . . . Fans of *Matched* and *Divergent* will enjoy this series."   —*Compass Book Ratings*

"A fascinating read that had me up until 1 a.m."   —*Fiction Freak*

"A great book that's easy to fall in love with." —*Books to Remember*

ALSO BY THEO LAWRENCE

MYSTIC CITY

TOXIC
HEART

THEO LAWRENCE

EMBER

Text copyright © 2014 by The Inkhouse
Cover art copyright © 2014 by Cliff Nielsen

randomhouseteens.com

Educators and librarians, for a variety of teaching tools, visit us at RHTeachersLibrarians.com

The Library of Congress has cataloged the hardcover edition of this work as follows:
Lawrence, Theo.
Toxic heart : a Mystic City novel / Theo Lawrence. — First edition.
pages cm. — (Mystic city trilogy)
Summary: Aria believes she can bring together the warring elite and the magic-wielding mystics, save Mystic City, and win back Hunter's love but first she must risk everything to find the missing heart of a dead mystic that would give her untold powers.
ISBN 978-0-385-74162-0 (hardback) — ISBN 978-0-375-98643-7 (ebook)
[1. Supernatural—Fiction. 2. Wealth—Fiction. 3. Love—Fiction. 4. New York (N.Y.)—Fiction. 5. Science fiction.] I. Title.
PZ7.L4378Tox 2014
[Fic]—dc23
2013049642

ISBN 978-0-385-74163-7 (trade pbk.)

Printed in the United States of America

10 9 8 7 6 5 4 3 2 1

First Ember Edition 2015

*For my family, who read the
first one and liked it, and for
Michael Stearns, who has
many good ideas*

TOXIC
HEART

·PROLOGUE·

"You've got nowhere to go!" someone shouts behind us.

Kyle.

I glance back at my older brother. He's limping toward us, a silver pistol in his hand. Behind him, soldiers with the Rose insignia on their black uniforms are marching steadily. Up ahead, more soldiers have created a wall that neither Turk nor I will be able to break.

I look to the side. The fragile railings of the bridge—gleaming metal beams that seem to float in midair—would be easy enough to jump over, but then what?

We would fall, swiftly and desperately, into the Depths.

For a second, I see something shimmering in the air nearby. Something that looks an awful lot like a face.

Flanked by his soldiers, Kyle approaches. "This is the end of the road, Aria."

I stare again at the dark blue sky.

Inhale deeply.

And run straight for the railing of the bridge.

"Aria, no!" my brother screams.

I jump.

The breath is sucked out of me as I tumble toward the dirty canals hundreds of stories below.

To my death.

PART ONE

Life contains but two tragedies.
One is not to get your heart's desire;
the other is to get it.

—GEORGE BERNARD SHAW

Every Rose Has Its Thorn. . . .

For Johnny and Melinda Rose, it seems that thorn is their daughter, socialite Aria Rose, with her mystic boyfriend, Hunter Brooks, son of the late mayoral candidate Violet Brooks.

The Roses are no strangers to controversy. They made headlines this summer when they announced that seventeen-year-old Aria was to wed Thomas Foster, son of George and Erica Foster and younger brother of Garland Foster. The Roses and the Fosters have been political rivals for generations. The marriage between Aria and Thomas would have united their families just in time for the August mayoral election, which Garland Foster was favored to win against Violet Brooks, the registered mystic who many felt was the voice of the poor people of the Depths, mystics and nonmystics alike.

Of course, after the discovery and subsequent ravaging of the secret underground tunnels where rebel mystics have been hiding for decades, and the deaths of both mayoral candidates, the election—and the wedding—were canceled. Hunter Brooks is now leading the rebel cause in the Depths, and the united Rose and Foster families are leading the Aeries dwellers.

The surprise here has been Aria Rose's shifting alliance. Her engagement to Thomas Foster seemingly broken, she has publicly declared her love for Hunter Brooks and her support for the mystic party.

With city morale at an all-time low, Aria Rose's support for the mystics makes one wonder if more Aeries residents will shift loyalties, and if that will affect the outcome of the most devastating war the city has ever known.

Meanwhile, we're waiting for the lovely Aria's next move. . . .

—from *Manhattan View,* an Aeries society
e-column, 19 September

"And block," Shannon says.

She's standing a few feet in front of me, a long wooden kendo stick at her side. Without hesitation, she lifts the stick and swings it at my head.

I raise my right elbow to block her, but she's too fast.

All I see is a flash of color before I'm on the ground, staring up at the blazing, white-hot sun, my head throbbing. It is oppressively hot—so hot I can barely think.

At least the grass is soft. Sort of.

"Get up!" Shannon bends over me. "Man. It's like you've never fought before in your life."

"I *haven't*," I reply, rubbing the side of my head, making sure I'm not bleeding. Until a few weeks ago, the only physical activity I'd ever really done was a handful of squash matches in the Florence Academy gym. And dancing, of course, at various debutante balls in the Aeries.

"Oh?" Shannon says, poking my leg with her stick. "I seem to recall your being in a pretty huge battle recently. Then again, you did end up in the hospital. So I would say you lost."

The tone of her voice is teasing, which bothers me. That entire night is a blur: my parents' army raided the underground hideout of the rebel mystics, who retaliated with mighty displays of their powers. It ended with Violet Brooks's death and my hospitalization—and a war that continues to this day.

Shannon pokes me again. "What are you going to do if someone attacks you and you fall? Just lie there? Get up and strike back."

I groan, pushing myself into a seated position. The surrounding field is an open square of land, though in the not-too-far distance are dozens of trees, clumped together like knots of hair, stretching their bare limbs up toward the clouds. This area—once prime farming land in Upstate New York—is nothing like the shiny skyscrapers that I'm used to in Manhattan.

Of course, none of the land is prime anything anymore: the sweltering heat has left the grass brown and yellow and stiff. There's been no respite for the past two weeks, ever since I left the hospital. Shannon has been drilling me every day. According to her, I'm a terrible student.

I brush the sweat from my forehead and wipe my hands on my training gear, stretchy black fabric engineered to reflect heat. It can't possibly be working. I'm so hot I could explode.

"Now watch me." Shannon drops the kendo stick to the ground and holds up her hands. She tucks her fingers into her palms and makes two fists. Then she brings her arms into her chest until her fists are just under her chin. "This is the correct position."

I mimic her. "Okay."

"Let's say I'm running toward you, ready to attack. You don't have time to run away, so you have to defend yourself. You get into this position . . . then what?"

I think for a second. "Punch?"

Shannon shakes her head. Her red ponytail flicks from side to side. She's barely broken a sweat.

"Why not?"

There's a flicker of light in her eyes. "Try to punch me."

Shannon rushes toward me. I extend one fist in what I think is a solid punch, but she smacks it out of the way, jabbing her knee into my stomach. There's a sharp pain and I'm on the ground again.

"Ow!" I cover my abdomen with my hands. "What's wrong with you? Do you get off on hurting me?"

Shannon gives me a wide grin. "*That's* why you don't try to punch your opponent. You're too weak, Aria. What do they teach you up there?" She lifts her chin and stares off into the sky. We can't see the silvery bridges and magnificent skyscrapers of the Aeries from here, but I know what she's referring to.

"Not to fight." I roll to my side and push myself up, wiping my hands on the backs of my legs. If Shannon only knew what my life was like just a few weeks ago—shopping with my friends Kiki and Bennie, parties and dinners every night, servants to administer to my every need—she'd hate me even more than she does now. "At least, not physically."

Shannon laughs. "I can tell." She reaches out and yanks on the chain around my neck, which holds the heart-shaped locket given to me by Patrick Benedict. Another ally, now dead and gone.

"Dull," she says, running her fingers over the tarnished silver. "I would have expected something fancier from you."

"Sorry to disappoint you," I say, suddenly tired and sore. "I didn't realize this was a fashion show."

I glance back at the converted farmhouse, a tall white structure with three stories. You could never tell that more than fifty mystics are crammed inside. This is one of several rebel army command centers outside New York City. Like the others, it is a refuge and a place to prepare provisions to be sent to the mystics who remain in the city—men and women who are fighting to overcome the Aeries and restore equality to the city. Though we haven't been given much information about the ongoing war, we *do* know that many people have died, that the Depths have nearly been destroyed. Manhattan is no longer the city I remember.

"Are we done for the day?"

"Absolutely not." Shannon picks up her kendo stick as if it were a feather. "Let's do leg blocks."

I don't even want to know what those are.

"Pretend I'm attacking." Shannon shifts her weight back and raises the pole behind her head. There's a moment when the sun catches her brown eyes, making them sparkle, and she looks almost . . . friendly.

Too bad she's not.

"If you anticipate my strike," she says, "you can deflect the blow and knock away my weapon. Let's try."

I raise my arm to shade out the sun. "Try what?"

Without answering, Shannon swings her arm down, striking me in the left shin.

"What in the Aeries—"

"Again." She narrows her eyes. "Too slow. If I'd hit you with any actual force, you'd be a goner." She pauses, then adds, "A plucked Rose."

Shannon cocks her head at me. It's easy to hate her. Aside from her perpetual smugness, she's beautiful in a way that I will never be. I barely know anything about her—where she's from, who her family is, what she likes, whether she has a boyfriend. She's managed to avoid answering any personal questions these past weeks.

Instead, she's focused on beating me up—*for the sake of the rebellion.*

I point to the yellowish-blue bruises on my arms from our session a few days ago. "I don't think this is what Hunter had in mind when he left me here for training."

"This is *exactly* what Hunter had in mind," Shannon says angrily. "Hunter has a rebellion to lead now. You barely escaped Manhattan with your life, Aria. You have to learn how to protect yourself."

"I know all that," I tell her.

I've avoided thinking about the battle that killed my boyfriend's mother, Violet Brooks. She was the mystic hope, the voice of the poor who lived in the Depths, the champion of the oppressed. She stood for everything my parents and the Fosters do not.

I have tried to erase the memory of the gun in my hands as I pulled the trigger and aimed directly at my ex-fiancé, Thomas Foster, then gazed in horror as he dropped to the muddy ground.

I have tried and I have failed. I defended myself that night, and

I certainly don't need Shannon, whoever she is, throwing it all back in my face.

My eyes travel across the dead grass, away from the peeling white paint of the farmhouse. Behind the field is what used to be an apple orchard. The trees are victims of global warming, their life sucked out by the sweltering heat.

I shift my attention back to Shannon. "Why are you here, anyway?" I ask. "Don't you have more important things to do?"

Shannon draws back her lips like some kind of feral animal. "You think I want to be here? Training some spoiled little rich girl when I should be off fighting?" She yanks the elastic from her ponytail, letting her thick red hair cascade around her face. "I'm here because Hunter asked me to help you. Unlike you, I wasn't born into a family of privilege. I never knew my mother. . . . My father is all I have, and he's back in Manhattan. Fighting a war *you* started." She glares at me with a look that chills me to the bone. I've known all along that Shannon doesn't like me—but now I realize she actually hates me. "I should be there." She spits on the dry ground. "Now run."

The sun is glowing red and pink. "Aren't we done?"

"We're done when I say we're done," Shannon says. She points in the opposite direction from the house, where a cluster of dying trees marks the edge of the farmland. "There and back. *Now.*"

"Okay, okay." I shoot her a dirty look. "I'm going."

My heart thumps loudly in my chest as I grit my teeth and run. I've nearly reached the training ground and am about to black out when I see a figure approaching me. "Here, Aria," a timid voice says. "Water."

I stop running and double over as I catch my breath. "Walk it off, Rose!" Shannon yells. "Walk it off."

I glance up: it's a boy, nine or ten at the most. Markus. The only one in the entire compound who's been kind to me since I arrived. He's holding out a glass of water.

I kiss his cheek with gratitude, then take the glass and gulp. Some of the cool water spills down my chin, but I don't care.

Markus laughs. He has floppy brown hair, big eyes, and dark freckles scattered across his skin. He's adorable.

"That was just what I needed, Markus. Thank you."

"I figured," he says, taking the empty glass. "I was watching you from the kitchen. You looked thirsty."

Shannon struts over to us. "Did Aria make a new friend? *So* sweet."

Markus is already skipping back to the farmhouse, my empty glass raised high in the air like a trophy. "Bye, Aria!" he shouts.

"Bye!" I shout back, waving until he's out of sight. Then I turn to Shannon, who is staring at me disapprovingly. "What?" I say. "He's sweet." Shannon shrugs. "He's an orphan. Well, I guess not technically. His dad is alive. But in the city, fighting. Like mine. His mother died in the underground battle."

"That's . . . so sad," I say, my eyes still on Markus.

"We all try to watch over him," Shannon says. "He's not the only kid on this compound with no parents around. We're all one big family." She pauses. "Except for you."

"Gee, thanks."

She purses her lips. "Well, it's true. Anyway. Tired?"

I nod.

"Good," she says. "Now do it again."

"No." I shake my head and push past her, starting toward the farmhouse. "I'm done, Shannon."

"Aria!" she calls. "Get back here. Now! Or I'm telling Hunter."

"I'll tell him myself," I call back. I hear a pattering of footsteps and Markus is right beside me. The sunset has darkened to a mixture of black and blue and deep red. The air is hot but slightly more bearable than it was.

I catch up to Markus. "You hungry?" I ask him.

"Yep." He rubs his belly. "Starving."

"Me too," I say. "Let's go eat."

In the two weeks I've been at the compound, there has never been a formal meal—something I'm still getting used to. My parents are fond of proper dinners: everyone in their finest clothes, seated around a perfectly laid table, silver glistening, the servants bringing in platters of elegant food. The cooking is done in the kitchen, which is in a separate wing, and no one sees the effort that goes into preparing a meal, only the glorious outcome.

Here, it's exactly the opposite. People come and go, sometimes staying only a few hours. Bread is baked in the morning and smuggled off the compound and into the city by afternoon. Sometimes there's a delivery of chicken or fish, and sometimes there isn't and we eat only vegetables and clear soup.

Tonight there are a few hunks of goat cheese, rolls, and some cold meats spread on an island in the middle of the kitchen, as well as bowls filled with nuts and boiled potatoes. Markus heaps food on his plate, then rushes into the other room to start eating.

I find a plate and slice a few bits of cheese. Then I grab a roll. I've lost more than a few pounds, and it's not only because I've been training and eating less. I've also been worrying more. Everyone here has.

Through the kitchen is a dining area with an oval wooden table. Markus is at the far end with a couple of other kids. A few women are eating, but they don't look up at me when I pass by.

I nod to them. "Hello."

But no one responds. Everyone here supports Hunter and the rebel cause, but they don't all support *me*. In their eyes, I'm the reason their loved ones are dying, the reason they've had to flee the city their powers helped build. Most have been here only slightly longer than I have. Signs that they have recently been drained linger in the dark green circles under their eyes, their chalky skin as thin as rice paper. They're waiting in this refuge until their powers have regenerated so they can fight alongside the rebels.

"Aria, come sit!" Markus says, but one of the women shushes him.

"That's okay," I say. "I'm gonna go upstairs and relax. I'll see you later."

He nods, focusing on his food.

I take my plate and leave the room, the floorboards creaking with each step. It's almost seven-thirty.

This farmhouse was built over a century ago, and everything inside it is part of a life and a time that I know nothing about.

The walls are beige, accented with mystic symbols for protection and health: Metal and wood carvings of large, open eyes, inlaid with turquoise and ruby-colored stones where the pupils should be. Dozens of charcoal drawings of silhouetted female figures, waves of hair cascading down their backs, palms pressed together—the Sisters, one of the older mystics told me when I asked her who they were, but she didn't elaborate.

The furniture here is simple and rustic: wooden chairs and stools; cots stacked against the walls in case unexpected visitors show up, needing a place to stay. Before the war, the farmhouse was a place where rebels could rest for a night or two. Because the rebels are mystics who refuse to register with the government to have their powers drained, if they're ever caught, they are jailed and then executed.

There are some unexpected touches to the farmhouse: the ceiling has exposed wooden beams with brown knots and whorls that look even darker against the stark white paint. It's the exact opposite of the décor I was used to in the Aeries—rich, exotic colors, gorgeous imported tapestries, sleek silver buildings and bridges. Still, there's a quaint charm here that I admire.

I pass a room where a few sick-looking elderly mystics are tucked into narrow cots, covered to their necks with blankets. A mystic with blond hair down to her waist is crouched on her knees, feeding a woman from a soup bowl. I seem to recall hearing that the blonde's name is Sylvia.

"Can I help?" I ask when she sees me staring.

The mystic shakes her head and returns to feeding the woman.

I continue down the hall, wondering how many other injured mystics there are back in Manhattan, not strong enough to fight or flee.

To the right is a door I have never opened; it's bolted shut and supposedly leads to a musty basement with an underground tunnel to the other side of the farm. *In case we're ever raided,* Shannon told me the first day I got here. She hasn't spoken of it since. Because mystic power is detectable, even when the women here do regain their powers, they're not allowed to use them in the compound for fear that my family or the Fosters will track the energy and locate the hideout. If there ever is a raid, I hope the tunnel is big enough for everyone.

At the end of the hallway is a steep staircase. My room is on the top floor of the house, and I share it with a girl named Nelsa, who seems two or three years younger than me. I don't know for sure because she has never spoken a word to me. Not even *hello.*

When I reach my door, I knock gently in case Nelsa's there, then enter the room. It's empty.

I place my food on a simple brown desk with an ancient computer on it. The monitor is twice the size of my head, maybe even three times, thick and boxy and gray. It makes me miss my TouchMe.

I press a button on the back and the screen comes to life. There's only one thing I look forward to each day, one thing that has made the past few weeks bearable: my seven-thirty p.m. video chat with Hunter. For these few minutes I can see his face and ask him how he's doing.

And when I can return to the city.

I wait impatiently as the computer whirs to life, rumbling the way a dinosaur might upon waking after a long slumber. I key in my username and passcode and wait.

Ding. Hunter is online. And he's messaged me. I click on the message and the screen opens up. There he is.

"Aria? Can you hear me?"

He's wearing a bright blue shirt with an open collar, exposing his neck and the top of his tanned chest. His blond hair is typically messy. He pushes it back and smiles. "Aria?"

"Yes," I say, feeling the familiar fluttering in my stomach that happens whenever I see Hunter.

His blue eyes seem to lighten as he leans forward. "Hey, you."

"Hey yourself," I say. "How are you? How was your day?"

He frowns. "Not great. But it's better now that I see your smiling face. Gosh, I miss you." Behind him are the things I've gotten used to seeing each time we talk: a bookshelf filled with ancient leather-bound books, a rectangular wooden table piled with topographical maps and TouchMes and coffee cups.

Where this room *is,* I don't know.

"I miss you, too. So much," I say. "Are you still not going to tell me where you're living these days?"

He nods. "It's for your own safety." In case we're hacked.

When Hunter dropped me off here at the compound, he promised that we would speak every day until it was safe for me to return to Manhattan. Just thinking about the day he brought me here—his sweet kisses on my lips, the urgent goodbye—makes me miss him even more.

"I know it's only been two weeks since we've been together," Hunter says, "but it feels like two years."

"I was just thinking the same thing," I tell him. "Why was your day not so great?"

"Your father." Hunter clasps his hands behind his head.

My father. I picture Johnny Rose in my head: the strong, stern face that rarely smiles, the slicked-back hair, the crisp tailored suits. A successful businessman who owns half the city. He's also a drug runner and a thug. When he found out I was seeing Hunter behind his back, he had a doctor erase my memories of our relationship and replace them with fake memories of Thomas Foster, trying to make me believe I had always loved him.

"He's not backing down," Hunter says. "I'm trying to recruit mystics from outside New York to come and help, but people are hesitant to get involved. They think it's too dangerous, that Manhattan is a lost cause for the rebels. That I should move on." Hunter's lips are drawn into a tight frown, his brow furrowed and tense, but he's still the handsomest thing I've ever seen. He takes my breath away—even on an old, fuzzy computer screen. Thank God I found my memories and realized that it was Hunter I had loved all along, not Thomas.

And now we are together.

And yet . . . still apart.

"When are you going to let me come back to the city?" I ask.

"I know you want to help, Aria. And that's great. But it's safer for you there. The city has changed. It's dangerous. Kyle is acting as the Rose front man—and we both know how he feels about you."

"Yes," I say. "My brother hates me."

"I didn't mean that. He doesn't *understand* you."

"He doesn't want to," I reply. "He's happy being my father's lackey. But what does he have to do with me coming back to Manhattan?"

Hunter thinks about this for a second. Instead of answering me directly, he says, "Do you think the rebels should win this war, Aria?"

The question catches me off guard. "Of course," I say. "You know I do." Ever since I found out that mystics aren't horrible, thieving criminals like I've been taught my whole life. I no longer support my parents' politics.

Hunter unclasps his hands and leans forward, a serious expression on his face. "Say that you do."

"Say what?"

"That you want the rebels to win the war. Please." He sucks in a breath of air. "I need to know that you believe in me, in what I'm trying to do." The pools of his blue eyes make me want to melt. "Please?"

"Okay, I want the rebels to win the war."

Hunter's expression changes—there's a hint of the crooked smile I've grown to love. "And that you renounce your parents."

"Why do you want me to say that?"

"*Please,*" Hunter says urgently, leaning forward in his chair.

"All right," I tell him. "I renounce my parents. Hunter, what is this all about?"

"I just need to hear you say it, Aria. I know that sounds weird, but . . . you make me feel like I can do anything."

He's made requests like this before. I figure he simply needs support from his girlfriend, which is understandable. His mother just died, and now all these rebels are relying on him to lead them against the people of the Aeries. If hearing me say that I hate my parents—which, for the record, I do—will help him, then I'm all for it.

"I *loathe* what my parents have done to the mystics and to the poor people of Manhattan," I say. "You know that. I would do anything to help you defeat them."

Hunter's entire face brightens, and I see the boy I defied my family for. I fought so hard for the memories my parents erased—how Hunter and I met, our first kiss, the way my hand felt in his, how he made me laugh so hard that it hurt—that now I cherish every second with him.

But this isn't enough.

"I have to see you or I'll go crazy," I say.

Hunter laughs. "I know how you feel." He presses a hand over his heart. "I miss you so badly it hurts. But now that you know the truth about me, about us . . . now that you feel everything you used to feel, we have all the time in the world. I know it might not seem that way right this instant, Aria, but it's true." He pauses, and for a second it seems like he gets teary-eyed. "We fought your parents and we won. We got your memories back. Now we need to fight *this* battle."

"I agree with you completely!" I say. "That's why I want to come to the city."

He shakes his head. "Aria, we've been over this—"

"Come on, Hunter. Nobody even wants me here anyway. Shannon is an evil—"

"Be nice to Shannon," Hunter tells me. "She has your best interests at heart. I know she can be a little—"

"Rude?" I interrupt. "Heinous?"

Hunter sighs. "I was going to say prickly. But that's just her way. It's not personal."

"It *feels* personal."

"She's just trying to help," Hunter says. "I swear. And when you're back in Manhattan, the first thing I'll do is sweep you into my arms and kiss you like a madman. Until then, this will have to do." He blows a kiss into the computer screen. "I've gotta go, Aria. We have another meeting in a few minutes. A bit of good news: we've been in communication with some of the mystics in Chicago. They want to help us."

"That would be great," I say. "But I still want to be with you."

"I know," he says. "I want that, too. I just can't bear to put you in danger. After my mom . . . if something happened to you, I'd never forgive myself." He gets silent for a moment, and I can tell he's hurting. "You understand that, right?"

"I love you, Hunter," I say. "I . . . understand."

"I love you, too. Until tomorrow," he says. "Good night."

My screen goes dark. I stare at it, wishing Hunter would return, but all I can see is the shadowy reflection of my own face, alone.

After a too-brief shower, I dry off and put on a fresh pair of sweatpants and a clean white T-shirt. I step into the hall and find the rest of the house bustling with activity: I can hear children whining as their mothers ready them for bed, and from the kitchen a teakettle wails like a siren. Tall fans stand by the walls, barely moving the humid air.

I pass a few bedrooms, stopping when I see a short, thin woman standing in the doorway of my room.

Frieda.

She looks *old*, her skin weathered and faded. She's wearing a shapeless dress that flows down to her ankles. It was white once, but now it's torn and stained, making her look like a sickly ghost. She is staring at me with her mouth gaping, her pink-yellow gums exposed. Her eyes are so dark that it's impossible to tell the difference between her pupils and her irises—they look like dull black buttons.

"Who are you?" Her voice is rough, like it's been mixed with rocks.

"It's okay, Frieda," I say. "I'm Aria. And remember, this isn't your room." I point to the open door a few feet away. "*That's* your room."

I gather she has dementia of some sort, though she's actually one of the healthier elders at the compound. She doesn't move.

"Is everything okay, Frieda?" I ask gently. "Would you like me to help you?"

Frieda just stares at me. She doesn't even blink. "What did you do with her heart?"

I take a small step forward. The poor woman has really lost it. "Come on, Frieda. Let's get you back to bed." I reach out to take her arm, but she jerks away violently.

"The heart. You didn't just leave it there, did you?" says Frieda, visibly distraught. "It is the source of her power! And Davida was one of the most promising young mystics. . . ."

I stiffen at the mention of Davida. My former servant. My friend who sacrificed her life so that Hunter and I could be together.

I peer into Frieda's eyes. Maybe she isn't as crazy as she seems. "Did you know her?" I ask.

For a moment, Frieda seems incredibly lucid, and then her eyes glaze over. "The heart," she mutters. "Where is the heart?"

"Her heart was in her body," I say, thinking back to that night, when Davida took on Hunter's appearance and allowed my father to shoot her, saving Hunter's life.

"Her body was lost," I add. "In one of the canals."

"No!" Frieda shouts. Her black eyes are open wide as she presses her frail hands to her cheeks. "A mystic's heart is never lost. You must find it."

I'm about to ask her what she means when the floor starts to shake.

I cover my ears as a burst of red explodes around me and the farmhouse goes up in flames.

· II ·

Red quickly morphs to black.

All the bulbs in the ceiling have burst, bathing us in total darkness. Glass fragments shower down on me; they cut my skin as I wipe them from my arms. I can't see anything. I feel hot—hotter than I ever have before. Smoke fills my nostrils and I start to cough, so hard that it's painful. My back drips with sweat. I can't breathe, I can't see, I don't know what's happening, and all I hear is screaming.

"Frieda?" I shout, but I can barely hear my own voice over the chaos. Orders are being shouted—*"Come quick, Tamra, execute the plan!" "This way! Hold on to my arm and follow me!"*—and the high-pitched screams of children fill my ears.

We're being raided.

My skin begins to burn. My lungs feel raw. The air around me is thick, black. It envelops me. I narrow my eyes to slits and stumble forward, feeling for Frieda, but instead I crash into a wall.

"Frieda? Anyone?"

I feel my way along the wall until I bang into a door. Which should mean the stairs are right in front of me.

"We've found them!" a male voice shouts. "Arthur! Here!"

It's not the only male voice I hear. The house is full of intruders, and they're coming from below. I don't want to head downstairs, but where else can I go? I can smell burning flesh, and a not-so-distant roar lets me know the fire is spreading.

I have to get out of here.

I drop to the floor, crawling, searching for the staircase. The floorboards are hot under my fingertips.

I hear a round of gunshots, then a shriek. It's too late to try for the secret basement tunnel. I have to get outside, past the trees Shannon made me run to this afternoon.

I find the stairs and begin to drag myself down. The screaming is louder, the smoke thicker. Behind me, red and yellow flames lick the doors of the bedrooms and engulf the walls, racing toward the staircase.

"Find her!" shouts a throaty baritone. "Get her out of here *alive!*"

I know immediately that whoever said those words is talking about me.

There's a snap and I flick my head upward. The floor above me is caving in.

"Aria!"

It's Shannon. She's popped her head out of one of the second-floor bedrooms. I can barely see her face, but I know the sound of her voice.

"Get in here. Now."

"But—"

"Now!"

I stand up and rush into the bedroom where Shannon is standing. My throat and lungs feel raw from coughing.

"Come on." Shannon pulls me toward an open window on the far wall.

"I'm not jumping out a window, Shannon!"

"How else are we going to get out of here? I promised Hunter I would keep you safe. So if I say jump out a window, you don't say no. You say *How quickly?* Get it?"

Shannon doesn't wait for a reply. She yanks my arm until I'm at the window and pushes me through. "There's a ladder welded to the side of the house," she says. "Grab it."

I feel for a metal handle and find one. The air outside is cool as I swing my legs around until they find the rungs.

"Move!" Shannon barks.

I begin to climb down the back of the farmhouse. Behind us is a ramshackle barn and, in the near distance, rows and rows of dead apple trees, their white-gray branches gnarled and reaching into the night sky.

This must be where we'll hide.

My feet hit the bottom rung and I jump to the ground, Shannon right behind me. I can see that the roof of the farmhouse has collapsed. Orange flames shoot into the sky as black smoke pours out of every window, mixing with the hazy air.

The darkness is absolute, so different from the city—there's no green glow of the tall mystic spires, full of the energy that fuels Manhattan. There is only black night—marred by flames, by the sounds of gunfire and the shrill voices of women and children under fire. I hear a child weeping, and the harsh calls of the men who have attacked, yelling *"Where is she?"* over and over.

And then there are sharp green rays of mystic energy that shoot into the sky like laser beams.

Some of the women and visiting rebels are fighting.

Now that we're being raided, there's no reason for them to hold back their powers. Through a window on the ground floor, I see the figure of a mystic surrounded by smoke. She throws her hands in front of her: razor-thin rays of green energy fly from her finger-tips, swirling together into one massive beam and pummeling a soldier in the stomach, knocking him out of view.

"Wear this," Shannon says as she slips something over my mouth. A mask.

"Shouldn't we stay and help?" I ask, my voice muffled.

"We're under attack," she says, leading me toward the trees. "Your family has found us. We have to go."

"What about the underground passageway?" I ask.

"Too dangerous. It's probably sealed up by now anyway," Shannon says. "Let's go, Aria."

I follow her farther into the darkness. Grass crunches beneath our feet as we run, but I know we're not loud enough for anyone to hear—not over the cries and crashes coming from the house.

"Faster," Shannon hisses. "Faster!"

Instead, I stop for a moment and turn around. The house is still standing, but not for long—the fire inside is unstoppable, bursts of red and orange and black shooting out of the windows, licking the walls and roof like an angry tongue. Suddenly, a soldier catapults through a wall like a cannonball and collapses on the ground.

The blond mystic Sylvia follows through the hole in the wall, which she must have made with her energy. Backlit by flames, she blasts the fallen soldier with rays of electric green energy. I can hear the crunching of bricks and smell the sizzling of human flesh.

I'm relieved to know that some of the mystics are still fighting.

An image of Frieda strikes me. Did she make it out of the house?

Then, over the battle, I hear it: a child's voice. *"Mama!"*

"Come on." Shannon's eyes gleam against the blackened sky. "Why did you stop?"

"Mama!"

That voice—I recognize it. Markus. Sweet face, floppy brown hair. He was so nice to me. And he has no mother to keep him safe.

The right thing to do is to keep running. To escape. But how can I leave him? "Markus is still in there," I tell Shannon. "I can hear him. And there are others—"

"This is no time to be a martyr, Aria. It's them or you."

"This attack is my fault," I say. "It's happening because *I'm* here. I have to help."

"If they haven't gotten out by now, they're goners," Shannon says urgently, grabbing for my arm. "There's nothing you can do to help. There's nothing—"

But I can't hear her anymore.

Because I'm leaving her, running back toward the house.

The mask I'm wearing blocks the smoke as I enter the kitchen. I can barely see an inch in front of me. There's less screaming—it sounds like most of the attackers have moved outside and are battling the remaining mystics on the lawn.

"Markus?"

No response. My hands begin to shake, and I move forward slowly, knocking over a ceramic bowl. It makes a high-pitched crash as it shatters on the floor.

Then I hear it.

"Mama! Mama!"

He cries again, and I follow his voice. I feel my way through the kitchen along the cabinets, heading for the dining area. *"Mama!"*

I drop to my hands and knees, creeping across the planks until I find a leg of the table. "Markus? Is that you?"

I see him a few feet away from me, curled into a tiny ball under the table. For a second I see a flash of floppy brown hair through the smoke.

"It's me, Aria," I say. "Hold out your hand. I'm going to help you."

The smoke has overtaken us again, and I grab for him. I feel nothing but air—until I make contact with a set of fingers. I clasp his hand and tug. "Crawl. And close your eyes," I tell him. "Come to me."

He does, and then I have one arm draped over him, edging him out from underneath the table. "Stay down, Markus. And follow me."

Softly, I hear him say, "Aria."

I rip off my mask as soon as we're outside and place it over Markus's head. It's too big for him, but it's better than nothing.

As we run, I hear a series of pops that sound like fireworks, but I know better. The field echoes with gunshots, with shouts and hisses, as the attackers who have come for me search in vain.

"Burn it all down!" I hear someone call.

"I said *alive*," someone screams back. "We need her alive!"

I doubt they'll rest until they find what they're looking for.

We're not moving fast enough. I see the apple trees in the distance. No Shannon. Markus is too slow. I stop and lift him onto my back. "Come on, guy. Hold on."

I hope Shannon is hiding in the trees, waiting for me. "Shannon!" I call.

There's no answer, and I keep moving. My arms tire. Markus is getting heavier.

Just then, I see glistening white—a pair of eyes.

Only they're not Shannon's.

"We've found her!" A man who is nearly twice my size and thick as a barrel shoots a round into the sky. "Guys!"

I try to zigzag away from him, but it's too hard to run and carry Markus at the same time.

A pair of hands grabs me from the side, and I lurch forward. Markus falls off my back, onto the ground. "Run!" I yell.

A sweaty hand covers my mouth. The grip on my shoulders tightens. I think back to my training with Shannon. What did she tell me to do when an attacker came at me from behind?

I bite down and catch one of the man's fingers with my teeth. I kick back my right leg, jamming my heel into his groin. "Aw, shit," the man groans, his hand falling away.

I stumble forward, trying to run, but it's so dark. Where did

Markus go? I don't dare glance back to see how many men are behind me. I search for the white eyes that were in front of me, but I don't see them anymore.

Until I do. And a matching pair of smaller eyes. *Markus.*

"Stop!" the man shouts. I look around frantically: I can't be more than a quarter mile from the trees. Is Shannon watching?

"Help!" I scream. "Someone help me!"

"Nobody is here to help you," the man says. His voice is husky and terrifying. For a second, there is a flare of green light in the sky. It illuminates the man's face, and I can see that he's barely older than I am. Red cheeks, blond hair, skin slick with sweat. A tight silver uniform. His hand is curled tightly around Markus's neck.

"Let him go," I plead. I can barely speak I'm so nervous; my heart is beating furiously. "Please."

"Okay." He uncurls his fingers, but Markus doesn't move an inch, frozen with fear.

The soldier raises his gun and aims it at Markus's head.

My heart stops. "Markus, run!"

The man unlocks the safety and shoots.

It's a soft sound compared to the chaos going on around us. There's a second shot and a thud as Markus topples to the earth.

I scream something into the night, barely recognizing my own voice. Tears stream down my face as the soldier shifts his focus. Now the gun is pointed directly at me. *No no no no no no no—*

There's a rush of air behind me and then someone else's hands are on my shoulders. I struggle with all my might but can't break his grip.

"We were told not to kill you," the soldier with the gun says.

"But we're happy to cripple you if that's what it takes." He moves his aim from my head to my leg. The Foster crest—a five-pointed star—glistens on the front of his uniform. "Or to kill everyone around you. Your call."

The man behind me kicks my legs out from under me, and I drop like a bag of bricks, slamming my head on the rough soil. I stare up at the burning sky, defeated.

"Cuff her."

My arms are nearly ripped out of their sockets as a pair of metal cuffs finds its way around my wrists. Everything seems lost.

I should have listened to Shannon.

· III ·

The guards' voices echo loudly in my head as I'm shoved into a metal chair, my arms yanked tightly behind me. My wrists are raw from rubbing against the cuffs. It feels like we've been traveling for hours.

"Stop moving!" comes a high-pitched voice, not one of the men who captured me back at the compound.

The dirty blindfold someone tied around my head in the copter is still in place. There's a click as the cuff on my right hand is unlocked. For a second I foolishly think they're letting me go, but then I hear the cuff being locked around my chair.

I leap forward blindly, attempting to pull the chair with me, out of the room, but it's bolted to the floor. There are a few hearty laughs; then someone strikes me across the cheek.

"I said, stop moving."

My mouth fills with the tang of blood. I try to spit it out but end up swallowing most of it.

Just breathe, I tell myself. *In and out.*

I suppose I'm back in the Aeries—judging from the time I spent in the helicopter and the elevator ride afterward—though really, I could be anywhere. The air around me is cool. I can actually smell the air-conditioning, which I always thought was crisp and clean, like freshly laundered clothing. Now that I've been in the countryside, though, I know what truly clean air smells like. This is overprocessed and fake. Much like everything else in the Aeries.

Suddenly, the blindfold is pulled off my face. I blink, letting my eyes adjust to the light after what feels like hours in the dark. It looks like I'm in some sort of warehouse, with exposed piping and cement-block ceilings and floors. There are dozens of windows, but they're completely blacked out, giving no clues to my whereabouts.

Ten guards—five men, five women—are spread out across the room. They are dressed in silver Lycra uniforms with black stripes running down the sides. Their chests are covered with metallic bulletproof vests, the Foster crest imprinted above their hearts.

Each of them holds a shiny pistol.

Pointed at my head.

An eleventh guard steps out from behind me. He's holding the blindfold in his hand. His head is shaved, his scalp as pink and smooth as a baby's. "Hello."

I stare straight ahead.

He walks around me in a circle. The Foster crest is inked in navy blue on the right side of his neck. "I'm surprised Johnny Rose didn't teach you better manners."

"Right," I say. "Because kidnapping me, handcuffing me to a chair, and beating me up is a sign of a really good upbringing."

I'm expecting to be hit again. Instead, he laughs. All his teeth are silver.

"Where am I?"

No answer.

I glance over my shoulder and see a long black table set for two—dinner plates, glasses, silverware, and all. Tall candlesticks that glisten with silver etching are positioned in the center.

The silver-toothed guard motions to me. "Tasha, Helen"—two female guards step forward—"take Ms. Rose to get cleaned up."

One of the guards—Helen—unlocks my cuff from the chair while the other—Tasha—aims her gun at my forehead. "Get up and walk," she says.

I do as I'm told.

I'm marched past the other guards, past the blackened windows, until I reach a cement wall with an empty space where a door should be.

On the other side are the bare essentials of someone's sleeping quarters: A bed that seems freshly made with cream-colored linens. Two pillows covered with stark white shams. A tall mirror resting against one of the concrete walls. More wide windows that have been blacked out but that I assume look over the bridges of the Aeries.

On top of the mattress are clothes that are clearly meant for me: a plain red dress and a pair of sandals covered with crushed gems, so bright they look like diamonds.

"Hold still," Helen says. She removes a razor blade from her pocket and I wince. Is she going to cut me? In one swoop, she slices down my back, opening up the T-shirt I'm wearing and stripping it off me.

Along with my bra. Another quick motion and my sweatpants and underwear are gone.

I'm completely naked now. The cuffs are relocked behind my back. Tasha points to the wall opposite the blacked-out windows, where there is a door that must lead to a bathroom. "Wash up," she says. "Quickly. When you're done, we'll help you dress."

"Wash up?" I say. "I'm handcuffed. How exactly is that going to work?"

The guards smirk. "Figure it out," Tasha says.

They leave. Helen presses a touchpad and a door slides into place, sealing me in.

I look around for a way to escape, but it's all walls and windows. Worse, my body feels like it has taken a thousand-foot fall. I'm bruised and sore all over. For the first time, I wish it were because of Shannon's training.

Shannon. I wonder if she saw them take me. If anyone is going to rescue me.

Was she captured, too? Is she still alive? And if she is . . . will she get word to Hunter about where I've been taken?

I walk over to the bathroom door and nudge the touchpad with my shoulder. The door whizzes open and I am in a space that looks like it could be in my parents' apartment: a glass shower stall, a porcelain self-flushing toilet, a sink like an enormous soup bowl.

I step into the shower. It's so unlike the stall back at the mystic compound it's almost funny. So Aeries: sleek black marble with white flecks, shined spotless. No showerhead is visible; there's a button that I press with my elbow, and immediately I'm doused with warm water. I let it rush over my face and down my back, soothing my swollen skin and washing away the blood, until my body no longer aches.

What happened back there? I thought we were safe, that no one would be able to find us—that's what Hunter said. Clearly he was wrong. Who's after me—my parents? Kyle? I clench my hands and pound the wall. It doesn't make me feel any better. Poor, sweet Markus is dead, and it's all my fault. If I hadn't been at the compound, they never would have gotten raided. Nobody would have died.

I lean back against the shower door. I feel useless and scared and responsible. I close my eyes and wish that everything would stop, go back to normal. But what's normal anymore?

The guards return and uncuff me so I can towel off.

I'm uncomfortable being naked in front of them; I didn't even like when Davida saw me naked after a shower, and she was my servant. My friend. These women are strangers. George Foster's soldiers. Enemies.

As I pick up the red dress that was left on the bed for me, I realize it's not as plain as I thought. The color is electric, a stop-in-your-tracks kind of red. *Look but don't touch.* The material is fine silk, though there's not much of it; sleeveless and backless, with deep cleavage and a halter tie that goes around my neck. There is no bra. A fine black beaded fringe rustles above my knees as I turn around and catch a glimpse of myself in the standing mirror.

This is a party dress—something I would have worn to an

event with my parents or on a date with Thomas before the war. Definitely a dress for an Aeries girl. But it's a frightening ensemble for a prisoner.

"Come on," Helen says. "Let's go."

My two new best friends usher me through the main room. My hair is still wet, heavy on the back of my neck, and I shiver from the cold.

The candles on the table have been lit, and there is a man sitting at the far end, his head down. He's dressed in a white linen suit and a white dress shirt with a navy tie. His brown hair is hanging down, covering his face.

Tasha pulls out a chair for me and I sit down. "If you try to run away, I will shoot you," she says. I don't doubt her sincerity.

I lean back to study the man in front of me. He raises his head and I can't help myself. I gasp.

Thomas Foster.

Light from the candles plays across the table and flickers over his face. It strikes the bottom of his chin, then fans upward, accenting the hollows of his cheeks and giving his familiar brown eyes a spooky glint.

My stomach does a flip. He's supposed to be dead.

On his plate is a hunk of meat so rare it might as well be raw. He cuts into the steak and blood pours from it, filling the air with a sticky-sweet smell. He takes a bite and tilts up his head.

My ex-fiancé swallows. Winks at me. "Hello, Aria."

I can't seem to form a coherent sentence. "But you—I saw you . . . you were—"

"Dead?" The look in his eyes shifts. "No. Though you did shoot me." He pats his chest, just under his heart. "Fortunately, you're not much of a shot."

My mind races back to the battle the night of the underground raid, when Thomas was about to kill Hunter and I shot him. Left him for dead. How many nights since then have I lost sleep, thinking I murdered him? And now here he is. Very much alive.

"I know." Thomas takes a sip of red wine. "You're speechless at the sight of me. Most women are." He pauses. "Though you never seemed to think so."

"Cut it out, Thomas," I say. "You never liked me. You cheated on me with Gretchen Monasty and lied about how we met. You're no better than my parents. A child was *killed* tonight because of what you've done. And countless others, I'm sure."

Thomas chuckles. "It's a pity I can't say I've missed the sound of your voice, Aria. Or anything about you, really."

His gaze focuses on my cleavage. I feel vulnerable, exposed. I want to strangle him.

"What we had could have worked, you know," Thomas says. "But you had to go and ruin it with that . . . *mongrel.*"

My stomach churns. I know he's referring to Hunter. "We didn't *have* anything," I say. "My parents wiped my memory clean and tried to trick me into believing I was in love with you. And it didn't work. Our whole relationship was based on a lie."

I let my words sink in and wait for a reaction. Thomas never loved me—that much I know. Our engagement was a scheme. He was a player in the alliance between my parents and the Fosters:

Get rid of Hunter.

Unite our families.

Make sure Garland wins the mayoral election against Violet Brooks.

Unfortunately, the only thing they succeeded at was murdering Violet. The traitor Elissa Genevieve did that, the mystic who works for my father and took advantage of me to gain access to the rebels' underground hideout.

"Look, Aria. What do you want me to say? That I'm sorry?" Thomas wipes his mouth with his napkin. He looks exactly the same as he did when we first met, on the night of our engagement party. Despite his recuperation from a serious bullet wound, he's well built and still picture-perfect handsome—smooth cheeks, a multimillion-dollar smile.

He'd be a great catch if he weren't such a jerk.

"I'm not sorry," he continues.

"How did you find me?" I ask. "Hunter told me— I thought I was—"

"Safe?" His eyes seem to glimmer. "We tracked you."

"How?"

"God, you're daft," Thomas snarls. "With a tracker."

"But how—"

"I have bigger concerns than you figuring out how I found you, Aria."

"Oh?" I say. "And what are those?"

He stabs a finger at me. "Your family has turned against mine. Again. And vice versa. Now that Garland is dead, it's every man for himself."

This doesn't surprise me. It was nearly impossible to believe that my father, crime lord of the West Side, would have wanted to unite with George Foster, his East Side equivalent, in the first place. The families have been enemies for generations.

Now that Thomas's older brother, Garland, is gone, and marrying me off to Thomas didn't work out . . . both Dad and George Foster must figure they're better off alone.

"This isn't a game, Aria," Thomas says sternly. "Do you have any idea what this boyfriend of yours is actually doing?"

"Fighting for equality," I say. "For what's right. Which is more than I can say for you."

Thomas gives me a wolfish smile. "And what do you think I'm doing?"

I shrug, once again acutely aware of how much of my skin he can see in this dress. "Probably selling Stic on the black market. Just like your father does. And mine."

Thomas laughs at me, loosening his tie and unbuttoning the top button of his dress shirt. His cheeks are flushed from the wine. "Wrong. The mystics are *rebelling.* Which means they're no longer being drained. Which means no more mystic energy to make into Stic and sell."

"I know that," I say. "But surely you have some hidden supply."

"Why?" He leans back and quirks an eyebrow. "Want some?"

"Of course not. You're disgusting."

Thomas licks his lips, which are stained a dark purple. "I love it when you talk dirty to me."

"We're in a war, Thomas," I say, growing more and more exasperated. "Your brother died. People are out there right now fighting for equality—"

"Screw equality." Thomas throws his napkin on the table and pushes back his chair. "This city is an absolute mess. Manhattan has never seen a problem like this before. We've always been a city-state that the rest of the country looks up to. Our parents might not like each other, but we're mostly equal in power and wealth. More importantly, we've always taken care of our business on the inside."

He steps toward me; I can smell the wine on his breath. "'Don't show weakness, Tommy.' That's what my father always taught me. Because once somebody sees a weak spot, they know exactly where to attack."

"Who are you talking about, Thomas? The mystics?"

He shakes his head. "People outside . . . they're watching us. Word has started to spread about the rebellion. We've tried to limit press access, but there have been leaks."

I don't understand. "So?"

"So," Thomas says, "Los Angeles, Chicago . . . pretty soon they're going to offer us their 'help,' which really means they're going to move in their own troops and take over."

"Why would they do that?" I ask.

"Imagine how it would look to the rest of the world if the rebels win. Mystics everywhere will start demanding all sorts of crazy rights. There will be more wars. No one wants that to happen, so New York will be vanquished by foreigners and the entire city will be wiped clean, everything hushed up. And then we'll all be slaves."

Thomas moves over to one of the blacked-out windows and gazes out as though he can see Manhattan. "The Aeries must win this war. If we don't, it will mean the worst for all of us—mystics, humans, Aeries, Depths. . . . *Everyone* will suffer." He turns to me, suddenly looking exhausted. "Can't you see what you've done?"

I avert my eyes, not wanting to feel sympathy for him. Truthfully, I haven't thought about how outsiders might be watching our city, waiting to pounce on us, to infiltrate. To conquer.

Still, who cares what the rest of the world is thinking? Don't mystics deserve the same chances for health and happiness as anyone else?

That is what Hunter is fighting for. What I am fighting for.

Thomas is the cruel one. He sent troops to kidnap me, troops who murdered innocent women and children. Children like Markus.

"You're being selfish, Thomas," I say. "This is bigger than just us. It's bigger than Manhattan. Let me go. *Please.* If you ever cared about me at all—"

"You don't get it, do you?" Thomas says scornfully. "I never cared about you, ever. I used you to get what I wanted, Aria, and because of your stupid mystic boyfriend I never even got that." He approaches me and grabs my shoulders. "You disgust me. You're tainted goods, Aria Rose. And don't act like you're above doing whatever it takes to get what you want. You're just as conniving as I am."

I'm aghast. "I am nothing like you."

Thomas raises his eyebrows. "No? Then what's with all the video propaganda?"

I have no idea what he's talking about. "Are you drunk?"

"Don't pretend to be dumb, Aria. It's not flattering. Besides, you're not that smart to begin with." Thomas walks over to one wall and presses a nearly invisible touchpad. A large square of gray cement retracts into the ceiling, revealing a TouchMe screen that must be two or three feet high and just as wide.

Thomas keys in a password and the screen comes to life. "Search Aria Rose," he instructs the TouchMe.

"Searching," the automated voice replies.

A queue of over a dozen videos appears instantly. Thomas selects the first one. It's me, back in my room at the compound, mere hours ago, before the fire, saying something.

I hate what my parents have done to the mystics and the poor people of Manhattan. I would do anything to defeat them.

Thomas clicks on another video. I recognize the shirt I'm wearing. That was almost a week ago.

My parents want to exploit everyone in Manhattan. To side with them is to deny yourself basic rights. Join the rebels.

Thomas pauses the video. His eyebrows pinch together as he watches my expression. "Should I keep going?"

My mouth is suddenly dry. Hunter has been recording our chat sessions, editing them down to short clips. I remember the times he asked me to tell him how much I hated my parents, how I supported the rebels. A sour taste fills my mouth, and I feel like I'm going to throw up.

Since the mystics are already with us, I can only assume the videos are being broadcast across the Depths as a way to rally the nonmystic poor in our favor.

Hunter has been using me. I can't believe it.

I keep my features blank. I don't want Thomas to see the surprise on my face. The guards are still lined up against the far wall of the room, watching us. I wonder what they think of me. Dumb little rich girl.

"Don't pretend that isn't you, Aria," he says.

"I won't." I cross my arms in front of my chest, wishing I weren't wearing an expensive red party dress, especially one with a plunging neckline and no back.

"How about one more?" Thomas scrolls through the screen until he finds a video that looks like it was posted almost two weeks ago—one of my first nights at the compound. I look upset. *I hate my family,* I hear myself say. *Don't trust anyone in the Aeries!*

"Those are quite some professions of hatred for your family," Thomas says. He presses a button and the TouchMe disappears into the wall. "And mine."

"Well," I find myself saying, "you all did terrible things."

He cocks his head. "Did we? Here's the thing, Aria: as naive as you are, people in Manhattan seem to like you. They relate to you. Not only in the Depths, but in the Aeries as well. Somehow, I came out as a bad guy in all this—"

"Gee, I wonder why," I say.

Thomas grabs my shoulders again. He's about an inch from my face, the tip of his nose practically touching mine. His breath smells of Cabernet. "Don't," he says, "interrupt me."

Then he kisses me.

I slap him across the cheek. He pulls away and rubs his jaw. I wait for him to order his guards to move in on me, but he doesn't. He just laughs.

"You always were feisty, Aria. I like that. Even though you sicken me."

"So why am I here? Why do you care about any of these videos?" I stare down at the shimmering skirt of my dress. It feels impossible to be taken seriously when I'm dressed this way. If I get out of here alive, I will never wear a dress again. "Let me go."

"Tell me where Hunter is," Thomas says.

"I don't know. He hasn't told me." I cross my arms. "And even if he had, I wouldn't tell you."

Thomas says nothing as he sits down again and takes a sip from his wineglass. "You know what? I believe you."

"You do?" I glance around, looking for an exit.

"You probably don't know anything."

"I don't," I tell him. Does this mean he's going to let me go? "Honestly."

Thomas smacks his lips. "My father wanted to blow up your little mystic hideout. Kill you. But I convinced him not to because I think you'll be useful. And if you don't have any information to share, then we have nothing to lose by wiping the slate clean."

I keep my eyes trained on Thomas, but I sense the guards moving behind me. Coming closer. "What?"

"Your memory," Thomas says. "We erased it before, and we can do it again. This time, though, we don't need you to believe you're just a dumb rich girl who OD'd on Stic; we need someone we can *use*. Like what you're doing for Hunter. Only we need you to do it for us.

"You will tell the people of Manhattan that you have changed your mind," Thomas orders. "You'll say that the rebels are wrong. Selfish. Dangerous. Then we will be married and unite the Aeries— just as we planned. *That's* how the Fosters will beat the Roses and the rebels." He pauses to take another sip of wine. "And I think the less there is in that stupid little head of yours, the better."

Thomas places his wineglass on the table. Then he snaps his fingers.

Before I can move, hands grab me from either side.

· IV ·

I am dragged into an adjoining room.

Unlike what I've seen so far, this new space looks lived-in and enjoyed: there are glossy paneled walls, huge impressionist paintings in gilt frames, soft golden lights embedded in the ceiling, and—on the far end—a cushioned black leather couch. Next to the couch is a bar topped with brightly colored glass bottles, and next to that is a silver refrigerator.

The only thing out of place is the chair, surrounded by a terrifying metal apparatus in the center of the room.

"Let go of me!" I scream, struggling against the guards, but I already know it's no use. I'm outnumbered by men and woman who would gladly kill me. And worse, now I know Thomas's sinister plan is to wipe my memory clean. Again.

I won't escape.

The chair looks like it belongs to another, older era. It reminds me of the mystic draining chair in my father's office, only wider, with thin metal spikes across the top and long, thick armrests that curl at the ends with straps. There is a black footrest with straps as well, and all along the back the metal has been polished so that it's as shiny as a mirror.

I squint and see my reflection.

I look terrified.

"Do you like the paintings?" Thomas asks, strolling into the room as though he hasn't a care in the world. He motions to the frames. "Only the best for Daddy's new office. His last one was destroyed by rebels, as was our apartment. Thanks for that, by the way."

I stare at the paintings and realize they are mystic-enhanced, like the ones the Fosters used to have in their home. The colors swirl together like something in Renoir's worst nightmare. One work in particular catches my eye. It's Van Gogh–ish; the bold colors and rough beauty are like his *Starry Night* painting. I watch as the sky darkens from afternoon to sunset.

The guard to my left twists my arm—a jolt of pain shoots up into my neck. "Yes," I say. "Beautiful."

"Don't forget expensive. Hunter couldn't buy you even one of these." Thomas sits down on the couch and crosses his legs at the ankles, relaxing into the soft leather. "Those freaks are good for something: art."

Behind Thomas's head is a six-foot-square pointillist painting that seems to vibrate. It's like Van Gogh's outdoor café painting, only it's set during the day instead of at night; the sky is a light blue, the cobblestone pavement bright and sunny. The colors ripple, suggesting a breeze.

"So . . . you like art?" I say, trying for a distraction.

Thomas rolls his eyes. "Oh, shut up, Aria. You're just stalling, hoping that I won't strap you into this medieval chair and wash your brain." He stands and punches a few numbers into a keypad on the wall. "Well . . . sorry. Because strapping you into this medieval chair and washing your brain is precisely what I'm going to do."

Two women in bleached-white lab coats appear. I can tell they're mystics by the green circles underneath their eyes and the yellow pallor of their skin, so thin that the blue veins underneath are prominent—they've been drained of their energy.

This bothers me. Why, during a rebellion, would anyone still submit to the barbaric ways of the Fosters? Or the Roses?

The traitor mystics don't make eye contact with me. They look at the guards, who bring me over to the chair and strap me in.

I try to pull away, but it's no use. The leather straps wrap around my ankles and my wrists, digging into my already chafed skin. One of the mystics opens a black suitcase full of syringes loaded with multicolored liquids.

It's like what happened in Dr. May's office—where my memories were initially erased.

"I've been told this process hurts," Thomas says. "A lot."

As he's talking, the mystic with the needles swabs my arms and begins a series of injections. Red. Orange. Yellow.

"So I thought I'd hang around and watch," Thomas continues.

"That's nice of you," I manage to say before the other mystic mutes me with a mouth guard. Something is placed over my head and I feel intense pressure against my temples.

"Because I have to say, Aria, you've caused me a lot of pain." Thomas gives me a wicked smile. "I offered to marry you, to be your husband. And you just threw it in my face like you were too good for me."

I am too good for you, I want to say, but the mouthpiece stops me.

I wiggle my arms, which feel swollen from the shots, trying to see if there's any slack in the restraints. I can no longer move my head or my neck, and I am staring straight ahead at one of Thomas's stupid mystic paintings. I want to leap out of this chair and rip it off the wall.

"Almost ready, Mr. Foster," one of the traitor mystics says.

"Good, good," Thomas replies. He turns to the silver-clad guards. "That's all for now. You are dismissed." They leave the room, and Thomas turns his attention back to me. "Soon you'll be a whole new girl, Aria. A nice girl who does what she's told. Doesn't that sound wonderful?"

I refuse to look at him. I focus on the painting instead. It's of a cluster of water lilies that seem to sway in an invisible wind. The colors melt from purple to pink to a darkish red, then back to purple. Thomas is still talking. *Tune him out,* I tell myself. *Just tune him out.*

I may only have a few moments left as myself. As Aria Rose. I fought so hard to regain the memories that were stolen from me. It's not fair that I will lose them again.

No more Hunter. There's no Patrick Benedict around this time to save my memories of the boy I love and store them away in a silvery heart locket.

No more memories of Kyle or my parents. No more of my friends Kiki and Bennie. No more Shannon. Names and faces of people I will probably never think about again flood my brain, saying their goodbyes. I picture Markus—his shooting makes me think of my father, of how carelessly he shot that gondolier the night he found me in Thomas's apartment.

Will I miss him? My mother? Kyle?

I don't know. The easy answer is no, of course—not after what they did to me. How they betrayed me. But it's more complicated than that. They're still my family. I once loved them. Maybe I still do.

Why did Hunter make those videos without telling me? Why didn't he just ask me to make a statement? Is that why he didn't want me coming back to the city? So I wouldn't be able to speak for myself?

A wave of nausea overtakes me and I retch. I haven't eaten since back at the compound, though, and nothing comes up. My throat is sore and I start to cry, even though I want to seem strong.

Maybe Thomas is right, and I have been naive. Thanks to my chats with Hunter, I may even have made things worse here in the city. Maybe not knowing anymore will be for the best, a blessing in disguise.

My eyelids are incredibly heavy, and I fight the urge to close them.

"Once your head is empty, we will turn you into our little spokesperson," Thomas is saying. "Might as well get some use out of you. And maybe we'll figure out a way to use the rest of you, too. Why waste such a nice body?"

I cringe. So it won't be a blessing.

This is it. This is the end.

My eyes find the café painting again.

"Mr. Foster," one of the mystics says. "We're ready to begin."

At least the last thing I look at as myself will be pretty. The yellow awning over the café tables turns to orange to a perfectly baked brown, and I see figures moving, drinking coffee. A dot in the distance—a red circle, maybe a light from a window—begins to burn brightly and expand.

It grows from a tiny speck to the size of my thumbnail, and then even larger, stretching out like taffy until it is no longer a circle but more of an oval. A head pops out, followed by arms, then legs.

It's a human figure, glowing red.

It rushes toward me from the back of the street in the painting, dodging figures who turn their heads as this red man surges forward.

Then it grows again and shifts. Changes from red to silvery-white.

It's no longer a person, I realize. The shape becomes so large that it's almost too big for the frame. It's a motorcycle.

One that, despite being made up of painted dots, clearly belongs to someone I know.

Turk.

My body seems to fight off whatever stuff the mystics have been injecting me with. I feel *alive.*

There's a roar as the motorcycle blasts out of the painting and into the room, and it is indeed Hunter's best friend astride the bike, which stops on the expensive-looking Oriental rug. Turk has the same black Mohawk I remember, sheared close to his scalp at the sides and spreading up toward the ceiling, the platinum tips so bright they make my eyes hurt. His tattoos pulse, and the fire-breathing dragon on his right arm actually seems to be billowing smoke from its mouth.

There's a familiar glint in Turk's eyes and a wide smile across his face.

Thomas's eyes nearly bulge out of their sockets. "What the—"

But Turk cuts him off by slewing his bike sideways. The white motorcycle pivots on its wheels, and the chrome-covered back knocks Thomas right on his pretty-boy face, slamming him to the floor. He goes stiff and I know he's unconscious. No one comes running into the room, which means the guards must be out of earshot.

Turk hops off the bike and frowns in my direction. Then he stares down the two mystics, who have frozen in fear. He pulls out a long black pistol and raises it in the air. It's as narrow as my pinky and nearly twice the length of any handgun I've ever seen—there's no hammer, only a barrel, a stock, and a trigger. Can it even hold a bullet?

"You two are on the wrong side." He moves the gun between the mystics. One of them drops the needle she's holding and trembles with fear.

Turk pulls the trigger.

He shoots.

Instead of bullets, thin green rays of mystic energy appear, spiraling out to connect with each mystic right in the center of their chests.

There's a loud clap as their skin flashes a sickly yellow color.

Their eyes roll back.

And they drop to the floor next to Thomas, unconscious.

"Sweet," Turk says. "I hate traitors."

He rushes over and removes the strange helmet from my head. "You okay?"

I nod. He undoes the bands around my wrists, then my legs. I sigh with relief as I flex my fingers and toes and fill my lungs with air. My body feels lethargic from the injections, but otherwise, I'm all right.

"Thought I might find you here," Turk says. I am so happy to see him I could cry. Again.

"How?" I ask.

He nods toward one of the pictures. "We've worked hard to get our mystic paintings into the homes of all the best and brightest of the Aeries. It makes it easier to spy on people. And," he adds, "it allows us to sneak in through the occasional loophole."

I can't help but laugh. Thomas was right when he said mystics are good at art—he just didn't know *how* right he was.

"Come on," Turk says, helping me out of the chair. His touch jolts me at first—the mystic energy running through him could kill me—but I watch his expression and I can tell that he's controlling himself. That he won't hurt me.

"Hunter told me this business of touching humans takes getting used to," he says. "Didn't realize how right he was."

Hunter. Hearing his name makes me thankful that my memory hasn't been erased but incredibly upset that he lied to me. I need to see him.

"I've missed you," Turk says softly. He grips the handlebars of his bike and throws one leg over the seat. He pushes a button and a metal rod comes out from one side of the bike. Turk yanks it into his hands, and his fingertips glow green as he stretches the metal, working it like putty, forming a . . .

Helmet.

"Safety first, dude," he says, tossing me the helmet. I put it on and climb onto the bike in front of him, adjusting my barely-there dress so that I'm as covered up as possible and digging my sparkling sandals into the sides of the motorcycle. There's only one seat, so I'm pretty much in his lap. I think back to the first time I met him, when he gave me a lift from Java River after Hunter saved my life. How scared I was of him, of mystics in general. How little I knew about my history with Hunter, thanks to my stolen memories.

So much has changed.

And yet Turk hasn't. I remember that night at Java River, when Hunter told me I should stay in the Aeries where I belong. He was only trying to protect me—I know that now—but Turk was kind to me from the start.

Unlike the other men in my life, Turk doesn't want to use me. He only wants to help. And at the moment, that's pretty damn comforting.

"Time for us to go," Turk says, reaching around me to grab the handlebars. He guns the engine, and we leap back into the painting.

· V ·

The first thing I notice is the stench.

We're going so fast I have to close my eyes so I won't scream. It's like I'm being sucked through a vacuum; there's pressure on either side of me, then an audible *pop!*

Suddenly, the pressure is gone. "You can open your eyes now," Turk says. I feel us slowing down to a more normal speed.

I follow his instructions. The motorcycle descends and lands easily on one of the streets of the Depths. Any lethargy from the injections is gone. I'm completely, incredibly awake.

In some ways the Depths are exactly as I remember them: dark, hot, dirty. Manhattan's streets are flooded by soupy brown water, which broke up the island's foundation and formed canals between the century-old buildings. It's been this way since before I was born. The air is heavy and smells sour, musty, like the back of an old closet.

The sun is up now. Gondoliers idle in clusters by the waterways, waiting in their small, agile boats for passengers, while people hurry over the canals on the raised walkways, moving from building to decrepit building.

This part of Manhattan is bleaker now than when it was when I first saw it, just a few weeks ago. It was never nice—with its broken shop windows, façades covered with swirls of graffiti—but it was never this devastated. Gone are the brightly colored shirts that used to hang on clotheslines outside the apartment buildings to dry in the hot, salty air. There are no children running alongside the canals, teetering dangerously on the edges as they peel oranges and stuff bits of bread into their mouths, yelling *Wait up!* to their friends.

As we travel through the bottom reaches of Manhattan, toward I-don't-know-where, I realize exactly how much has changed. The buildings here were always grimy, the cobblestones were always broken beyond repair, but there was still an overwhelming sense of *life*.

Now all I see is death.

Tiny shops have been decimated, pillars of rubble and rock left in their place. Entire buildings have crumbled and fallen into the canals, and certain streets are blocked off by piles of debris.

A few girls whiz past us on rusty-looking bicycles—the only real form of transportation that can squeeze through the narrow alleyways of the Depths.

Except, of course, for a souped-up mystic motorcycle.

"Miss it?" Turk asks as he maneuvers over the narrow stone bridges and along twisting streets. I glance over my shoulder: tiny green flames of mystic energy buzz out from the chrome exhaust pipes behind us.

"Yes," I say, and I mean it. The Depths are where I met Hunter. I feel more at home here than I would back in the Aeries with my parents. "Where are we going?"

"Even though we use paintings as loopholes," Turk explains, referring to the indirect route we're taking, "there aren't any direct connections to rebel hideouts from the Aeries."

A mystic loophole—like the one on my old balcony that Hunter used to transport himself from the underground to the Aeries without being noticed. That explains how we got from Thomas's hideout to the Depths so quickly.

"As it is," Turk continues, "we can't use the subway tunnels for hideouts anymore, since they've been flooded. It'd be too dangerous to link our new hideouts with any loopholes. If they were somehow accessed by your family or the Fosters . . ." Turk trails off as we shoot up a walkway, crossing a wide canal that runs alongside a string of battered buildings. His words make me think back to the night Elissa Genevieve shot Turk and betrayed us by using my passkey to enter the underground rebel hideouts.

Turk flinches; I can tell he's remembering the same thing. "So we'll have to get there another way," he says.

Soon, I see land, the outline of one of Manhattan's older streets rising above the water. "Hold on," Turk whispers, then flies off the walkway, landing solidly on the street. A few scraggly passersby turn their heads, but we're already gone, rounding a corner into a shady alley.

Turk skips us around too-full garbage cans and an uneven line of potholes. Then he slows down and comes to a stop. "Where are we?" I ask.

He lowers the kickstand and hops off the bike, extending his hand for me as I slide off the seat. "Just going to meet a friend of mine real quick."

The shadowy alley is cooler than the street, which is baking with morning sun, but it's still unbearably hot. Even though it's backless, the red dress I'm wearing is soaked with sweat. The straps of the glittering sandals dig roughly into my skin.

Turk wheels the bike slowly to the end of the alleyway. He glances out at the street, then waves me forward. "Come on, slowpoke."

I take off my helmet and hand it to Turk as we turn onto the street, which is mostly deserted save for a tiny flower stall with a tattered blue awning and buckets of dried-up daisies. Within a few seconds, he manages to reduce the helmet to the simple metal rod it was before.

At the corner, a woman with long blond hair and leathery skin is manning the flower stall. She wears oversized sunglasses and a pea-green dress, and she's incredibly thin—her arms can't be any thicker than my wrists. "Seems like a waste to be selling flowers down here," I say, thinking of the Aeries greenhouses full of exotic mystic-enhanced greenery.

"Everyone can do with a bit of beauty," Turk says. He reaches the woman and taps her on the shoulder.

"You!" She throws her arms out and pulls him into a hug. "Where have you been, stranger?"

"Here and there," Turk says. He gives the woman a kiss on the cheek, and I feel slightly uncomfortable, like I'm watching something I shouldn't be.

"You don't call, you don't write . . . I thought maybe you'd left the city," she says.

Turk shakes his head. "Leave Manhattan? Nah. You know me.

I'm just lying low." He motions to his bike. "Lock her up for me, will ya?"

The woman shakes her head and—even though she's wearing sunglasses—I can tell she's rolling her eyes. "So that's why you came to visit. I thought you missed me."

Turk chuckles. "I do miss you. But can you help a brother out?"

"Yeah, yeah." The woman pulls a tarp from underneath the stall, unfolds it, and throws it over the bike. "Don't worry. I'll take good care of it."

"I know," says Turk. He reaches into the front pocket of his jeans and removes a gray bag the size of his palm. It jingles. Coins.

She pockets the money and kisses Turk again on the cheek. Then she looks past him, at me, and frowns. She reaches back underneath the stall and pulls out a wad of folded black fabric. "For your friend," she says. "Bye now."

"Bye," Turk says, taking the clothing and tossing it to me.

I unfold the fabric. It's a cloak—not unlike the one Davida gave me that I lost. I drape it around my shoulders and pull up the hood, relieved to not be so exposed.

Turk grabs my hand and leads me down the street, away from the leering gondoliers smoking hand-rolled cigarettes and calling out for customers, away from the mothers hustling their children down the grimy sidewalk.

Who was that woman? How does she know Turk?

"Hey, Aria," Turk says, eyeing the cloak.

"Yeah?"

He smirks. "You look good in black."

As we walk, Turk gives me a tour of war-ravaged Manhattan. "Violet's death was a huge turning point," he tells me. "In a lot of ways, it finally united the mystics and the poor in the Depths. They've always been at odds, ya know?"

I nod. In the past, the poor despised the mystics the same way the rich in the Aeries did. They blamed mystics for the deaths in the Mother's Day Conflagration and feared their powers. The mystics resented the poor for not accepting them as part of the city when they were abiding by the rules, registering with the government and submitting themselves to be drained.

"Where'd you go?" Turk asks.

"Hmm?"

"You drifted off. What were you just thinking about?"

"The night we met," I say. "Back at Java River." Hunter had left me at the coffee shop, sending for Turk to pick me up and drive me home. "I was so scared to be near the Magnificent Block, where the registered mystics were. . . . I'd been taught to fear them. Fear you." I wipe my hair back from my forehead. "I'm glad the poor and the mystics have reconciled."

Turk gives me a wink that lets me know he agrees. "Violet wanted the best for *everyone* in the Depths. Not just the mystics. When she died, everyone felt the loss, realized they need to team up if they're ever going to defeat the Aeries. Your father and brother, though"—Turk frowns—"took it an as opportunity to kick us when we were down."

Around us, the light spires, which were once full of green

mystic energy, are dark and empty. The city has been overdraining the mystics for years; I'm sure there's a fair energy reserve to run Manhattan for the time being, but what will happen once it's gone?

I can't tell how many hours have passed since my abduction from the compound, but I have definitely lost an entire night: the sun is up, people are awake.

And I'm exhausted.

"Just after Hunter took you to the hospital, your loving father and Elissa Genevieve bribed a few mystics to help create mystic bombs—like the one she used in the Mother's Day Conflagration," Turk says, referencing the attack over twenty years ago that took hundreds of human lives. Initially, this was blamed on the mystics, and was the impetus for the city to drain their powers—to prevent them from hurting any more ordinary humans, to stop them from overthrowing us.

In fact, Elissa was the one responsible: she had offered up her energy to my father in return for a place on his staff, along with privileges no other mystic would receive—like keeping her powers—and, I'm sure, a good deal of money. She created the bomb that caused the Conflagration, betraying her own kind and killing hundreds of innocent people. She fooled people back then just like she fooled me into trusting her this summer. She told me she was a double agent, working for the rebels, and that she needed my help to gain access to the underground.

Well, it turned out that she did need my help. But she was no double agent. Patrick Benedict, another mystic who worked for my father, was the good one, actually trying to help the rebels from the inside. Elissa was working solely for my father, and she used me to help him wage war on the mystics. I still don't understand her motives entirely, why she would betray her people time and time again.

Now Benedict is dead and Elissa is . . . well, I'm not sure where she is.

"Why would any mystic help her?" I ask. "It makes no sense. She's pure evil."

Turk shrugs. "Some mystics and humans are exactly the same. It all comes down to money. They'd sell their own mother down the river for a couple of bucks." He laughs. "I'm not sure what that expression means, exactly. Where do people sell people down a river? *Which* river? Doesn't make sense. Aside from being offensive on so many levels."

I smile. Even amid all this destruction, Turk can find a way to lighten the mood.

We walk past Times Square, which has been bombed out completely—leaving a hauntingly quiet wasteland. Just a few weeks ago, I was here with my father as he dragged Hunter along the streets on a search for the entrance to the rebels' underground hideout. I remember thinking how seedy Times Square was, old theaters and faded marquees, buildings practically on top of each other, trash and dirt and rats everywhere.

But at least there was something.

Now there is nothing. Just a pit of blackness on a stretch of old land, bisected by filthy canals clogged with brick and plaster and scraps of metal. All I can smell is dust and dirt and death.

It almost doesn't seem real.

Then I see us.

Scattered across the ground are posters of me and Hunter—huge glossy pictures that read SUPPORT THE NEW MANHATTAN. The images make it seem like we're standing next to one another, even though we've never been photographed together. Hunter is dressed all in black, no smile, very serious. His dirty-blond hair, which is usually messy and just long enough that I can run my fingers through it, has been clipped and sheared close to his head on the sides. He looks older this way, more intense.

The picture of me is from a charity event last fall: I'm wearing a baby-doll dress the color of a ripe plum, with a soft-pink sash around the waist. My dark hair is up in an elegant twist, and I'm smiling like a little girl on her birthday. The image makes me feel uncomfortable, fake. I want to gather all the posters and tear them to shreds, but there are dozens and dozens of them.

So I just turn away.

"Anyway," Turk continues. "The good thing that has come from all this is that most mystics now refuse to be drained. Pretty much all of us have joined up with the rebel cause, and we can defend ourselves and fight."

"How can you support yourselves, though?" I ask. Most registered mystics were city workers or servants in the Aeries.

"It's tough," Turk says. "It's definitely tough. Some people have set up shops around the Depths. We still need to eat, need clothes. Most of the men are driving gondolas. We're surviving . . . barely."

"But you're surviving," I say. "That's what's important. Once everyone has had time to regenerate their powers, they'll be able to fight . . . and then we'll have a chance of winning. My parents and the Fosters can't compete with mystic energy. That's why they had mystics drained in the first place: they were scared of their power."

"Yeah, but . . ."

"But what?" I ask.

"It's not as simple as all that." Turk leads me over a stone bridge that looks like it could fall apart any second—there's a gaping hole in the center. "Money still rules the world."

We turn down another street and pass a row of mangled brownstones, the street overflowing with chunks of cement and broken stone.

I begin to recognize the area. It's near where the mystic Lyrica lives—which means we must be nearing the Magnificent Block. As we walk, Turk pulls out his TouchMe and sends a quick text.

"Was that to Hunter?" I ask as he stuffs it into his back pocket.

"No," he says. "Nosy."

"I need to see him, Turk. Now."

Turk shakes his head as if to say *C'est la vie!* "No can do. Not at the moment. But soon."

"This is ridiculous," I say, walking ahead of him. "Why is he hiding from me?"

"Aria, wait up," Turk says, but I'm already practically running—even though I have no idea where I'm going. It feels like everyone is keeping things from me. More nauseating posters of Hunter and me are plastered all over the place—on the sides of buildings, even on the pavement. I stare at myself smiling and holding on to Hunter. I look like an idiot.

We hurry up Broadway, scurrying underneath empty clothes-lines and deadened mystic spires. Homeless people with dirt-caked faces and ratty hair line the streets, their palms open for change. I pull my cloak tighter.

"Aria, come on!" Turk says. But I don't feel like talking to him.

The street opens up onto a major road where a series of bridges cover a wide, circular canal, and now I know exactly where I am.

The Magnificent Block.

Only instead of a towering wall, there's simply . . . water.

No mystic tenements peeking over a stone blockade. No stilted walkways leading to the center of the Block, because there is no center.

The entire place has been destroyed. This section of Manhattan—what used to be Central Park and then was inhabited by the mystics—has been completely obliterated. The individual waterways and drained areas where the buildings were have been wiped out, leaving a sad, watery mess.

"Sad," Turk says from behind me.

I turn to him, shocked. "What happened?"

He doesn't respond for a few minutes, his broad shoulders slumped, his tattoos washed out by the sun. Even his Mohawk looks droopy.

"When the mystics refused to be drained, your family bombed the Block," Turk says. "Hundreds were killed. Some escaped and are hiding out around the Depths. But here, your father wiped everything clean."

I stare out at the massive lake that has taken the Block's place.

Tenement ruins rise from the water, haunting reminders of what used to be.

"This is horrible," I say.

"I know," Turk replies. Gently he rests a hand on my shoulder. "Come on. Let's go."

We make our way to a gondola, and Turk pays the gondolier to let us use the boat alone, promising to return it when he comes back to pick up his bike.

"How does he know he can trust you?" I ask as Turk pilots us down a canal. The movement of the boat and the wind across my face feel nice, offering slight relief from the hot, sticky air.

"We go way back," Turk says. He's seated in the boat, facing me, one hand grasping the gondola's motorized steering wheel, the other arm resting on the side of the boat. "His name is Monroe. I've loaned him money in the past."

I'm silent for a moment, watching the ripples in the murky water. "Who are you?"

Turk raises his eyebrows. "What do you mean?"

"You just live a very wild life," I say.

"Because I lent a gondolier some cash?"

"And where does this money come from?" I ask, removing my hood. I quickly run my fingers through my hair.

"MYOB," Turk says, turning us left, onto a smaller canal. We pass a group of buildings that seem more or less intact, with gates that cover their doors, the bottom layers of stone stained green and brown from the water.

"What's that? Some sort of bank?"

Turk sticks out his tongue at me. "Yeah. The bank of mind your own beeswax." He laughs.

"Oh, that's mature," I say, but I can't help it. I'm laughing, too.

"This part of Manhattan used to be called Harlem back in the day," Turk says.

We've been riding the canals for the better part of an hour, and we're now in an area of broken-down brownstones, like jagged teeth rising from the waters.

"And why are we here?" I ask.

"You'll see." He pulls the boat up to a sagging dock and ties it to a rotting wooden post.

We leave the gondola and step onto the street. We're truly in the middle of nowhere. No people. No signs of life. Just abandoned buildings and the remains of old warehouses.

Turk guides me to a street corner—but it's the corner of nothing and nowhere. There isn't a building in sight that looks remotely livable. Just an empty lot that takes up nearly an entire city block, surrounded by a rusty chain-link fence. At least it's still morning and the sun is shining through the smog. Otherwise, this place would be absolutely frightening. There is a stillness that makes me feel like something awful is about to happen.

"Please don't tell me this is it," I say.

"This is it!" Turk says, smiling.

I scan the street for a loophole or a portal like the old subway entrance at the South Street Seaport. "Where?"

"Just relax," Turk says. Then he raises a hand in the air and points.

He closes his eyes, and his creamy skin begins to glow green. The color starts at the tips of his fingers and bleeds down, like wet paint, until his entire hand is pulsing with mystic energy.

And then there's a shift.

I feel it first—a sort of rumbling beneath my feet.

Glancing down at the cracked pavement, I see a tiny fissure. The jagged crack slips forward like a fish, lengthening until I can no longer see the end of it.

And then the pavement begins to part.

"Watch out," Turk says as the street beneath our feet expands.

We both move to the side as—in less than a second—a structure shoots up from the opening in the ground and a new wedge of building appears in the center of the empty lot.

"Wow," I say. "Impressive."

It's oddly reminiscent of the historic Flatiron Building, which I learned about at school. The triangle-shaped building is about five stories high and covered in red bricks. There are a few steps leading up to a red door that glistens in the sun.

Even though I saw a mystic home appear out of nowhere once before, when I visited Lyrica, watching such a large building pop into place like this still takes my breath away.

I step forward, but Turk blocks me with this arm. "There's a force field around this place," he says. "Anyone can leave, but only a person with mystic energy in his blood can pass through it to enter. If you take one more step, you'll be fried."

I stare at the building. "I don't see anything."

"Watch," Turk says.

Then he lets out a deep breath.

All of a sudden, there's an iridescent ripple in the air. It's the slightest movement—like the surface of the bubbles my brother and I used to play with when we were younger. "Hold on to me and you'll be fine," Turk says, grabbing my hand. I feel a tiny shock in my palm as our fingers intertwine. "I promise."

We pass through the force field. It's more intense than using a loophole—it feels a bit like when Hunter took me through a wall. There's a fierce squeezing sensation, like my entire body is being gripped in a vise, and then a quick release.

"See?" Turk says. "Now let's go inside. There are some people I want you to meet. And one is—"

"*You*," Shannon says before Turk can finish his sentence, striding down the steps and slapping me on the cheek.

"Ow!" I say. "What was that for?"

"*You* got Markus killed. I saw it all." Shannon glares at me, and I can see that she's exhausted: the circles under her bloodshot eyes are so dark it looks as though she was punched. Her red hair is unwashed, and she's wearing loose-fitting blue sweatpants and a T-shirt that's grimy with ash—the same clothes she was wearing when I saw her last. I bet she's been up all night, too.

I don't know how to respond, so I don't. I doubt that anything Shannon says could possibly make me feel worse.

"Shannon, calm down," Turk says.

"I will *not* calm down!" she says angrily. "I blame you for every death last night, Aria. So if you thought your training was tough before, it's only going to get tougher. The sooner you're in shape and able to defend yourself, the sooner the rest of our team isn't getting killed as collateral damage. And children. *Markus!*"

"You think I don't feel guilty?" I scream. "Because I do. I will have to live with this for the rest of my life."

There's an awkward silence as Shannon and I stare at each other.

"Sooo . . . ," Turk says. "Shannon, it appears you got my text and you're excited to see Aria." He turns to me. "Shannon is a little . . . touchy this morning. We're all on edge."

Shannon abruptly turns on her heels and heads back to the town house. "Well, come on," she says, motioning for us to follow her up the steps.

I step inside and the air is immediately cool—a welcome relief. A simple oval mirror hangs near the front door in a foyer with a mahogany-stained wood floor, bright yellow walls, and an old-looking chandelier with dozens of glittering crystals overhead. There's a pile of sneakers in front of a closet with a few hooded cloaks hanging inside.

The foyer leads into some sort of living room, but my view is blocked by three people standing in front of me with their arms crossed, a girl and two boys who look around my age. I assume they're mystics, because they're here, but there's no real way to tell. They look healthy and fit, which lets me know they haven't been drained of their powers, or at least, not recently.

The girl is standing between the boys. She's tiny, much shorter than I am, with a shock of blue hair. She's wearing cut-off jean shorts and a pink T-shirt with a picture of an elephant on it. The boys are both handsome in their own way. They're wearing shorts and dark shirts that expose their arms.

They do not seem particularly excited to see me.

"Aria," Turk says with forced enthusiasm, "meet your new friends!"

"Um, hello," I say.

No one responds.

I give a little wave. "Nice to meet you."

In response, the boy on the right extends his hand. At first, I think it's for a handshake.

But then a flaming ball of mystic energy bursts from his fingers, shooting rays of electric green up into the ceiling, and I realize I am wrong.

There's a harsh buzz and a flash of green, and a loud smash as the chandelier crashes to the floor and shatters.

This boy doesn't want to be my friend. He wants to kill me.

· VI ·

"Landon!" the tiny blue-haired girl says to the boy. "What are you trying to do, scare her to death?"

"Not a bad idea," Shannon mutters.

The kid with the glowing hand—Landon—gives a dramatic sigh. He shakes his wrist and the glowing stops, his fingers turning back to their natural tawny color. "Oops," he says dryly.

I can play this one of two ways: be upset, or kill him with kindness. I go for the latter.

"I've seen a lot worse than a broken chandelier," I say. "Happens to the best of us."

Landon raises his thick eyebrows. I can tell he thought I'd be scared.

Blue Hair shoots Landon a disgusted look. "You're like a little dog, marking your territory. It's stupid." Her voice is high-pitched, and she's a fast talker. She reminds me of a peppier version of Kiki. I like her immediately. "Grow up."

She turns to me and says, "Sorry. Not exactly the welcome you were expecting, I'm sure. I'm Ryah." She points to the guy on her left, who's been silent the entire time. "And this is Jarek."

"Hi, Jarek," I say, but I don't get any response.

Jarek is tall, even taller than Turk, with wide shoulders. From the thickness of his tan arms and the way his T-shirt clings to his body, I can tell that his chest, and probably the rest of him, is made entirely of hard muscle. His long brown hair is pulled back into a ponytail, and he has thin, arched eyebrows that suit his sculpted face. His nose is straight and wide, his jaw square. There's a soft slant to his eyes, and I wonder if he is of Asian descent. He's no Hunter, but he's still very handsome.

"He doesn't say much," Ryah says. She gives me a smile and I can see her dimples. "But his heart is in the right place. And this is Landon." She points to the boy who tried to scare me. "He's . . . sort of an ass."

"He's actually not that bad once you get to know him," Turk chimes in. "Right, Landon?"

Landon doesn't reply. His black hair is buzzed close to his scalp, and he's about half the size of Jarek—both in height and width. He looks strong and lithe, with a cocky expression and smooth coffee-colored skin. It's pretty clear he doesn't like me.

"Now clean this mess up." Turk motions to the fallen chandelier. "Stop destroying the place where you live. That's no way to treat your home."

Landon shakes his head and slopes down the hallway. I assume he's getting a broom.

"He's very moody," Ryah whispers. "It's not you. Well, it's a *little bit* you. . . ."

"Let's get you set up, Aria," Turk says, steering me around the broken chandelier. There's a staircase along the left wall leading to the next level, a living room with couches and a fireplace to the right. Straight ahead is a large, open kitchen.

The décor is homier than I expected from the outside, and the space looks lived-in—the couches are frayed, their cushions indented; the yellow paint is dirtied and scratched; the hardwood floors are scuffed. Cheap-looking multicolored area rugs dot the floor, and carvings like the ones back at the compound adorn the walls.

Turk turns to Shannon and Ryah. "Can you point Aria toward her room?"

Ryah says, "Absolutely, Turk," in a way that makes me wonder if she has a thing for him. She turns to me. "You're going to be staying with me, Aria! But first—a tour." She links her arm with mine. "We're going to be *great* friends. I can already tell."

I glance back at Shannon, who is miming sticking her finger down her throat and puking.

"Okay," I say to Ryah. "Let's go."

I'm surprised by how large the house is. Outside, I could see only the narrow façade; inside, the rebel hideout seems to have the depth of an entire city block.

Ryah takes me through the kitchen and the pantry, which is full of canned fruits and vegetables. The floor here is made up of large black and white tiles, and the gas range and cabinets seem fairly new and well polished.

"There's a walk-in freezer with meat and fish." Ryah points to a metal door. "We don't get a fresh supply now because of the war, so we have to use it sparingly. Are you vegetarian?"

"No," I say. "Are you?"

"Oh, *God,* no. I love me some beef." She leads me out of the kitchen, down a hallway with sunshine-yellow walls and black track lighting along the ceiling. "I try to eat my weight in protein. But since we have to be careful to leave enough meat for everyone, I just wind up eating a lot of peanut butter."

She stops outside an open door. "So this is the armory," she says, motioning for me to look inside. Stacked on shelves and against the wall are more weapons than I've seen in my life: rifles, pistols, ray guns, stacks and stacks of bullets and ammo clips.

There is also a fair amount of weaponry I don't recognize, which must be unique to the mystics: bronze pistols that look like miniature trumpets and gloves made of silver and gold twists of metal; black headgear with purple lenses over the eyeholes and vests covered with tiny lightbulbs; rows of knives in various shapes, their clear handles filled with deep-green liquid.

She points to the far wall, where a dozen or so axes are hanging. "Those are Damascus steel," she says. "And there are swords and knives—all mystic-enhanced."

This word is familiar: *Damascus.* I learned it from Hunter; it's steel that has been welded by the mystics, able to support unbelievable weight, nearly impossible to break. It is how the mystics helped build the Aeries, forming the foundation of its skyscrapers.

It strikes me as ironic and unfair that most mystics seem to live in old stone buildings instead of the ones they helped create.

"Come on," Ryah says, pressing a touchpad and sealing the armory door. I follow her down the hall to another doorway, which opens onto a flight of stairs leading to a basement. Old-looking brass sconces hang on the wall, burning with bits of green mystic energy and casting a luminescent glow. I hear grunting sounds and breaking glass.

"A shooting range," Ryah says before I can ask. "It's basically a training area." As she says that, the bottom of the stairs brightens with green light. "I'd show you, but whoever is practicing isn't expecting us, and you *don't* want to catch a mystic off guard when he's training."

"Who's down there?" I ask.

"Right now? I'm not sure." Ryah shrugs. "Mystics sort of come and go as they please around here. But this is where Jarek and Landon and I do our training."

I think of my sessions with Shannon back at the compound. How impossible my training was—and that didn't even involve actual *powers*.

"You need to train?" I ask.

"Of course, silly!" Ryah says, chuckling. "Why wouldn't we?"

I'm actually not sure. Turk and Hunter have always seemed so confident with their powers. It never struck me that they had to, well, practice.

"I'm only sixteen," Ryah says. "I came into my powers three years ago, so they're still new. There are some things you can do inherently, but most of it you have to learn."

"Who teaches you?" I ask, relieved to have someone who is willing to answer all my questions.

"Parents. Friends. Registered mystics never get to learn, really, because they're drained as soon as they hit puberty. I grew up underground, though, so I've had a few years of practice. My dad taught me a lot before he died."

"I'm sorry," I say. "I didn't know."

"How could you?" Ryah blinks. "We just met. He was killed in an attack about two years ago. My mom passed soon after him. . . . She got sick and just never got better. I've been on my own ever since."

It shocks me that someone who has lost both parents can be so cheerful.

"We're all sort of misfits," Ryah says. "That's why we're here. Landon's parents are still alive, actually. His mom is in a compound outside the city, taking care of his younger sister. His dad is somewhere, but I'm not sure where."

"What about Jarek?" I ask.

"He's an orphan, too," Ryah says. "Us kids with dead parents gotta stick together." She runs her fingers through her blue hair, then takes a step away from me, heading down the hall.

"To our right is an infirmary." She points to a large black door. "There's no nurse or anything, but there are bandages and pretty much anything you'd need if you got hurt."

Mystics heal incredibly fast, so I wonder how much this room gets used.

"Here's where we eat," Ryah says. The hallway opens up to a utilitarian dining area with four long tables and benches for dozens of people.

At the back of the dining room is a staircase. Ryah skips up, and I follow her more slowly. "This floor is the library," she says, leading me into a room that is simply crammed with books. Physical books are such a rarity that seeing so many of them in one place is a unique experience—even in the Aeries, only the biggest libraries and richest families have collections, and they don't nearly rival this.

The shelves are practically bursting. The books look old, some of them falling apart. A tall ladder is attached to a metal rod that runs around the top of the room, allowing access to the books near the ceiling.

"This is where most of the strategy meetings happen." Ryah motions to the long wooden conference table, its planks different lengths fitted together neatly with a glossy, varnished top.

"Those books . . . ," I say.

"I know. *Old,*" she says. "Most of them are from before the Aeries even existed. Crazy, huh?"

"Wow." I think back to my video calls with Hunter—he was always in a meeting room that had books. "Is Hunter here?"

Ryah shakes her head. "No. Sorry." She leads me out of the library to another staircase. "Girls' rooms are on the third floor, boys' are on the fourth."

"How long have you lived here?" I ask as we head upstairs.

"We don't exactly *live* here," Ryah says. "More like . . . we're staying here. There are a few concealed rebel hideouts in the city, and people move between them now that the underground has been blown out. This is our home base for the moment, but it could change at any time."

We reach the third floor and Ryah leads me into a room with three beds. It's nice but pretty minimal. "The color is called *rose,*" she says, referring to the light pink walls. "Do you like it? I painted it myself. Pretty fitting, right?"

"Right," I say.

She smiles broadly. "You know. Because your last name is Rose."

"Yes. It is."

"Funny," Ryah says, perching on one of the beds. "I didn't even know you were going to be living here when I chose this color. And some people don't believe in fate!" She laughs. "Life. It's really something, huh?"

"It sure is," I say, standing in the middle of the room. There are three of everything: beds, dressers, and desks, each with its own TouchMe. One of the desks has a clear vase with a few weeds sticking out the top, pretending to be more exotic flowers. I'm betting it's Ryah's.

"That one is yours," Ryah says, pointing to the bed by the window, with a purple comforter and matching pillows. She walks over to one of the desks and picks up a TouchMe. "And this is yours, too. Same number, new gadget."

She hands it to me and I scroll through the menus. None of my saved texts have been transferred over, or any of my family or friends' information. The new TouchMe is a clean slate, a fresh start.

"Great," I say. "Thanks."

"Turk made sure to enter us all as contacts, so you have our numbers—just in case." She goes over to the closet and opens it with the press of a touchpad. Then she starts flipping through the clothes. "We're not the same size, exactly, but you can borrow whatever clothes of mine you want. And Shannon's."

"Shannon is sleeping in here, too?" I ask.

Ryah nods and points to the bed by the door.

"Well, I'm not sure that Shannon would like me borrowing any of her clothes," I say. "We're not exactly friends."

"Don't mind her," Ryah says, waving her hand in the air. "Shannon likes to put on a bold front, but really she's a sweetheart. She's just tense. Everybody is."

We stand in silence for a moment. "The bathroom is down the hall," Ryah tells me. "And here's where we keep some emergency funds." She runs her hands along the wall next to the door. I can see a faint square outline; she grabs a knob that's painted the same color as the wall and pulls, revealing an alcove full of tiny leather pouches.

"Coins," she says.

I nod. In the Aeries, everything runs on credit, but here in the Depths, you need physical money to pay for things.

"You probably won't need them," Ryah says. "But just in case." She closes the hidden safe and turns back to me. "We're going to have dinner in a bit. Why don't you rest up, put on some fresh clothes, and come down? Really, take anything in the closet you want. We're family now."

She trots out of the bedroom, calling "Later!" over her shoulder.

Family.

What a loaded word.

After a catnap, I pull some underwear from a dresser and a navy-blue tank and pair of slim-fitting jeans from the closet. Then I find a pair of old sneakers that look as if they haven't been worn recently.

I go downstairs to the dining room and slide onto the bench at the table where Turk and Ryah are sitting. It was a pleasure to throw the red dress Thomas made me wear into the garbage, though it feels strange to be wearing borrowed clothing.

Jarek and Shannon are at the table, too. They seem to be in the middle of a conversation, but once I sit down, they stop talking and avert their eyes.

The rest of the dining room is empty, except for a group of men older than my father who are huddled together at another table, not paying us any attention. The walls are covered with some of the same mystic charms that were at the compound: beautiful hamsas with intricate beading, and other symbols I don't recognize, inlaid with colored stones and pieces of ceramic. There's also a silhouetted image of one of the female figures that were on the walls of the farmhouse, with nearly identical curls down her back: a Sister.

"Hope you don't mind that we aren't going to have a feast," Turk says. "A bunch of rebels who were pretty good cooks just left, so we'll have to make do."

There are empty plates and utensils in front of us; in the middle of the table is a pitcher of ice water. "That's fine," I say. "I'm not picky."

"Did you find everything okay?" Ryah asks.

"Yeah, thanks again for the tour," I say.

"No problem," Ryah says. "My pleasure."

"Is that my shirt?" Shannon asks, studying my tank top.

"Chill out, Shannon," Ryah says. "Seriously." She tilts her head and smiles at me. "Aria, I *love* that shirt on you."

Just as I'm about to ask what's for dinner, Landon rushes into the room balancing a circular platter on one hand. "Dinner is served," he says, coming around to the table and dropping a slab of raw meat onto everyone's plate. He saves mine for last and, I notice, gives me the smallest one.

I glance up at him and smile. "Thank you so much, Landon."

"Whatever," he says. "Bon appétit." Then he heads back into the kitchen with the empty tray.

I stare at the raw meat on my plate, remembering Thomas's barely cooked steak.

"Is something wrong?" Ryah asks in a concerned voice. "Do you like your meat well done?"

"I like it more done than this," I say.

Turk laughs as Ryah lets out a high-pitched giggle. "Obviously!" She slams the table with her fist.

"Just cook the meat already," Shannon snaps.

"I'll second that," Turk says.

Ryah holds out her hand and I hear the familiar buzz of mystic energy. Thin, delicate green rays shoot out from her fingertips, bathing the table with light; she curls her fingers into a ball and the rays blend together, becoming less intense, changing color from an electric green to something much softer.

The rays connect with the steak on my plate and I watch it cook right before my eyes, like a barbecue without smoke. A delicious charcoal-blackened-meat aroma fills the room.

"Poor Ryah," says Jarek. It's the first time I've heard him speak—he has the rich baritone of an opera singer. "She wanted to be powerful and mighty, but all she can do is act as a microwave oven."

"Oh, Jarek," Ryah says. "You know as well as I do that I could light your entire body on fire before you had time to blink." As she uncurls her fingers, the rays dissipate, and I am left with a perfectly cooked piece of meat. "Not that I would ever do that."

"Not to me," Jarek says as Ryah turns her energy to Shannon's plate. "But seriously, Aria, you should see this girl go."

"It's true," Ryah says matter-of-factly. "I'm incredibly powerful." She flexes her fingers. "There's danger in these hands."

Hunter once told me that a mystic's power is as individual as his personality. Some powers are incredibly tepid, like being able to heat tea with your fingertip. But Hunter can walk through walls and drop through ceilings. And Davida could take on the appearance of another person—a talent that is extraordinarily rare.

"What's your power?" I ask Jarek.

Before he can answer, Landon comes back into the dining room with a bowl of sautéed greens and a pair of tongs, taking a seat on the other side of Turk. "Well," he says to Jarek, "aren't you going to tell her?"

Shannon has a strange expression on her face, like she wants to say something but she's holding back.

"Tell me what?" I ask.

Before Jarek can show me his power, whatever it is, Landon holds out his right hand and presses his fingertips together: a green ray of mystic energy the size of his wrist shoots out of his hand and strikes the center of my water glass.

I think it's going to explode, but it doesn't.

The water instantly freezes, leaving the glass intact.

"I can solidify liquids," Landon says, puffing out his skinny chest. "And vice versa." He shoots another ray of energy at the glass, and the water reverts to liquid form. "Including lakes, rivers, rainwater . . . you name it. But poor Jarek here"—he says in a mocking tone—"can't do much of anything."

"Leave Jarek alone," Turk says. "Just be quiet and eat, Landon."

"Is that true?" I say, turning to Jarek.

He rolls his eyes. "Of course not." He reaches over and punches Landon's shoulder. "Landon is just being . . . Landon."

Ryah finishes cooking and takes her seat at the table. "Dig in, everyone!"

I cut into my meat—it's perfect. I don't know whether it's because of shock or exhaustion or the fact that I haven't had any food since yesterday, but it's the most delicious thing I've ever eaten.

"So what *is* your power, Jarek?" I ask.

Jarek swallows and pounds his chest, letting out a huge burp.

"Nice," Shannon says. "Really nice."

"I can . . . disappear," Jarek says cryptically.

I gasp. "You can turn invisible?"

Landon laughs. "Hardly. Jarek is just really good at camouflage."

"Oh," I say. "Well, that's . . . useful."

Turk gives me a sideways grin.

"Here," Jarek says. He stands up, and I'm quickly reminded how tall he is—well over six feet. He takes a deep breath, then closes his eyes. I wait for something to happen, but nothing does. "See," he says. "You can't see me."

I look to Ryah for help, but she's purposely not paying attention. "Actually, I can," I say.

Jarek opens his eyes. "That's just because you know I'm here. But if you didn't, then I would have blended into the wall."

"Oh. Well, I think that's . . . impressive," I say, focusing my attention on my dinner.

He shakes his head, sitting back down and rounding his shoulders. "No. It's not," he says with a hint of despair. "Not compared to what most people can do."

"Jarek is excellent at camouflaging himself," Turk chimes in. "I've even seen him blend right into a brick wall. It's just harder to demonstrate than most powers."

"Wars aren't won by hiding," Shannon says, putting down her fork. "They're won by fighting. No offense, Jarek."

"I know," Jarek says. "I agree with you. I wish I could do more, but . . . I can't."

"Sucks to be you," Landon mutters under his breath.

"Be nice," Ryah says.

"Hunter once told me about some guy who can hold his breath for hours," I say. "Michael? Marty? I don't remember. That sounds pretty cool, though."

"Marty Fuller," Landon says with a hefty sigh. "He's quite a piece of work."

"What do you mean?" I ask.

Landon snaps a finger at me. "Never mind. Whatever. So he can hold his breath for a few hours. This isn't Atlantis. It's Manhattan. We don't need to go swimming." Landon raises a fist to the ceiling and shakes it. "Damn you, Marty Fuller! I hope you choke on that water and die!"

"What's going on?" I whisper to Turk.

"Landon used to have a thing for Marty," Turk whispers back. "It didn't end well."

Across the table, Shannon lets out a tiny laugh. It catches me off guard; I've never seen Shannon smile or actually be nice to anyone, but surely she must have friends. It's just *me* she doesn't like. Which is a shame, because as Shannon smiles, her entire face glows.

"Hey." She looks at me, her smile disappearing. "What are you staring at?"

"Nothing," I say, taking another bite. "So what's your power, Shannon? Having no sense of compassion?"

At this, Landon lets out a loud *"Ohhhh."* He snaps, then adds, "She *went* there."

Shannon fixes her lips into a tight red line and clenches her jaw. "Aside from being an incredible fighter, Aria," she says, "something you are *not*, I'm a tracker."

"Trackers are very rare," Ryah chimes in. "Shannon is truly one of a kind." She thinks for a moment. "Actually, I had an aunt Nelly who was a tracker. It's still rare, though."

"What does a tracker do?" I ask.

Shannon brushes a few strands of hair out of her eyes. "You wouldn't understand."

"Try me," I say.

"Girl fight, girl fight!" Landon says loudly. "Somebody slap somebody!"

We all stare at him.

"What?" he says defensively, holding up his hands.

"Basically, I can hunt down a physical object by visualizing it," Shannon says. "It has to be something I've owned or touched. Something I know inside out."

I immediately think of my locket—the silvery heart hanging around my neck on a thin chain. It doesn't have magic anymore, but at one point it was the capsule where Benedict stored my memories of Hunter—the ones my parents tried to erase—for safekeeping.

"Give us an example," Turk suggests.

Shannon shrugs, but I can tell she's enjoying being the center of attention. "Let's say I wanted to find my mother. I would close my eyes and envision this brooch that she used to wear all the time. It was gorgeous: handcrafted, studded with pearls and pink diamonds. So I would focus on an image of that brooch, re-creating it in my mind." Shannon closes her eyes to demonstrate, and the room goes silent. "And then I would cast out a ray of energy that would function sort of like a homing device."

Shannon flicks back her wrist and then shoots her hand forward, almost like she's casting a fishing rod. There's a flash as five green rays jet out of her fingertips. They shoot up to the ceiling, and she squeezes her fingers together so that they're touching. The rays braid together into one thicker ray pulsing with electric energy. Then she turns her hand over so her palm is facing the ceiling. The ray of energy coils like a corkscrew.

"Whoa," says Jarek. "I've never seen you do that before."

She twists her hand in the air and the ray begins to shrink, growing brighter but thinner until it's practically invisible, so thin it could fit through the eye of a needle.

Shannon opens her eyes. "I would then follow this line of energy, and it would lead me to the brooch."

The entire group is still, watching her. "Does it work with

people?" I ask. "Imagine your mom instead of the brooch—would your energy lead you to her?"

"Not so much," Shannon says. "People move around too much, and they're nearly impossible to track without using a much stronger sort of energy that I don't possess. Besides"—she shakes out her hand and the ray disappears—"my mother is dead. So tracking her wouldn't do me much good."

Another orphan, I think.

"Aria, you haven't asked *me* what *my* power is," Turk says, breaking the silence.

"Sorry, Turk," I say. "What's your power?"

He raises an eyebrow. "Aside from being hot?" he asks through a mouthful of steak. "I have a very good sense of modesty."

Landon snorts water out his nose, onto his pants.

"Gross," Ryah says.

"It's just water." Landon pats his crotch with a napkin. "Chill."

The tension broken, the conversation switches to the rebellion. Everyone catches Shannon up on the gossip, as she's been out of the loop training me—something she doesn't hesitate to complain about.

"Where's Hunter?" I ask Turk while Ryah is telling some story about the Fosters to Jarek, Landon, and Shannon. "Why isn't he here?"

Turk swipes his hand over his Mohawk and fiddles with one of the silver hoops in his ears. "Hunter is off doing VIP shit," he says. "But he'll be here tomorrow. Bright and early. Don't you worry, Aria."

"Hunter's coming tomorrow?" Shannon asks, suddenly alert.

"Indeed," Turk says.

I'm confused. Surely Hunter must know about what happened at the compound. How Turk saved me. Where I am at this exact moment.

So why isn't he here?

· VII ·

I wake up the next morning to the sharp scent of coffee and a whole lot of noise.

I glance at the clock. Is it really noon? I stretch my arms over my head, looking from side to side—both Shannon's and Ryah's beds are perfectly made. They must have been up for hours.

I slip out of bed and remind myself that this is a new day. The tragedy of Markus and the compound, my cruel interaction with Thomas, my introduction to the rebel hideout—all that is behind me now.

Today I will see Hunter. And I will find out what exactly what is going on between us.

I pull back the curtains, thankful for the sun that filters into the bedroom. There's a commotion downstairs: voices, what sounds like dozens of people. I quickly throw on the jeans from yesterday and a yellow shirt that fits me snugly. I pull back my hair with a tie I find on Ryah's desk, then open the bedroom door.

"Halt!" A mystic I don't recognize is positioned at the top of the staircase. He's dressed in a skintight black uniform with a wide green eye on the chest.

"What do you mean, 'halt'?" I say.

The mystic broadens his chest. "You're not allowed to move until Hunter is secure."

"I'm his girlfriend," I say.

"Doesn't matter." The mystic holds out his hand, flexing his fingers as though he's about to attack. "Stay back."

"It should only take a few minutes," Ryah says, coming out of the bathroom.

"Oh. You're stuck up here, too?"

"Yep," Ryah says. She's wearing a pair of tan overalls that have paint splattered all over them—you can barely see the original color underneath the splotches of green and orange. Her hair seems especially blue today, gelled and spiked. "My need to pee apparently coincided with Hunter's arrival." She sighs. "Oh well. At least I got to do my hair."

"It's very pointy," I say.

"Thank you," she says sweetly. She turns to the guard. "You know, Adam, you don't have to be so fierce all the time. Lighten up."

He doesn't move a muscle. "We're in the middle of a war, Ryah. There's nothing to be light about."

"War, schmore," Ryah says, reminding me more and more of Kiki every second. "It's Aria's first full day here, and she hasn't seen Hunter in what—three weeks or so?" Ryah turns to me, and I nod. *Three weeks,* she repeats. "So be nice."

The guard's face softens. "Let me see if he's ready yet." He spins around and heads down the stairs.

"You know him?" I say to Ryah.

She furrows her forehead. "Not intimately, if that's what you're implying."

"No, I wasn't—"

"Our parents are friends. He's harmless. All these kids think they're hotshots now that they're in uniform. Anyway, I'm sure Hunter is in the library by now. That's where they have their meetings."

I *knew* that library looked familiar.

"Did you sleep well?" Ryah asks, seeming genuinely concerned. "You were out like a light!"

"Yeah . . . I was tired."

"Understandable." Ryah claps her hands together. "I know this place isn't the same as home, but since your home is, well . . . with your parents, and they're awful, I hope you're happy here." Her smile turns into a frown. "I didn't mean to say that about your parents. I mean, they *are* awful, but I didn't mean—" She bites her bottom lip. "Yeesh. I keep digging the hole deeper and deeper."

"It's fine," I say, laughing genuinely—the first real laugh I've had in I can't remember how long. "They are pretty bad."

"The worst," Ryah agrees.

There are footsteps as the guard—Adam—reaches the top of the stairs and waves us forward. "Hunter will see you now."

I expect him to be cold as I enter the library alone. Where was he when Thomas almost transformed me into a walking zombie? The Hunter I fell in love with would have been at my side the moment he heard something had happened, would have protected me or died trying.

Not that I want him to die, of course.

I shake the thought from my head. That's selfish. And ridiculous. Still, I'm upset that I've been in the Depths and he obviously knows, and he hasn't come to see me or even sent me a message on my TouchMe. And I'm still pissed about the videos and the posters.

The library looks different with so many people in it. Smaller.

Hunter is seated at the head of the conference table, with four large bodyguards behind him, two on either side. Positioned like this, he reminds me of my father, though these bodyguards are nothing like Stiggson and Klartino, my father's thick-necked, red-faced goons. They're taller and leaner, and they can't be older than twenty.

Hunter still has the same rugged beauty that took my breath away the first time I saw him. The same tousled dirty-blond hair, the same slightly crooked nose, light-blond stubble, and piercing cerulean eyes.

He's leaner, that's for sure; he must weigh ten pounds less than he did a month ago, and he was thin then. But he's so handsome it's unbelievable. It's almost unreal that he's mine. That he's in love with me.

He *is* still in love with me, right?

"Aria!" Hunter shoots up from his seat and rushes toward me.

I suddenly feel awkward, like I'm on display. Everyone is watching our reunion: Hunter's bodyguards, the inner circle of mystics—men nearly twice his age with mustaches and beards and cropped hair and hardened faces—Shannon, who's off to the side, glaring at me, and Turk, whose shiny Mohawk is standing at full attention, his colorful tattoos and ripped arms exposed in a sleeve-less gray tank.

I wish this were a private thing.

Hunter pulls me tightly into his arms. He smells like cinna-mon and smoke. "I'm sorry about all this," he says in a low voice. "Everyone is just being very careful after what happened to my mom." He leans back slightly and looks into my eyes. "I don't get much alone time."

"I can see that."

"I'm so happy to see you." He kisses me, but before I can even register the taste and feel of his lips on mine, they're gone. "Are you okay? I heard what happened with Thomas. That bastard." He lets go of my arms, looking furious. "I'm going to make sure he never hurts you again. I promise."

I want to believe him. Really, I do. But there's something else, something he's not telling me.

"Don't make promises you can't keep," I say.

Deep creases form along his forehead. "What's that supposed to mean?"

"It means I could have *died*, Hunter. How can you possibly promise to keep me safe when you don't even see me? If it weren't for Turk—"

"Who do you think *sent* Turk?" Hunter says. His face colors, and I can tell he's getting angry. "I want to be with you all the time, Aria. Every second of every day. But I have people counting on me, thousands of them. And until they're safe, I can't rest."

He steps away from me and addresses the entire room. "Mystics: we must do whatever we can to depose the people in the Aeries from their power so that everyone can be free. This is not news, but it must be repeated—especially in light of Aria's kidnapping. We will do anything it takes to defeat the Aeries."

For some reason, Thomas's voice rings in my ears: *People outside . . . they're watching us. If the rebels win . . . New York will be taken over. We'll be slaves to other people's desires.*

"Anything?" I ask.

Hunter smiles at me, and in spite of my anger, I smile back. "Right," he says. "We all know that there can be no peace while those in the Aeries exploit the mystics." The men around Hunter nod, and Hunter sweeps an arm toward them. "Aria, these are the men who were helping my mother run her campaign. They've chosen me to be the face of the rebellion because I believe that anything less than equal rights and freedom for mystics is unacceptable."

A few of the men make sounds of agreement, and Hunter continues. "There are very specific keys to warfare," he says to me. "Tactics that we have been employing and will continue to employ until the Aeries has no choice but to submit. Your family and the Fosters and their allies are our opponents, and we will decimate them." He turns to include the men of his inner circle. "We will wipe out the Aeries completely and rebuild, from the ground up—a new Manhattan."

There's a round of applause from everyone except me. "Hunter, don't you think you're being a little . . . extreme?" I ask.

He shifts his attention back to me. "Extreme? Your father is extreme, Aria. He has no respect for life, human or mystic. He worships nothing except money and power. He is a weed that is strangling our entire society."

"I know my father is a bad man," I say, "but there are many people in the Aeries who don't agree with him. Or who agree with him because they don't know any better. I used to be that way before I met you. Not everyone is so lucky. Shouldn't they be given the benefit of the doubt?"

I wait for Hunter to reply. Where is the sensitive, sweet guy who wrote me love letters and signed them as Romeo?

Instead of answering me, he motions to his men. "There are some plans I have to go over," he says. "I'll have to see you later."

"I'm not finished, Hunter." I lead him to a corner of the room. "There's a lot more we have to talk about."

He sighs and rubs his forehead. "Later, Aria—"

"What's with the ads?" I blurt out. "The videos. I saw them, Hunter. Thomas played them for me."

Hunter grows ten years younger in a second. He looks like a child who was just caught breaking one of his parents' rules.

"Why are you using clips of me for your campaign? That stuff is private."

"They need something to believe in, Aria," he says. "So I gave them something. *Us.*" He takes my hands in his; they feel like a stranger's. "Together we can convince the people here in the Depths that we can offer something different. Something better."

"But you should have told me. You should have asked—"

"I did what I thought was best," Hunter says. "I'm sorry if I hurt you." He pauses, studying me. "I have work to do." He kisses me on the forehead. "We'll talk more later. I promise."

Then he goes back to his men.

Did Hunter just . . . dismiss me?

Shannon walks past me and stops before leaving the room. She stares at my—*her*—shirt. "I honestly don't remember telling you that you could borrow my clothes."

"What else am I supposed to wear?" I ask. "Besides, don't you have bigger concerns?"

Shannon blinks. "Like what?"

"Like this war," I say.

"What do *you* know about *my* concerns?" Shannon asks me. "Let's get one thing straight, Aria: you don't belong here. You're not one of us—no matter what Hunter thinks."

"So now you don't even trust Hunter?" I ask.

"I trust him about most things, but not everything. He's not *perfect*." She looks me up and down, then rolls her eyes. "After all, he's dating you."

Before I can respond, Turk makes a beeline for me and grabs my arm. "Come on," he says, "let's go to the kitchen and get you something to eat. Breakfast is the meal of champions and all that."

Shannon smirks and tosses back her hair. "I think there's some leftover humble pie, Aria. I wouldn't eat too much of it, though. You're practically popping out of that shirt as it is." Then she exits the room.

Stay calm, I tell myself. *Don't go after her and start a fight.*

"Can you get me away from that girl?" I ask Turk. "Fast?"

He bows. "Aria Rose?" he says with a mischievous twinkle in his eye. "I am at your service."

· VIII ·

Turk and I are soaring down the Broadway canal on his mystic-powered motorcycle, cruising through the Depths just above the surface of the dimpled water.

We left the hideout without telling anyone, not even Hunter, where we're going. Though Hunter's so preoccupied with his followers and his plans that I doubt he'll even notice we're gone.

"You're a good driver," I say. Turk picked his bike up from the woman he left it with yesterday, and I'm surprised by how comfortable I am on it. "Normally, I'd be scared going so fast . . . but I'm not with you."

Turk weaves around gondolas and larger water taxis, which are big and inexpensive enough for dozens of people to use at once. The wind whips the back of my hair, and the wet, salty smell of the canals fills my nostrils. The bike itself hovers a few inches over the water, and we're going so fast it barely feels like we're moving.

"I used to race this thing when I was younger," Turk says loudly enough that I can hear him over the wind. "I earned a lot of cash that way."

"Really? You never mentioned it."

"I don't give away all my secrets at once," Turk says. "If I'd told you that I was a super-crazy driver and my bike was powered by mystic energy and could actually *fly* the second you met me, you would have been all, 'Fly, Turk, fly!' and I don't like to take instructions." We veer off the main canal and head east, farther downtown. "I like to give them."

"Okay," I say, laughing. "Where are you taking me?"

Turk's legs grip the bike tightly behind me as we duck under a stone bridge. Water sprays up and soaks the edges of the jeans I borrowed from Shannon. "I figure if we're gonna come down here, we might as well do some good," he says.

"Meaning . . ."

"Chill, Aria. You'll see. Patience is a virtue, you know?"

"So I hear. You know, you never did say what your power is at dinner last night."

"Ah," Turk says. "That."

"Is it a secret?" I ask.

"No," he says. "If you must know, I'm a healer."

"I thought all mystics could use their powers to heal people."

"Some more than others," Turk says. "And I happen to have that gift. So if you ever get injured—I'm your man."

He doesn't say more than this, which surprises me. I don't press him, though—instead, while we ride, I tell Turk about Frieda and what she said about finding Davida's heart. It's been on my mind ever since the fire. Were her words merely senile ramblings, or did they have any merit? And did she survive the raid?

"I'm really not sure," Turk says, making a few quick turns past a row of dinged-up brownstones. "Though that's definitely intense."

We rush past an area that used to be known as Rockefeller Center, now a blown-out circle of rubble and waste, and find ourselves approaching a square of land that looks like a miniature island. It's surrounded by thin canals and has dinky metal docks that jut out into the brown water and bob up and down, loose in their cement foundations. Twenty or so pointy white tents are scattered around the area. Just beyond the square is a JumboTron flashing commercial advertisements and images of Hunter and me for all the Depths to view.

"Madison Square Park," Turk says, spreading out his arms. His light gray tank contrasts nicely with his dark jeans. His Mohawk hasn't flattened at all from the ride. I take off my helmet; unfortunately, my hair is practically plastered to my head. I try brushing it back with my fingers, but it ends up sticking out in weird places. I wish I had a hat.

There's activity all around us: people rushing between tents and speaking in hurried voices, pushing open the flaps and carrying IV drips, bottles of water, and trays of what look like medical instruments.

"This is sort of a mass triage center," Turk says. "A place the poor can go to receive medical attention. Pretty much all the hospitals in the Depths were bombed out by your parents and the Fosters, so these makeshift places are all that's left." Turk takes off his sunglasses and stuffs them into one of his pockets. "There are mystics and nonmystics mixed together here. A bipartisan hospital, if you will.

"Come on." Turk slings his arm around me and leads me into the middle of the chaos. A woman around my mother's age spots us almost immediately. "Turk!" Her arms are overflowing with towels and bandages. "I'd give you a hug but my arms are full."

"Let me help you with those, Nancy." Turk skips over to the woman and grabs the bandages from her. "Where are you heading?"

"That way," she says, nodding toward one of the tents. "And fast. We've got a bleeder."

She and Turk rush off, and I do my best to keep up with them. Turk glances over his shoulder and smiles at me. "Move it, slowpoke!"

I pick up my pace and follow them into the tent. I'm shocked by what I see:

Rows and rows of flimsy metal cots are stacked up like bunk beds, with barely an inch of space between them. There's a baby crying somewhere, though I don't see any children, and the entire tent is burning hot—there are only two fans to cool at least a hundred people.

"This way," Nancy says, leading us down the middle of the tent. Other women—nurses?—seem to be coming and going as well, bringing food and drinks and medical supplies to the people in the beds. They wear white masks over their mouths, latex gloves on their hands, and white caps covering their heads.

"To help stop the transfer of diseases," Nancy says, catching me staring. "You're Aria Rose, aren't you?"

I nod. "Nice to meet you."

"And you." Nancy leads us all the way to the back of the tent and squeezes herself between two beds. On the bottom bunk is a man in his late twenties. He has a buzz cut, and his face is drawn in pain.

I glance down and see a wedge of steel sticking out of the middle of his thigh. Blood is seeping from the wound, staining the white sheets red.

Nancy hands me the towels. "This is going to be painful, young man," she says, "but it will save your life."

He nods at her, a world of hurt in his eyes.

"Poor thing," Nancy says to Turk. "There was an explosion in a building on the Lower East Side, near the river. Some of the shrapnel got him." She grips a clamp in one of her gloved hands, fastens it around the jagged piece of steel, and pulls.

I close my eyes.

The man lets out an excruciating scream.

I open my eyes and watch as Nancy struggles with the metal. The piece of steel won't come out, and she's forced to twist it almost ninety degrees before there's a squishing sound and the metal pops out of the man's leg and into her palm.

Immediately, the blood begins to flow like a river.

"Quick," Nancy says to me. "A towel."

I press one of the white towels to the man's wound. It sops up the blood like a sponge, but he doesn't stop bleeding. "What should I do?" I say to Nancy, terrified. "The blood . . . there's too much. . . ."

"Aria, stand back," Turk says. He holds out his hand and locks his fingers; I watch the tiniest speck of green form in the center of his palm and spiral out until his entire hand is radiating mystic energy.

Pulling back the soaked towel, Turk presses his hand to the man's wound. The blood begins to bubble and coalesce, hardening into a clump of reddish-brown. The man's eyes open in shock as he watches his wound heal before his very eyes.

Turk removes his hand and shakes it, like he just put down a heavy weight. The energy dissipates and his hand returns to its normal olive color. "Nancy, do you have any water?"

She bends down and pulls a bowl from underneath the bed. I hand Turk a clean towel; he dips it into the water, then washes the dried blood from the man's thigh. Beneath it, the wound has healed completely—the skin is pink and fresh. There isn't even a scar.

"Thank you," whispers the man, who still seems weak, maybe from loss of blood.

"You're welcome," Turk says, wiping his hands clean. "All in a day's work."

"Now you get some rest," Nancy tells the man, leading us back into the aisle. "I'm so glad you're here, Turk. If you weren't, well . . . I don't think he would have been so lucky."

"With a nurse like you?" Turk says to Nancy, giving her a kiss on the cheek. "He would have been fine."

I'm surprised by this tender side of Turk. He truly is gifted at healing, and at putting those around him at ease. It's a quality I wish I had myself. I tend to alienate people, it seems.

"Who else needs help?" Turk says, curling his fingers. "The doctor is in the house." He follows Nancy as she motions to another patient. "Aria," he says to me. "Be useful."

Then he hurries down a row of beds.

Be useful. Sure. I can be useful.

I spot a young woman wearing a white nurse's cap and tap her on the shoulder. She spins around. "Emily, I need those syringes an—"

She cuts off as she realizes that I'm not Emily.

"Oh!" she says. "You're . . . you're . . ."

"Aria," I say.

"Of course!" She blushes. "I'm Kerry. I just, I didn't expect to see you here, and Emily, well, she hasn't been much of a help . . . not that that's any of your concern. Thank you for visiting the square." She glances behind me. "Is Hunter Brooks here with you?"

"No," I say. "Just me. What can I do?"

The girl looks confused. "You've helped so much already. You and Hunter, you're so inspiring."

I *really* don't deserve her compliments. "There must be something I can do," I say, feeling uncomfortable.

Kerry looks around. "There," she says, gesturing to a bed. "I was going to bring her one of these." She extends the tray she's holding; it's full of plastic cups of water. "But I'm sure she would appreciate it more coming from you."

I take one of the cups and walk over to the bed, where a sickly-looking bald girl is resting on a dirty white sheet. Her eyes have a milky film over them, and she's frail—as skinny as a toothpick. I can't tell if she's mystic or human.

"Hello," I say. "Would you like some water?"

The girl turns her head. "Yes, please."

"You should probably sit up so you don't spill."

The girl strains her neck, but she doesn't move. She's too weak.

With my free hand, I reach behind her head and gently guide her to a seated position. "Thank you," she says to me.

"You're welcome." I hand her the water. "Drink up."

She takes the cup. "You're Aria Rose," she says.

"I am. What's your name?"

"Yolie."

"That's pretty," I say.

"I've seen you on TV," Yolie says to me. She looks sicker than any drained mystic I've ever seen. I wonder what happened to her.

"Oh?"

"Your boyfriend is *mag*," she says, giving me the slightest hint of a smile.

I laugh at her use of Aeries slang. "You think?"

"That's what my older sister, Lorda, says," Yolie says.

"Where is Lorda?" I ask.

Yolie sits still. "I don't know," she says. She cranes her neck, looking around the tent. "Maybe here."

My heart goes out to this poor little girl.

"I'm cold," Yolie says. Her twiggy arms are covered with goose pimples, and her teeth have begun to chatter.

"Let me get you a blanket," I say. "I'll be right back."

I leave her bedside and walk back to the main aisle. Across the tent, there's a flash of green energy. Turk must be working his healing magic. If only there were something he could do for Yolie . . .

"Kerry," I say, rushing up to a nurse. "I think Yolie is—"

The nurse turns around and makes a face at me. "I'm not Kerry."

"I can see that," I say, taken aback. This girl has a tense face and coarse skin; her cheeks look like they've been roughened with sandpaper. "Well, um, Kerry told me to give that little girl Yolie some water, and she's cold. She needs a blanket."

"Look around, *Aria Rose*." The girl says my name as though

it's poisonous. "Do you see a hiding place for blankets? No. That's because we don't have any."

"You don't have any blankets?" I ask, shocked.

The girl clucks her tongue. "You come off a lot more eloquent on TV."

"Why don't you have blankets?" I ask.

"Ask your boyfriend," she says, walking away. "We're missing a lot of stuff."

"Genna isn't exactly the sugariest cookie in the batch," says Kerry, coming up beside me. "Sorry."

"That's okay," I say. "She doesn't like me."

"It's not that," Kerry says, offering me a look of sympathy. "It's just . . . well, war does funny things to people."

"I understand," I say. "But that's not important right now. It's Yolie. She's cold, and—"

"I just gave her something to help her sleep. Do you mind?" She holds out the tray, still half filled with cups of water. "Just for a moment. My arms are getting tired."

"Of course," I say. "What happened to Yolie? And where is her sister?"

Kerry considers my question. "Let's walk and talk."

"Yolie's family used to live in the Magnificent Block," Kerry tells me as she leads me down a row of beds. "They were registered mystics." I stop at each bunk, handing cups of water to injured men and women who are so appreciative, some of them even start weeping. "Aria Rose," they say. "Our savior. Where's Hunter? The two of you . . . so inspiring."

"When it was destroyed," Kerry says, "her parents were killed. She and her sister hid out there as long as they could with some other kids, but eventually they were hungry enough that they started stealing. A storekeeper caught them. She realized how thin and sickly they were and brought them here."

"But she still looks ill."

"She has dysentery," Kerry says. "We've been trying to treat her, but it's not working. If we had better medicine, maybe . . ."

"And her sister?"

Kerry frowns. "Dead. Nobody's had the heart to tell her yet."

I take a deep breath, trying to steady my hand as I give a young man a glass of water.

"Aria Rose," he says in a throaty whisper. "You're more beautiful than I could have imagined."

"This is Steve," Kerry says. "He's the Don Juan of tent four. A real lothario." She giggles and glances back at the young man. His face is practically burned off—one of his eyes is missing, and the skin around his nose and mouth is an angry red, overtaken by scar tissue.

"Well, thank you, Steve," I say. The corner of his lip twitches. I think he's trying to smile.

"What happened to him?" I ask once we've left his bed.

"He's a human injured by mystic fire," Kerry says. "The rebels set fire to a building in the Aeries that housed a number of Foster supporters." She pauses. "Unfortunately, because the power grid is out and they couldn't ascend to the Aeries in a POD, they ignited the building from its foundation. Steve's father had a shop on the lower level, and, well . . ."

"That's terrible!" I say, enraged. Since the Point of Descent elevators are the only way to travel between the Aeries and the Depths, extinguishing a building from the bottom up means death for everyone inside. No escape. "That is so irresponsible of the rebels."

Kerry nods. "There are others here, too . . . more than you'd think. Blasted with stray mystic energy. Collateral damage," she says. "No one intends to hurt them, but they get hurt anyway. That's what war does."

Outside, I take a seat on an empty wooden bench. I look around the square, overwhelmed by the idea that inside each of these tents are dozens of people just like Steve and Yolie—innocent casualties of war. People who did nothing wrong, who are losing their lives so that my parents and the Fosters and Hunter and the rebels can continue playing their dangerous killing games.

People stare at me as I sit. Most are nurses traveling from tent to tent, but there are a few mystics, too. Many of them recognize me and are gracious and introduce themselves. But some of them try to burn me with their eyes and make me feel invisible. Worse than invisible—evil.

"Monster!" a girl my own age screams at me. Her mother has to drag her away. "Selfish monster!"

It's clear that to some, I am the face of this war.

I stand up. There's only so much hostility I can take. The square is still bustling, and the air is threateningly hot, the sun beating down on us. There's a loud hum like a swarm of bees coming from one of the tents, and I head toward it, intrigued.

Outside the tent, men, women, and children are waiting in four lines. At the front of each line is a square metal stool and a nurse standing beside it with a buzzing electric razor.

People are getting their heads shaved.

"Excuse me," I say to a man in front of me. He's wearing tattered pants and a stained brown shirt. "What is this for?"

He doesn't even turn back to look at me. "Vermin," he says.

"Excuse me?"

"Rats. Everywhere." He turns, finally making eye contact. If he recognizes me, he doesn't let on. "And mice. And fleas. And lice. The mystic energy used to help keep 'em in check. But now the Depths are full of 'em. Better to shave your head so they don't have a place to nest."

Gross. My skin crawls.

"Yo!" shouts someone behind me. I turn around: it's Turk. "Did you see me back there?" He stretches out his arms. "I was like a healing ninja! I cast some *spells* on that shit."

"You're a weirdo," I say.

He sticks out his tongue. "Takes one to know one. Ready to go?"

"No." I move up in the line.

"Next!" one of the nurses shouts.

Turk widens his eyes. "Aria Rose. You're not waiting in line to have your head shaved, are you?"

I shrug. "What would you have to say about it if I were?"

Turk thinks for a moment. "I'd say you have some serious cojones. And that Hunter is going to *fliiiiip* when he sees you."

"Yeah, well, who knows when that will even be?" I'm practically at the front of the line.

Turk quirks an eyebrow. "Trouble in paradise?"

I don't bother answering him, because the nurse has shouted, "Next!" I take a seat on the stool, feeling the weight of my hair spilling onto my shoulders.

For a split second, I wonder what Hunter will say when he sees me, what it will feel like when the girl presses the razor to my scalp. Then I blink and say, "Take it all off."

She gulps. "Aria Rose? I don't think—"

"Please." I stare into her eyes. "All of it."

"If you say so," she says softly. She cleans the razor and mutters, "None of my friends are going to believe this."

I make two fists. I'm ready for something new.

"Hey!" someone says to my left. I turn my head and see Turk cutting in front of an older guy and stealing his spot on the stool next to me. "What's the rush?" Turk says, shooing him away. "It's just a haircut."

"What are you doing?" I ask, staring at his beautifully crafted Mohawk, his identifying feature. "Are you insane?"

"I'm not going to let you do this alone," Turk says. "It's that simple." He reaches out his hand, and I grab it. "Oh God," he says out loud. "What in the Aeries am I doing?"

"Close your eyes," I say. "It's just hair. It'll grow back."

"Yeah, yeah," Turk says, turning to the nurse at his side. "Just do it."

Turk looks totally different. Younger. Sweeter. You couldn't help but stare at his hair when you first met him—the sharp black spikes, the intense, hard edge the Mohawk gave him.

But now he doesn't look all that intimidating. Well, minus the piercings and the multicolored tattoos.

He looks good.

"It feels funny," I say, rubbing my hands over the soft fuzz covering my scalp. My head tingles—it feels pounds lighter without the hair, almost like a balloon full of helium that could pop off and drift away at any moment.

"I want you to remember that I did this for you," Turk says glumly. "Remember for the rest of your life."

Someone passes me a tiny wooden hand mirror.

I stare at my reflection. It's my face, only different. The brown locks are gone, and the buzz cut accentuates the shape of my skull—my cranium is pointer than I would have guessed, egg-shaped; my ears are more pronounced without my hair to hide them, my brown eyes more piercing, my dark eyebrows more severe. Everything is exaggerated. I don't look like the privileged daughter of one of the richest men in the Aeries. I look like a girl who has seen hard times.

I stand up and immediately the crowd of people waiting in line erupts into applause. I feel myself go red with embarrassment.

"Aria! Aria!" People are chanting, people who have just gotten their heads shaved, people who haven't, men, women, and kids, mystics and nonmystics. Even some of the nurses are clapping and laughing.

I feel like one of them. Accepted.

Just then, a new image flashes on the JumboTron just outside the square.

It's Kyle. My brother.

I haven't seen him since the night my father invaded the underground. He's wearing a navy suit and a tie, his hair parted neatly on one side. He stands behind a podium making a statement to the press, seeming much older than his twenty-one years. My mother and father are behind him, both looking proud. Seeing them is like an electric shock to my entire body: rage and fear mingle inside me, together with flashes of other emotions from when I was much younger—love, maybe.

"We will not rest until every mystic is found and destroyed," Kyle announces. People around me begin to hiss and boo, cursing at the screen. My brother looks up from his notes and stares directly into the camera. "And I am holding myself personally responsible for making sure that the Aeries are resurrected to their proper heights. The *true* Rose family has never disappointed this city, and we will continue to see it prosper and prevail."

Kyle. A fresh face for a troubled time. This must be a publicity stunt. My father has never trusted Kyle with much responsibility before now. No doubt Johnny Rose is still pulling the strings behind the scenes.

As Kyle continues to speak, I realize that he's actually quite poised. Passionate. Charming, even. I wonder if he's still a Stic junkie or if my father made him kick the habit.

Behind him, my mother purses her painted lips. She's wearing a white blouse with a black pencil skirt, her hair dyed blond and blown out so that it falls past her shoulders. She looks so put together. So elegant. I highly doubt that anyone would guess she had me handcuffed to my own bed, made me a prisoner in my own apartment.

"Your brother is such an ass," Turk says. "No offense."

"I know. None taken."

I scan the screen and see another familiar face: Elissa Genevieve. The supposedly reformed mystic who works in my father's office, who befriended me only to betray me.

She's at the edge of the screen, wearing a cream-colored suit with a soft-pink blouse underneath. Her blond curls are pinned back, and she has an easy smile on her face—pretending to be nice when she is anything but. Seeing her reminds me of how I trusted her, how she stood up for me when Patrick Benedict and my father were giving me a hard time.

I thought she was my ally.

But it was all an act. Some sort of sick game. Benedict was the one looking out for me—I just didn't know it then. Elissa was two-timing me, pretending to be on my side when really she was my father's secret weapon. I think about how I brought her along with me and Turk the night my parents abducted Hunter, how she shot Turk and stole the passkey to the underground, betraying her own kind to my father.

Pretty much everyone I hate most is being displayed on this screen. I look away.

Turk sees her, too, and lets out a sharp hiss. "I *hate* that woman," he says. "She's a vulture. A traitor. A mystic who used her own energy to make the bomb that caused the Conflagration—she told us that night! She's—"

"Terrible," I say, placing a hand on his shoulder. "I know. We both know."

"If I ever run into her . . ." Turk makes two fists. "She'll be sorry." Then he lets out a deep breath and rubs his palm over his head, letting some of his stress dissipate. "I don't think I'm ever going to get used to not having *hair.* Come on." He rubs his finger over my scalp. "Fuzzy," he says, then laughs. "Let's get back to the others. I'm sure they're wondering where we went."

"I doubt Shannon cares."

Turk takes back his hand. "She might surprise you, Aria. Shannon is a woman of mystery. But she has a good heart."

"Okay," I say. "You keep telling yourself that."

Turk says something in response, but I can't hear a word.

Because my ears are filled with a bomb blast.

· IX ·

Noxious gas is everywhere.

The toxic mist fills the square, creeping into my chest and making me cough viciously, like I'm hacking up a lung. I close my eyes but it's too late—they're burning, leaking tears.

"This is a safe zone!" one of the nurses screams. "A medical zone! Leave us alone!"

People rush past me like confused cattle, and I don't dare open my eyes for fear of the blinding gas. "Here," Turk says. He stuffs something thin and papery into my hand. "It's a surgical mask. Put it over your mouth."

I do as he says. The mask snaps around the back of my head. I inhale cautiously. My lungs are still raw, but at least I can breathe. "What's happening?"

"Tear gas," Turk says. "Not sure why."

An amplified voice pierces the din. *"Aria Rose is here."* The voice is channeled through what seems like a dozen speakers ringing through the triage area. *"We want her."*

"We're supposed to be safe here!" a woman hollers. People are pushing blindly through the crowd, some crying, "Aria Rose! Turn yourself in before we're all killed!"

"Don't listen to a word those fools say," Turk says, grabbing my arm. "Turning yourself in is the last thing you should do."

My eyes are still tightly shut against the tear gas. "Maybe I should," I say. "Maybe that would—"

"Win the war for your brother, that's what it would do."

Someone shrieks and falls into my back, nearly knocking me over. I open my eyes, and for a second I see the entire square in chaos: hundreds of people swarming together with nowhere to go, thanks to the crisscrossing of silver electrical wire that has quickly been put up around the perimeter.

Masked guards dressed in black are flooding the square now. A glowing red rose is stitched into the backs of their uniforms.

I recognize the uniform immediately. These are my father's men.

Then my eyes begin to burn and tear again, and I close them. All I see is black.

Somewhere nearby, I hear a painful howl and the smell of sizzling flesh. It reminds me of the attack at the mystic compound, the fire.

"Do not touch the blockade," the amplified voice says overhead. *"The wires are live. I repeat, Do not touch the blockade. You will be electrocuted."*

I can't believe my family is going to all this trouble to track me down. They don't love me, not since I betrayed them and chose Hunter. And yet they're looking for me. They think I'm going to help them win the war, that they can brainwash me or threaten me and make me their figurehead.

I will never support them. Too many fingers have already been pricked by the Roses' thorns.

By now, the worst effects of the gas have worn off, and we can open our eyes.

The square is stuffed with people. The tents have been emptied, and everyone has been divided into ten lines of probably more than a hundred people each. Some of the injured can't even stand, let alone walk, so the healthier people are carrying them. Two lines down from me, I see three men with gaunt eyes and crooked legs leaning against a nurse wearing a mask and gloves and holding two babies, one in each arm.

My father's soldiers spread out. Some stand facing us; others fan down the lines, making sure people stay standing. "Every single person needs to be checked," I hear one of them saying.

Another soldier chuckles. "Even the babies? And the men? Obviously *they're* not Aria Rose."

The first soldier growls. "Who knows what they can do with their mystic voodoo powers. Aria may have disguised herself."

"But if she's disguised herself, then how will we find her?"

The first solider smacks the other one's cheek. "It's amazing you can even talk, you moron. Her eyes will be the same. Look at the eyes."

On the JumboTron, the live footage has been stopped. Now there's a picture of me that takes up the entire screen. It's my senior picture from Florence Academy. My hair is down, framing my face, and I'm wearing a simple navy dress and the teardrop diamond necklace my parents gave me for my seventeenth birthday.

I am grinning like an idiot.

I think back to when the picture was taken—the beginning of the last school year. Almost an entire year ago. I hadn't met Hunter yet. Or Thomas. I didn't know anything about mystics or the Depths. My biggest problem in life was being photographed and speculated about on gossip blogs.

"Keep your eyes down," Turk whispers. "And don't say a word."

Soldiers are pushing people forward, up to the line of guards who are comparing each person to my picture. "Come on, come on!" one of them shouts at an old woman whose right leg has been amputated below the knee.

"But I've lost my other crutch," she replies, sobbing. "I only have one—"

"One'll do," the soldier says, pushing her forward. She loses her balance, and the crutch slips out from under her. She falls to the ground. "Get up!" the solider says, kicking her in the stomach. But the woman doesn't move.

"Aw, Christ," the solider says, cupping his hands over his mouth and calling out to one of the other men. "Someone come here and help me, would ya?"

Another soldier rushes over. I can't see his face, only the shiny red rose on his back. He takes out a pistol and shoots the old woman in the head. People in the line start shrieking, and one man steps out, fists clenched, mustache twitching, looking ready to attack the soldier.

The soldier shifts his pistol to the man. "Take one step closer and I'll blow your brains into the canal."

The man shakes his head and steps back in line.

Nobody even bothers to clean up the woman's body. She's just left there on the ground, and people step over her as the line surges forward.

Ahead, all I hear are rounds of "Next!" as the guards compare the people in the square to my picture. The people who pass inspection start filling up the empty tents. A dozen or so bodies still cling to the electric fence—people who tried to escape the blockade and were burned to a crisp.

"When they reach us," Turk instructs, speaking low, "just close your eyes and start crying. Say they burn from the tear gas. No one will recognize you. I promise."

I don't believe him. I'm bound to be recognized. And if I'm not, what if someone is mistaken for me? I don't want to be responsible for anyone else getting hurt.

The waiting is tedious. I am sweaty and tired and nervous. I clench my hands together in front of me to stop them from shaking, and before I know it, one of the soldiers butts me with the end of his rifle. "Move up, girlie. Watch it, now."

Turk is pushed off in a different direction, and one of the guards curls his finger at me. I walk toward him and close my eyes. "Name?"

"J-Jessica," I stutter.

"Open your eyes."

"They burn," I say, just as Turk told me to. "From the gas."

There's a sting against my cheek. The guard has slapped me. "Open your eyes."

I follow his order and stare at a soldier who can't be much older than I am. I've never seen him before, but he has my family crest tattooed on the side of his neck.

He holds up a picture of me—the same one from the

JumboTron. I watch as his eyes flick from the picture, to me, then back to the picture.

It seems to be taking forever.

The guard raises an eyebrow. Have I been found out?

He opens his mouth and calls out, "Next!"

Suddenly, I'm being shuffled forward. The line of guards is now behind me. "Our source must have been wrong," I hear one of the soldiers say. "Or else she left before we got here."

I search for Turk but it's hard to find him amid all these people—especially now that his Mohawk is gone.

I go into one tent, then another. Then I head toward the far end of the square. I'd like to stand on one of the benches to get a better look over the crowd, but I don't want to call attention to myself.

"Well, that was messed up."

I spin around and there's Turk. I'm so happy to see him that I throw my arms around him. He flinches, stiffening like a board.

"Let's hide in one of the tents until they're done and they cut down the wire," Turk suggests, gently pushing me away. "Then we'll head back uptown."

"How did they know I was here?" I ask. "Did someone at the triage center tell them?"

"Unlikely," Turk says. "Everyone here is sick—and the nurses would've wanted to prevent something like this from happening, even if they don't like you. It's possible that someone in the Depths saw us on the bike on our way here, but it's not likely, and anyway, they wouldn't have known where we were going."

"The only other people who could have known are back at the hideout," I say. "But we snuck out."

"Maybe one of them followed us."

"Even so," I say, "they're all on our side."

"Apparently not *all* of them," Turk says with a grimace. He gulps. "I hate to even *think* it, Aria, but . . . there must be a leak. And now we've gotta find out who it is."

Turk hasn't even closed the town house door behind us before Landon whistles. "Nice haircut," he says.

Landon and Shannon are standing in the foyer—waiting for us, I assume, since Turk texted them about the attack on our way uptown. "Aria shaved her head!" Landon shouts to whoever is listening, heading toward the kitchen. "She looks weird!"

Shannon is standing with her arms crossed over her chest, dressed in workout gear. She gives me a once-over. "I didn't think you could get any uglier," she says. "But I was wrong. You look like a Chihuahua."

"Shannon," Turk warns. "Be nice."

"I am being nice. She should know what she looks like."

I ignore her, pushing my way into the living room at the same time that Ryah and Jarek come tramping down the stairs. "Oh wow!" Ryah says. She's traded her overalls for a short-sleeved pink shirt and white leggings. "You look . . . different." She glances at Turk. "You too?"

Turk nods.

"But your Mohawk was a part of you. It was like a limb. Like another arm."

"It's just hair," Turk says. "It'll grow back."

Ryah carefully touches the tips of her blue spikes, which are gelled and pointed with precision. "Hair is not just hair," she says. "It's art. You of all people should know that." She shifts her attention back to me. "All those long brown waves . . . *gone* . . ." She places her hand over her heart. "I could just weep!" She leans into Jarek, who's standing right behind her. "Jarek, I'm weak! Catch me if I fall!"

He ignores her and says to me, "Aria, you should rest."

"I'm okay," I tell him. "Honestly."

Jarek shrugs. He's wearing a washed-out red henley shirt, his brown locks pulled into a ponytail. "Rest is good."

"Hair," Ryah whispers, talking to herself. "Gone." She rests the back of her hand on her forehead and sighs.

"You're okay *this time*," Shannon says in a voice as tough as leather. Then she picks up a lamp from a side table and throws it.

Right at my head.

It comes at me like an oversized ceramic bullet. I throw my hands up and catch it just before it meets my skull. "What's wrong with you?" I shout. "Why would you throw a lamp at my head?"

"To see if you managed to learn anything when I was teaching you to defend yourself," Shannon says, flicking her hair back. "You're rusty. You need to be more prepared, in case there's another attack. Am I right, Turk?"

Turk lowers his eyes. "Aria, you *do* need to be able to defend yourself—"

"I can defend myself."

Turk shakes his head at me. "Not well enough. It's nothing on you. But lots of people are after you, and we got lucky today. If they had recognized you, we would have had to fight them—us against a slew of soldiers. I can handle myself, but I can't take care of both of us. So tomorrow? We start training you hard-core, picking up where you left off with Shannon." Turk cocks his head at the staircase leading to the library. "But first, we've gotta talk to Hunter. I already texted him."

The guard posted outside the library lets us in, and there's Hunter, huddling over some printouts with the same group of men who were here yesterday.

I glance at the table. Maps of the Aeries, specifically the West Side. The man to Hunter's right sees me looking at the papers and flips them over.

No one's paying much attention to him, though. All eyes are on my hair.

Or rather, my head.

Hunter's expression is hard to read. "Guys, give me a moment with Aria and Turk." The men exchange glances, then stand, their chairs screeching as they pick up their TouchMes and coffee and shuffle out of the room.

Hunter stands, too, closing the door once they're all gone. The door clicks, and I suddenly feel odd, positioned between Hunter and Turk with a shaved head and a bucket full of questions.

Hunter struts up to me and places his hand on the side of my face. My entire body warms at his touch. Is he mad at me? Surprised? Disappointed?

He leans forward and kisses my fuzzy head. Then he smiles. "Smart."

"Hmm?"

"This will endear you to the poor even more."

I think back to the moment after I shaved my head—when I rose from the stool and people cheered. I didn't shave my head because I wanted them to do that. I did it in support of Steve and Yolie and Kerry and everyone else at the triage center.

Because it felt right.

"It wasn't so . . . calculated," I say to Hunter.

"Look, Hunter," Turk says, stepping beside me. "We were raided."

Hunter's eyebrows shoot up. "You were *what?*"

"Aria's family, they sent out troops. They closed off the square where the triage tents are and searched for Aria. They didn't recognize her because of her hair, and her eyes were pretty red from the tear gas—"

"Tear gas? Aria, are you all right?" Hunter asks, reaching for me and holding me tenderly. My heart beats faster at his touch.

"I'm okay," I say.

"The thing is," Turk says, "how did they know she was there? I can't imagine anyone caught a decent glimpse of Aria on my bike—we were going *fast*. The only people who saw us leave here, who could have followed us and guessed where we were going—"

"Are *inside* the hideout," Hunter says, finishing Turk's sentence. He pulls away from me and rubs his temples. "Damn. It's hard to believe." The color drains from his face, and it looks like he might topple over. He sinks into an empty chair at the head of the table.

"I've been working so hard," he says. "And it's all for nothing if one of my guys is leaking our plans to your family and the Fosters."

Hunter rests his head on the table, clearly upset. *My family and the Fosters . . .*

"Wait!" I cry. I turn to Turk. "When Thomas kidnapped me, he said that they were able to locate me at the compound. But he never said *how*. And now this incident with Kyle . . . What if there's some sort of *tracker* on me?"

Hunter looks straight at me, concerned. "Hmm," he says. "Seems like it's time for a trip to the infirmary."

Hunter and Turk lead me through the main floor, past the kitchen and the armory. They're both walking swiftly. Nervously.

At the end of the long hallway is the infirmary. Hunter punches the touchpad, and the door opens onto a small room painted white with three empty cots and a station full of medical supplies. Much like at the triage center, there are bandages and gauze, empty syringes and vials of antibiotics, rubbing alcohol and medical instruments.

Unlike at the triage center, though, there's a tall glass cabinet half the length of the wall that is full of bottled mystic energy: small vials glowing with green extracted energy that pulses and swirls, protected by thin layers of quicksilver.

Quicksilver, or mercury, is the only material that can contain mystic power. Elissa Genevieve told me this back in my father's office, when she and I hid in the draining room and watched a mystic's energy be stolen from her. I can still remember the piercing, painful sound of the mystic's cries as the life was torn from her body.

"Here," Hunter says. He points to a tall oval contraption fashioned out of glistening black metal.

"What's that?" I ask.

"A scanner," Turk replies. He presses his thumb to a touchpad built into the metal. There's a whirring noise as the machine comes to life and a slight hiss as an invisible lock is opened. The machine springs open like a clamshell. It's hollow, lined with soft-looking white padding.

"Step inside," Hunter says to me. He sits down at a narrow white desk and cues up a TouchMe. "If there *is* a tracker on you, this thing will detect it."

I shake my head, thinking of the coffinlike contraption back at Dr. May's office and the awful noise it used to make—*bang, bang, bang.*

"I really don't want to," I say. My lips begin to tremble; I touch my fingers to my mouth, trying to make the trembling stop, but I can't. "Please don't make me."

"Hey," Turk says. He places one hand on my lower back and a zip of mystic energy shoots up my spine—which only makes me more upset. "We're not going to let anything happen to you. Trust me. Okay?"

I take a deep breath. Of course Turk and Hunter won't let anything happen to me. "Okay," I say.

Hunter smiles. "Don't worry, Aria. It'll be over in a minute."

I nod, then step inside the machine as it closes around me.

Everything smells like lemon. Clean. Fresh. I close my eyes, try to think of happy things: the first time Hunter kissed me—the sweet taste of his tongue on my lips, the soft feel of his hair beneath my fingertips, the coiled muscles of his shoulders, the firmness of his chest. . . . We haven't kissed like that in so long.

Then I think of the sound of his laugh—the throaty scratch of his voice as he whispers in my ear. The stirring in my body every time we touch. The strong rays of energy that jet from his fingertips, shooting out green blazes that ignite the sky; the way his arms wrapped around me as we plummeted through the roof of my parents' apartment building. His magic. His power. His love for me—what he would do, has done to protect me. To save me.

There is no banging in this machine. There are no scary thoughts. There's just a soft, low hum as sensors scan me from the top of my bald head to the tips of my bare toes and I overflow with memories of Hunter, the boy I love.

The first thing I see when I step out of the machine is Turk.

Frowning.

"What's wrong?" I ask.

Hunter glances up from the TouchMe. "You're clean," he says. "No tracker."

"But . . . how did Kyle find me at the triage center, then? And Thomas back at the compound?"

Hunter sighs. "I have no idea. But I'm going to find out."

"Meanwhile," Turk says, "we have to assume this means there's a traitor after all. And it's up to us to figure out who he or she is." He glances at Hunter, then at me. It's shocking to see Turk so serious, with no jokes or witty remarks. "Nobody speak a word of this to anyone. If it gets out that we know someone at the hideout is betraying us, whoever it is might try to cover his tracks."

"Agreed," Hunter says.

Suddenly, I feel my eyes begin to flutter, and I realize I'm exhausted. "Guys? I'm going to go upstairs and rest."

"Of course," Hunter says, getting up from the desk and putting his arm around me. "I love you."

In my room, I take off my—no, *Shannon's* jeans and shirt and toss them into a pile of clothes next to the bed. *Must do laundry,* I remind myself. Though I don't want to admit to anyone here that I have no idea how.

I'm about to crawl into bed and get under the covers when there's a loud buzzing noise. A TouchMe.

Whipping my head around the room, I quickly realize that it's *my* TouchMe, which is on my desk. But who in the Aeries would be calling me?

I grab it and glance at the screen. Restricted. I slide the lock and press Accept with my thumb. "Hello?"

There's a second of silence. Then I hear someone breathing.

"Who is this?" I ask.

A familiar baritone says, "Well, hello there, little sister. I've been *dying* to hear your voice."

· X ·

Kyle.

The call from my older brother is so unexpected that I nearly drop my TouchMe. The last time I saw him in person he snapped a metal pipe in two, as if it were a twig—thanks to the superhuman strength that resulted from his Stic addiction. He also spied on me, turning me in to our parents and nearly getting me and Hunter killed.

Apparently, this endeared him to my father, who is now letting Kyle be a public figure, rallying the people of the Aeries in support of the Roses.

"Why are you calling me?" I ask him.

"Is that any way to greet your older brother?" he says. The familiarity of his voice is unsettling.

"You're right," I say. "I should have said, 'Why are you calling me, you lying traitor druggie?' I'm going to hang up on you now."

"Stop playing games, Aria. We both know you're not going to do that. You're too curious about what I want."

True.

When Kyle and I were children, we were nearly inseparable.

Even though I'm younger, I was always the strong one; whenever anything went wrong, I protected him. He was so scared of our parents, especially our father. But as we got older, we grew apart. Kyle graduated from high school, went off to see the world for a year, and entered college. The only reason I had anything to do with him recently is because he was dating one of my friends, Bennie. If he's still scared of my father, he's never let on.

I haven't spoken to Bennie and Kiki, my two best friends, in weeks. Bennie is likely back at college, but who knows what Kiki is up to—if she's even still in Manhattan or if she's off traveling, like most Aeries kids do before they enter college. And if she were . . . would she talk to me?

"Hello? Aeries to Aria?" Kyle chuckles.

"What is it, Kyle—why are you calling? It seems like you've been keeping yourself pretty busy these days."

He snorts. "Just biding my time, really," he says. "Today was fun."

Biding his time until what, I wonder? "I'd hardly call what you did *fun*, Kyle. Innocent people lost their lives because of you."

"See, that's where you're wrong, Aria. Innocent people lost their lives because of *you*. Because you wouldn't give yourself up."

He's making me angry. I walk over to the bedroom door, making sure it's locked so no one will walk in on this conversation. "That is not true and you know it," I say.

"Dad will be so happy to know that I've gotten in touch with you," Kyle says, a smirk in his voice. "Actually, he's the one who asked me to call."

This surprises me. "He did?"

"Indeed," Kyle says. "As you can imagine, he wasn't too thrilled with how today went down. He wants me to reach out. Make amends."

"Amends for what?" I say. "For almost killing me? For making my life unbearable?"

If my parents truly wanted to see me and apologize, they would reach out to me themselves. I could never convince them to change their minds about this war—but perhaps it's not too late to connect with Kyle. "Too many people are getting hurt. Surely you don't want to kill off all of Manhattan. There has to be some agreement everybody can come to."

"Agreement?" Kyle says, raising his voice. "With those animals? I think not."

"Kyle." I want to leap into the TouchMe and strangle him. "We all—I mean, you and Dad and the Fosters and Hunter and the mystics—need to sit down like civilized people and figure out a plan for the city. Innocent people are being hurt, even killed."

I think about what Thomas told me: how other cities are watching us, waiting to move in. Take over. Kyle must know this, must know how important it is to end this war—before *everyone* loses.

"And pretty soon," I add, "the Aeries will begin to truly suffer. There isn't enough stored mystic energy to run the city forever. You're going to need help. Or else your supporters are going to start turning on you. . . . Then what?"

There's a long silence between us.

Then I hear Kyle clear his throat. "Tell you what," he says. "I'll agree to meet with Hunter and discuss some sort of peace deal if you meet me privately first. I'll even phone Thomas Foster and include him. A peace summit, we can call it. I can't make any promises, but even Dad doesn't want a never-ending war. Maybe we *can* reach a compromise."

I think about this for a moment. I would have to persuade Hunter to meet with Kyle and Thomas, but that seems doable. Especially since, surprisingly, Kyle seems open to talking—a far cry from his declaration on the JumboTron only hours ago. "Why would I meet you alone?"

"Because I'm your brother," Kyle says, "and you owe me the chance to try to win you over to our side. Let me convince you why you should come home."

"You'd be wasting your breath, Kyle," I say. "I'm never coming home."

"This attitude is exactly what got you into trouble in the first place," Kyle says. "You're looking out for yourself and your boyfriend instead of your own flesh and blood."

"I'm looking out for what's *right*," I say.

Kyle laughs, a mean, angry sound. "Do you honestly think that's what Hunter is fighting for—what's right? These rebels are using you, Aria. Hunter is using you."

He pauses, and I hear him take a sip of something. "I have things to tell you about Davida."

Davida. Hearing the name of my old servant, my friend, strikes a chord of sadness in me. With everything that's happened, I haven't had time to properly mourn, to appreciate the sacrifice she made for us—giving up her life so that Hunter could live. So that we could be together. Especially since she was in love with Hunter herself, a fact I only learned after her death.

"Can you get away? Tomorrow morning, maybe?"

I don't want to meet with Kyle. I don't believe he cares about my well-being—he only cares about winning this war. But Hunter is so one-track-minded these days, he thinks there's no room for compromise with the people of the Aeries. If I present a peace summit as an idea that came from Kyle, though . . . maybe Hunter will accept the invitation. Take it seriously.

"Come on, Aria. I don't have all day."

"Fine," I say. "If you call Hunter and Thomas and arrange a peace summit, I'll meet with you privately beforehand. But I'm not going to let you take me hostage."

"I just want to have a conversation with my sister without other people listening in," Kyle says. "I used to be able to do that."

"You should have thought about that before you ratted me out."

"You were sneaking around with—" Kyle stops himself. "Never mind, Aria. We'll talk about all this in person. I'll call Hunter. After I talk to him, I'll text you the location and the time for our private rendezvous. Don't let me down." His voice cuts off and the TouchMe flashes. The call is over.

"Hello?" I step cautiously into the room.

I haven't been up to the fourth floor yet, where the guys sleep. The rooms are basically the same as ours, but the beds are made up sloppily, with sheets sticking out past the comforters. Pillows and clothes are scattered across the floor—jeans, dirty socks, and T-shirts crumpled into balls.

Nearly an hour has passed since my conversation with Kyle.

Hunter is sitting at one of the desks, leaning back with his feet up on Turk's bed, while Turk is lying on top of the covers, fully dressed, tossing a tennis ball against the white ceiling.

"Did you sleep well?" Hunter asks. His hair is sticking up in the back. I want to smooth it down, but I'm not sure he'd like that. I put my hands in my pockets instead.

"Not really," I say. After my chat with Kyle, I couldn't do anything except lie on the bed and stare at the ceiling. But I don't tell Hunter this.

"Naps are lame anyway," Turk says. Bounce, catch. Bounce, catch. "Makes it impossible to sleep at night. So then you're tired the next day and you take *another* nap. It's a vicious cycle."

"I guess," I say.

Hunter tilts his head. "Well, while you were resting, I received a very interesting phone call," he says.

"From who?"

"From *whom*," Turk says. "If you're going to lead this city one day, you need to have proper grammar."

"Bite me," I say. "Is that proper grammar?"

Turk chuckles and continues throwing the ball. Bounce, catch. Bounce, catch.

I turn my attention back to Hunter. "Anyway. From whom?"

"Your brother," Hunter says.

"Oh!" I say, feigning surprise. Just then, the tennis ball crashes to the floor.

"Sorry," Turk says. It's still bizarre to see him without his Mohawk—just a light layer of fuzz instead. He shifts his hands behind his head, and I see the green tail of the dragon tattoo that wraps around his left bicep, the scales outlined in black and dark blue.

"He wants to meet with me," Hunter says. "Can you believe that? What nerve. Wants us to have a *summit*, along with Thomas Foster." His blue eyes seem full of anger—I thought he would have been more intrigued by the proposition. "He suggested Thursday at noon."

"This Thursday?" I ask. "Are you going?"

"Yes, this Thursday. Barely enough time to organize any sort of plan . . ." His voice trails off. Then he looks at me and says, "Do you think I should?"

I'm relieved that he's asking my opinion. That he still cares what I think. "I do," I tell him. I'm nervous that I'll say the wrong thing—I want so badly for him to agree to meet with Kyle. "You'll be able to sit down and figure out how to end this war. No more fighting. No more innocent lives lost . . ." My throat is starting to go dry. "Don't you think?"

"I say screw him," Turk says.

Shut up, Turk, I think.

Hunter runs his fingers through his hair, making it even messier than it already was. He stands up and starts pacing. "How do I know I can trust him? He's a Stic junkie. And a liar. And a rat."

I take a few steps forward, until we're close enough to touch. Then I reach out my hand and press it to his cheek. I think of the Hunter who saved my life when I nearly fell from my balcony and plummeted into the inky darkness of the Depths.

He's warmer than I thought he would be. For a moment, even

though Turk is in the room, it's only the two of us: Hunter and me. Like it should be.

"You *don't* know that you can trust him. But it's worth a shot. Isn't it?"

Based on everything that's happened, I expect Hunter to give me some resistance. Instead, he seems to soften at my touch. "Okay," he whispers into my palm, kissing it tenderly.

"Okay? I thought you would take more convincing."

"What can I say?" Hunter says, wrapping his arms around my waist, his grip strong, demanding. "I'm a sucker for your charms."

My hand slips from his cheek to his shoulder, and he nuzzles my neck, giving me light butterfly kisses that make me feel frozen and on fire at once.

I try to empty my mind, to think only about Hunter's kisses, his touches, but I know how much he despises Kyle, how unwilling he is to compromise. So why isn't he putting up a fight about this summit?

Unless he's ready for the war to end. Maybe the raid on the triage center has motivated him to try to compromise with Kyle before more people die.

I push my concern to the back of my mind, shoving it into the deepest, darkest crevice. And then I plant my lips on his; they're familiar and foreign at the same time—it's been so long since we've been together.

But his entire body is stiff. Uninterested. His hands drop from my sides. I might as well be kissing a statue.

"Hunter?" I whisper. "Are you okay?"

He shakes himself like he's waking up from a bad dream. "I'm sorry," he says, staring at me with those beautiful blue eyes. "I have to go."

"Now?" I ask desperately.

He nods. "People are waiting for me."

Then he shuffles out the door, downstairs, away.

"Just so you know," Turk says loudly. I'd forgotten he was even there. I look over at him and he says, "PDA is *so* not cool. Unless you're the one doing the PDAing." Which I was not.

Then he leans over, picks up the dropped tennis ball, and lobs it at the ceiling with surprising force.

Hunter doesn't join us for dinner. After our conversation, he disappears into the library and emerges later with five or six of his men, each dressed completely in black with the green rebel eye in the center of their chests, their faces unreadable.

"We just got word that there's been an attack on the East Side in the Depths," Hunter tells me. "Led by the Fosters. We have to go."

He takes Shannon, Landon, Jarek, and the older mystics with him. "I'll make sure we all return in one piece," he says. "Turk, Ryah—you stay here with Aria."

"We can all go and help," I say. "I'm sure—"

"It's too dangerous," Hunter says. He gives me a brisk kiss on the forehead; then he's gone.

Left to our own devices, Turk, Ryah, and I have a simple dinner of pasta with grilled vegetables. Ryah tries to lighten the mood by telling us how she accidentally laundered her red bras with some of Jarek's white boxers and now all his underwear is pink. "Pink!" she says. "Can you believe it?"

"No," I say. "I really can't."

All I can think about, though, is what Hunter and the others are doing and whether they'll come back safely. I'm so upset that I can't even eat. Turk is deathly silent, which can mean only one thing: he's worried, too.

After we eat, I shower the grime from the Depths off my skin. At least having no hair means *a lot* less maintenance time.

I wipe my towel over my head, and I'm done.

Ryah is already asleep when I grab a cotton nightgown from Shannon's dresser and slip it on, burying myself under the covers. I can't believe that I spoke to Kyle, that I haven't spoken to my parents in nearly a month. I think back to a year ago, or two years, or five—when I still let my mother pick out my clothes and did my best to please her; when I thought my father was the strongest man in the world; when I thought Kyle and I would be on the same team—*our family*—forever.

Even if I wanted to, that's not a time I could ever return to. I know too much now. My parents have lied to me, stolen my memories, nearly killed me. Kyle has betrayed me. Hunter is my family now; the rebels are my friends. I should be happy . . . and yet suddenly, I find myself crying for everything I've lost, for everything I imagined the future would bring that will never come.

After about an hour of lying awake, my stomach begins to grumble, so I decide to go down to the kitchen and find something to eat.

I slip out of bed and close the door softly behind me. Shannon's bed is empty, which means she and Landon are still off somewhere with Hunter.

Downstairs it's mostly dark. Only the faint yellow glow from a lamp in the living room—the one Shannon threw at my head earlier—makes the hallway visible.

I rustle through the pantry and pour myself a bowl of granola. I'm heading back upstairs to eat it when I hear voices coming from the second floor.

I veer off the stairway, creeping toward the library door, careful not to make any noise. It's open just a sliver, and light filters out around the doorframe, casting an odd-looking shadow across the floor and up the opposite wall. It's two voices, I realize, a man and a woman. I lean against the wall until I can see through the open door.

Two figures are huddled at the end of the long conference table. One of them is Shannon. I can't see the other, but I know from the sound of his voice who it is.

Hunter.

"How many mystics have to die—or almost die—because of her?" Shannon is saying. "Why is she so important?"

I know Shannon dislikes me, but hearing her speak like this infuriates me. Who is she to hate me? What did I ever do to her?

"It doesn't matter *why*," Hunter says quietly. "She just is. And I don't want any more mystics to die. The . . . project we're working on won't harm any mystics. Trust me."

What project? I wonder. What's he working on with Shannon?

I lean in even closer, trying to hear what else Hunter is saying, when a warm hand slips dangerously over my mouth.

· XI ·

Mystic energy surges through my body, and my pulse skyrockets. I grip the bowl of granola so tightly I worry I might break it.

"Shh," the person says, pulling me away from the open door.

His hand comes off my mouth and I whip around, prepared to scream.

It's Turk.

He looks moody in the dark light. I catch the silver glint of an earring, but the rest of his face is hidden.

"No one likes a spy," he whispers.

"I'm allowed to spy," I say, beginning to calm down. "He's my boyfriend. And what *project* is Hunter talking about?"

Turk shakes his head. "Hunter doesn't tell me everything— something you obviously can relate to."

"I'm sorry," I whisper. "I'm just stressed."

He presses a finger to his mouth. "They'll hear us. Come with me."

I glance back at the library, where Shannon and Hunter are still talking, and jealousy floods through me. "Sure," I say. "Okay."

"I like coming up here to think," Turk says. He presses a touchpad and the door to the roof slides open. "You can see the Aeries from here. Well, some of it, anyway."

"I don't have much luck with rooftops," I say, remembering how my father tried to shoot Hunter and me on top of our apartment building on the West Side—until Hunter used his mystic powers to drop us through the roof so we could escape.

The first thing I notice when I step outside is how cool it is. "Amazing," I say.

"Part of the force field, the one I warned you about the other night," Turk says. "It hides us from view and protects us, *and* it's temperature controlled." He flashes me a smile. "Can't beat that. We can see out, but nobody can see in."

"How does it work, exactly?" I ask.

"Once it's set up, it pretty much does its own thing," Turk says. "Someone usually revitalizes it about once a week."

In the distance, I can see a scattering of old water towers that rise from the rooftops on thin, wired legs. The high windows of the buildings far above us in the Aeries are like hundreds of eyes, watching us, waiting, but everything below them, in the Depths, is masked by fog.

Turk plops down and pats a space next to him. "Take a load off, Ms. Rose."

I sit as he stretches out, resting his hands behind his head and staring up at the sky. I put my bowl of granola down, careful not to knock it over.

"If you look very carefully, you can see the force field," Turk says.

I lie back as well, stretching out my legs and resting my head on the roof, casting my gaze upward—only I don't see anything except the smog-swirled sky, gray over blue over black. If I squint, I can see the silvery glints of the Aeries light-rail. But no mystic force field.

"I don't see anything," I say.

"You will," Turk says. "Just wait."

He inches toward me. There's barely any space between us now. Our arms are practically touching. Amber light from some of the streetlamps filters onto the rooftop, outlining his nose and cheekbones in a warm glow.

Turk is nothing like Hunter. He doesn't have the sort of face that inspires confidence in hundreds of thousands of people. He's unrefined, rough around the edges. Turk says what he feels, does what he wants. He's real. He's not calculating like Thomas and Kyle and . . . even Hunter. It's sort of strange to realize this about Hunter, that he's not exactly who I thought he was.

Turk catches me staring. "Your head looks . . . different," he says.

I immediately cover my scalp with my hands. Earlier, having all my hair buzzed off seemed defiant. Now it just seems silly. "Hideous, I'm sure," I tell him, suddenly conscious that I'm wearing only a nightgown. "Don't look at me."

Turk reaches out, prying my hands off my head. His fingertips sizzle my skin. "No," he says. "Not hideous. Beautiful."

Turk's eyes seem to sparkle as he leans toward me as though he's going to kiss me.

I shoot back up to a seated position and Turk falls onto his elbow. "Thanks," I say. "You look . . . different, too. Better."

Turk rubs his elbow and looks at me strangely. "You didn't like the Mohawk?" He pouts. "Most girls do."

"Well, I'm not most girls."

Turk sighs. "Oh, believe me. I know."

An uneasy feeling settles in the pit of my stomach. Does Turk like me? I don't have any feelings for him. He saved me, that's all, and he's been looking out for me while Hunter is off fighting. There's nothing more to it.

"Are you okay?" Turk asks, resting a hand on my shoulder.

"Hmm?"

"You look deep in thought. . . . Is this about earlier . . . at the triage center?"

"Oh, um. Yes," I say, not wanting to admit what I was really thinking. "It was difficult."

Turk removes his hand and runs it over his head. "I imagine it would be—seeing your brother on the JumboTron after everything that's happened."

"Yeah," I say. *And you don't even know that I spoke to him.* "But really, it was seeing all those injured people—especially the children. It was all so . . . *sad.*" I wish I had a better word to describe how devastated I'd felt.

He doesn't respond, just stands up and steps toward the edge of the roof, thrusting his hands into his pockets. Without turning around, he asks, "Do you miss your parents?"

I laugh. "That's a random question."

He looks over his shoulder. "Is it?"

"Well, sure," I say. "They're terrible people."

Turk nods. "But they're still your parents. You don't get to choose your family, Aria. It's okay if you hate them *and* you miss them."

Childhood memories flicker before my eyes like scenes from a movie: trips to the Aeries greenhouses with my father, who loved to have me pick out the prettiest plants to bring back to our apartment; my mother showing me how to put on makeup, dabbing my face with creams and powders.

The good memories are far and few between—mostly what I remember is distance, coldness.

"I do think about them sometimes," I admit. "I wonder what they're doing. I wish they loved me unconditionally." I feel myself start to tense up. "But they don't. They love power and money. As far as I'm concerned, they're not my family anymore. You guys are."

Turk shoots me a tight-lipped smile. "That's how I've always felt about Hunter. My parents, they passed away forever ago. When I was five. It's always been me against the world. I was passed along from mystic family to mystic family . . . to anyone who would take me in and feed me. I could tell I was never really wanted, though. When I met Hunter, I felt like I'd finally found my brother. We've always had each other's backs. And now I have your back, too, Aria Rose. Always."

I feel myself flush with a feeling that's hard to describe. I'm sad that my parents and Kyle didn't turn out to be who I wanted them to be, and happy to have found people like Hunter and Turk.

I cross my arms over my chest, feeling the soft cotton of the nightgown against my skin. "I do miss Kiki and Bennie, though," I say. "Did you ever meet them?"

Turk shakes his head. "I know who they are, though. Hunter's told me all about them."

"Bennie was like an older sister to me. And Kiki reminds me of Ryah," I say. "A lot. They're both a little—"

"Animated?" Turk says, raising an eyebrow.

"That's a nice way of putting it," I say. "We have nothing in common anymore, though. Even if I saw them, I wouldn't know what to say. They'd be upset that I led a double life—Kiki especially. She's probably so incredibly pissed that I kept Hunter a secret. She was mad enough that I didn't tell her about Thomas—and that turned out not to be, you know . . . real."

"Why didn't you?" Turk asks. "Tell them about Hunter, I mean. I don't give a rat's ass about Foster."

"I didn't think they would understand. Or approve."

"Of Hunter?"

"Yeah," I say. "And of me." My lungs feel tight. Constricted. It's hard to think about Kiki and Bennie, about my family—everything I gave up to be with Hunter, who's been acting like I barely exist.

"I know what you're thinking," Turk says.

"You do?"

"Give him time." Turk bites his lower lip. It makes him look young, vulnerable even. "Hunter. He's going through a rough patch," Turk says. "He needs time to adjust to his new life. And we need time to adjust, too."

"Of course," I say. "I understand that. But there's a difference between mourning the death of someone you love and . . ."

Turk looks at me quizzically. "And what?"

"He's not even remotely the same." It doesn't feel right talking disparagingly about Hunter, but he's practically a new person. The old Hunter created a loophole from where he lived to my balcony so we could see each other whenever we wanted to. So we'd rarely have to be apart.

The new Hunter is actively keeping me away. Manipulating me for his own benefit.

"It's not you, Aria." Turk takes his hands out of his pockets. "Like you said, he hasn't had time to process Violet's death." Turk rocks back and forth on his feet; his shadow moves along with him, almost like it's dancing. "He does love you, you know. More than anything. I know he's not showing it right now, but give him time. Okay?"

I'm about to respond when I hear a sharp patter above us.

Rain.

It's a light splattering at first. I watch as the raindrops fall down, *around* us.

And then I see the force field. It's much more visible than when Turk first brought me to the mystic hideout: it rounds over our heads and down a few feet below us, covering the entire town house like a dome. A mystic dome.

The raindrops make tiny impressions on the iridescent force field, which I can see fully now. It shifts colors seamlessly between different shades of green, like thousands of butterfly wings sewn together. It ripples like the water in the canals, delicate but strong.

"Wow," I say.

Turk flashes me a bright smile. "Pretty cool, huh?"

I don't know why—maybe it's the soothing pitter-patter of the rain, or the raid, or our matching shaved heads . . . but I'm feeling incredibly simpatico with Turk. Like I can trust him—even more than I trust Hunter right now.

Just then, my TouchMe buzzes. I glance down: a text from Kyle.

Summit is a go. Meet me tomorrow outside Belvedere Castle. 7 a.m. Come alone.

"Who's that?" Turk asks. "Hunter."

I shake my head. "No. Listen, Turk . . ."

"Yeah?"

"I have to tell you something," I say.

His eyes glisten with curiosity. "Oh?"

"I know how close you and Hunter are. So if I tell you, you have to promise not to say anything to him."

Turk shrugs, looking uncomfortable. "I don't know what you're going to tell me," he says. "How can I promise?"

The rain is speeding up now, falling harder. "Forget it, then," I say. "Never mind."

Turk moves closer, then exhales a huge rush of air. "Fine. I've never kept a secret from Hunter for as long as I've known him . . . but I promise. Just don't tell me you're doing something crazy like jumping off a bridge in the Aeries. Because that would hurt. And you'd die. Like, for sure."

"No," I say. "Nothing like that. It's just that . . . my brother wants to meet me privately."

Turk throws up his hands in frustration. "I wish you *had* said you wanted to jump off a bridge! Aria, you can't meet up with Kyle—he's dangerous. A total loose cannon. Hunter will never go for that."

"I know," I say. "Which is why I'm telling you."

"Not cool," Turk mutters. "This is so not cool of you to unload on me."

I ignore this. "We're going to meet tomorrow morning at seven, near Belvedere Castle," I tell him. "And I want someone to have my back."

Turk's eyes narrow. "Aria, your brother is crazy and violent. He's a Stic addict. You can't trust him."

"I know. But he called and asked me to meet him. I said I would, but only if he called Hunter and Thomas to arrange a meeting."

Turk smacks his forehead. "So *that's* why he called Hunter."

"I know how resistant Hunter is to compromise," I say, "but he agreed to meet Kyle and Thomas—that's a start, right? Maybe they'll figure out a plan to end the war. And in order for the summit to happen, I need to meet Kyle first. It was part of the deal."

Turk doesn't respond. He looks away, up at the rain.

"You were there today, Turk. Too many people are getting hurt, dying, on both sides. If there's even a chance that a meeting will resolve things—"

"You have to do everything in your power to make it happen," Turk says, finishing my sentence.

"Yes," I say. "That's it exactly. *Please* say you'll show up tomorrow."

I hear the desperation in my voice, and I know Turk does, too. His face softens, and his shoulders slump in defeat. "Okay."

"Okay, what?" I say.

"I have your back, Aria," Turk says. "This is a terrible idea, but if you go to meet Kyle tomorrow, don't worry. I'll be there."

I can't sleep.

I'm full of jittery, anxious energy. What will I say to Kyle? Will he listen, or is he just showing up to preach the Rose family gospel?

Finally, careful not to wake Ryah and Shannon, I creep out of bed to gaze through the window at Manhattan. I'm so used to the view from the balcony in my parents' apartment—the majestic skyscrapers, their mirrored façades capturing the silvery bridges, the towering light posts practically bursting with stored mystic energy, pulsing with flashes of yellow and green and white.

But there is none of that here, in the flooded city beneath the Aeries. All I can see are the few surrounding buildings, wisps of canals, and the empty lot on either side of us. In the distance, a few spires that once contained mystic energy stand empty and broken—smashed by the rebels as a reminder to the Aeries of how much they need mystic power.

Follow the lights, I remember the mystic Tabitha telling me once. Without her, I never would have realized that the mystic light posts pulsed in patterns. Well, I followed those lights, all right, and they led me to Hunter. To love. To rebellion and now to war.

I close my eyes and see an image of Hunter. And then of Kyle.

I hope I'm making the right decision to meet him tomorrow.

I hope I won't regret it.

PART TWO

Beauty is in the heart of the beholder.

—H. G. Wells

· XII ·

The next morning, I wake up to the smell of bacon.

It's still dark in the bedroom, and early—the clock on my dresser reads 5:30 a.m. Next to me, Ryah is sound asleep, her head buried underneath two pillows. Beyond her, I can hear Shannon snoring lightly.

I glance toward the foot of my bed and see a tiny wooden table with a metal tray and a perfect breakfast arrangement: two eggs over easy, two crisp slices of bacon, toast, a glass of pulpy orange juice, and a ceramic vase with a clipped red rose.

And Hunter is hunched over it, arranging the utensils.

"Hunter?" I say quietly.

He looks up, startled, like a young child doing something he's been told not to do.

"I woke you," he says. "I wanted this to be a surprise."

He creeps over and sits down gently on the bed. I prop myself up on my elbows to get a better look at him.

"It's so early," I say. "What are you doing here?"

Hunter sweeps back his hair from his forehead. Even in the darkness, I can see the piercing blue of his eyes, staring straight at me. He is freshly shaved; I press a hand to his smooth cheek and feel a light buzz of mystic energy run through my fingertips and into my palm, stirring my blood.

"We received information about the location of one of the Foster bases on the East Side," he tells me, speaking softly as not to wake up Ryah and Shannon. "We're leaving to check it out, but first, I wanted to do something special for you."

I shift my gaze from Hunter to the breakfast he's prepared for me. "Thank you," I whisper back.

He leans down and presses his nose to mine, giving me a soft kiss on the lips before wrapping his strong arms around my waist. I scoot over to the side of the bed, making room for him; he rests his head on the pillow next to me. His breath warms my neck, and the way he's holding me makes me feel safe and secure.

"I've missed you," he says.

For a moment, I let myself forget how we haven't been connecting like we should, how neither of us has been completely honest, how the sheer number of questions I have about us and the rebels and the city and the war is enough to drive any sane person mad.

Instead, I focus on the simple things: the way Hunter's warm hand feels pressed against my stomach; the way our breaths mirror each other; the feel of the strong, capable muscles of his chest against my back; how he smells faintly of citrus shampoo; the gentle, ghostly kisses he's leaving along my shoulders.

"I've missed you, too," I say. "More than you know."

"I doubt that," he says softly. "I know I've been distant, Aria. Please just trust me. I promise things will work out in the end."

Trust me. Words that strike me like poisonous barbs.

Turk told me I should give Hunter time. Maybe Hunter is right. Maybe things will work out in the end.

"I've gotta go," he says. The sheets rustle as he gets up and plants a kiss on each of my cheeks. "I love you," he tells me. "I'll see you later."

I sit up and watch him disappear from the bedroom, his lingering scent the only reminder that he was here in the first place. Well, that and the breakfast in bed.

I reach over and sample the bacon. It's delicious—crunchy, just how I like it. Which makes me feel even worse about what I'm going to do next.

I've already picked out some clothes—more of Shannon's—and hidden them under my bed. A pair of black leggings and a stretchy midnight-blue shirt that might as well be black. I slip on my borrowed sneakers, sliding a plain gray cap over my shaved head. I stuff a pouch full of coins in my pocket, then grab a pair of sunglasses from Ryah's dresser, glancing at myself in the mirror.

I look nothing like myself. I could be anyone.

I send a message to Turk on my TouchMe, letting him know that I'm leaving. He won't travel with me in case I'm being followed. I hope he's still coming, that he's not going with Hunter to track down the Foster army instead.

Then I'm down the stairs and out the door and off to the Magnificent Block.

"This is good?"

"No." I yank on the brim of the cap, trying to cover my eyes. "*Inside* the Block."

The gondolier glances at the mounds of rubble towering in the water. "It's too dangerous," he says. He's about my father's age, with shaggy salt-and-pepper hair. He has a bruised eye and cracked lips and is missing most of his teeth.

We have slowed to a stop. "Here is as far as I will go," he says.

"Look," I say, yanking out the tiny pouch full of coins. "I have money. Please, just a bit farther." I open the pouch so he can see inside.

"Crazy," he says, gripping the wheel and steering us ahead, into the Block. "Crazy girl."

The imposing brick wall that used to line the Magnificent Block is nothing more than broken fragments of red and brown stone that poke out from the water. There is debris everywhere, and we have to inch along like snails to make sure the boat doesn't get snared on metal rods or the fallen pieces of lumber that dot the canals like tombstones.

The smell grows sour as we move forward, like a mixture of old milk and seaweed. I keep expecting there to be bursts of red and blue fireworks, like when Hunter took me to one of the mystic carnivals.

But this is different. The mazelike steel walkways that allowed people to traverse the Block by foot have all tumbled down after being bombed by my family and the Fosters; pieces have lodged in the muck at the bottom of the canals, sticking up like metal ghosts of what used to be.

None of the tenements, where the registered mystics were forced to live, remain. As we float farther toward the center of the Block, I can't imagine what the scene must have looked like when the Block was blasted apart and law-abiding mystics suddenly lost their homes and even their lives.

The dark, early-morning shadows are evaporating into soft light that trickles over everything, casting a gray sheen on the green-black water. Tiny ripples from the gondola sweep through the canal.

"Sort of pretty," I say to the gondolier. "Don't you think?"

He crosses his eyes at me, and I realize what a stupid thing I've just said. "Not the destruction, I mean, I was just talking about . . . Oh, never mind."

After a few minutes, we reach the point where, before the bombing, the land rose out of the water and blossomed into grass and trees and life. Where Hunter and I walked and he told me about his grandfather Ezra Brooks, who fought for mystic rights until he died and his daughter, Violet, took his place.

And now Violet is gone, leaving Hunter the only surviving member of his family.

What a huge burden.

We quickly approach a mound of brown earth solid enough to walk on and dotted with the remains of a handful of blackened trees.

A roundish piece of wood—likely one of the stilts the mystic tenements used to rest on—juts out of the water. "Can you tie up here and wait for me?" I ask.

The gondolier licks his dry lips. "No."

I glance around. There isn't a soul in sight. I don't want to be stranded here if Kyle doesn't show. "I won't be long. Fifteen minutes at the most." I shake the bag full of coins. "And if you take me back uptown, I'll give you everything that's here."

He lets out a low whistle. "Fifteen minutes. Then I'm gone. But I want half now."

I nod in agreement and stand up on shaky legs, careful not to topple into the water as the gondolier helps me onto the bank. I drop a handful of coins into his hand, then pocket the rest. "Good luck," he says as I plant a foot in the mud.

"Thank you," I say. I'll need it.

Kyle said he would meet me at Belvedere Castle—what remains of it, anyway. Turk hasn't replied to my text. Is he here yet? Hiding? Or has he changed his mind?

I head toward where the Great Lawn, the center of the Block, used to be. Or at least, where I *think* it used to be. It's hard to gauge where I am, since all the landmarks are gone. The Great Lawn is higher than the rest of the park, so it has never been underwater.

When I was here with Hunter for the carnival, there were rows of booths where mystics were selling their wares, and the air was scented with fresh muffins and cookies and breads. There was light everywhere—from the fireworks, from the jovial displays of power by the mystics themselves—and everything around me seemed to glow. I glowed, too, happy to be with Hunter, to hear about his powers and the mystic cause. And to beat him at the ring toss, of course.

But there are no more mystics here, and certainly no more

carnivals. Even the most recent time I was here, with Davida, for Violet Brooks's political rally, seems like a memory from someone else's life.

Now Davida is no longer alive, and neither is the Block: gone are the patches of yellow and brown grass, replaced with mucky brown goop. Gone are the lily pads in tiny pools of water and the ivy-covered iron bridge. The only things left are tiny clusters of rock. And there, past the rock, is Belvedere Castle.

I remember the first time I saw it. *It's falling apart,* Hunter told me. *Crazy unsafe. But sometimes I like to come here to sit and think. Probably sounds silly to you.*

But it didn't sound silly to me, certainly not that night, when I was falling in love with him—for the second time, unbeknownst to me. And now, well, I stare up at the maimed castle. The basic gray stone structure is still there, but there are craggy holes where the arched windows used to be, and the walls are uneven. The tower is missing its conical cap.

"I'm surprised it's still standing," comes a voice behind me.

Kyle.

I turn around and there's my brother. The blond hair that was always too light for my dark-haired, olive-skinned family; the green eyes, full of hatred; the pale skin, as though he's never spent a second in the sun. He would get so red as a child—our maid, Magdalena, used to slather him with sunscreen every morning before school.

"After what we did." Kyle smiles, as if proud of what my family has done to the Block. Which, I suppose, he is. "No more mystics here," he says.

I wipe sweat from my forehead with the back of my hand. "Yeah, you really showed them."

"So here we are," Kyle says, blinking the sun out of his eyes. He's wearing a navy suit and a white dress shirt, open at the neck. A tan satchel is slung over his shoulder, and a white circle the size of my thumb is stuck to his temple. Must be a mystic cooling patch, which explains why he isn't even sweating. "You look . . . *different*," he says, staring at my cap. I wonder if he suspects that my head is shaved underneath it.

"I *am* different," I say as boldly as I can. I motion to the cooling patch on his temple. "It's funny how you can hate a group of people so much and yet capitalize on them at the same time."

Kyle shakes his head. "That's where you're wrong, Aria. I don't hate mystics."

"But you've—"

"Mystics have their place," Kyle said. "And we have ours. What I *hate* is when the equilibrium that our parents and grandparents and great-grandparents have fought so hard to maintain is disturbed. By people like you and your mystic . . . *lover*."

He laughs, and the sound makes me queasy. "Are you still on Stic?" I ask.

Kyle straightens up. "Is that why you agreed to meet with me? To discuss my recreational drug use?"

"I don't care what you do on your own time, Kyle. You may be my brother by blood, but you're nothing to me. You sold me out to our parents and nearly got me killed—"

"*You* betrayed *us!*" Kyle's cheeks turn cherry red; a vein in his forehead begins to throb. "You have no idea what you've done to our family." He takes a few deep breaths. "You've made a lot of mistakes, Aria, but that can be forgiven. You were blinded by love—or however you want to label your time with that . . . mystic. Come home. We can spin it to the media that you were sucked in by the rebels, brainwashed, that you didn't know what you were doing—"

"But that's not true!"

Kyle sighs. "Who cares if it's true? It only matters whether people believe it. And besides, you know a whole lot less than you think you do."

Why does Kyle have to put me down? "I know that the mystic population wasn't responsible for the Mother's Day Conflagration," I say, "which is the main reason we started draining them in the first place. That was all Elissa Genevieve, who's still working with you and . . . our father." I'm so angry that I can't even bring myself to say *Dad*.

Kyle nods. "Elissa Genevieve is a mystic who understands that her own kind are a bunch of mongrels, and she's risen above them to secure a place within the Rose entourage."

"Elissa Genevieve is a traitor and a liar," I say. "She's with you now, but she'd betray you in a second if she thought someone else would offer her more." I clench my fists in frustration.

"Whatever you say, Aria. Are you coming with me or not?"

"The peace summit," I say. "You're going to follow through with it, right?"

"I said I would," he tells me. "And I called Thomas and your boyfriend. We're meeting two days from now—Thursday at noon, on the top deck of the Empire State Building. One bodyguard each. A lot of good it will do, though."

"Maybe it *could* do some good if you're open to it," I suggest. "If the city can get back to how things were before the drainings, before the Conflagration, maybe everything can work out."

Kyle tilts his head, curious. "And how will everything 'work out'?"

Think, Aria. Think.

"Maybe the mystics can agree to use their powers to help rebuild the city if they're promised equal rights. Everyone can live in the Aeries. . . . There'll be no more Depths, and—"

"No more Depths?" Kyle's eyes are nearly popping out of his head. "Aria, are you insane?"

"No."

"Where would all the people go? Where would they live? And you'd expect people in the Aeries to suddenly accept the fact that disgusting, smelly poor people and mystics are living in the same buildings as them? Eating at the same restaurants?" Kyle shakes a finger at me. "That would never work. Never in a million years."

"Then help us figure out something else!" I say, growing more aggravated by the second. "At least I'm offering suggestions. What are you doing—besides killing people and wearing suits that make you look like you're seventy-five years old?"

"I resent that," Kyle says. He brushes off his sleeves. "This was handmade for me in Italy." Behind him, in the mud, I think I see something moving. Turk?

Kyle adjusts the strap on his satchel. "You can still come home, Aria. You know how Dad gets when he's upset. He just wants you safe."

"I can't believe you're still defending him," I say. I think back to when my father called me into his office and told me that Manhattan was my city. That he and I were alike. "He thinks you're weak."

Kyle goes silent, and I can tell I've struck a nerve.

"Why do you even care if I come home?" I ask.

Kyle's left eye begins to twitch nervously. Suddenly, I understand what this meeting is really about.

"You *don't* care," I say. "You're just trying to get me to come home to save face with Dad. He must be pissed about the triage center bust, that you weren't able to get me. Did he threaten you?"

"Fine," he says, holding up his hands. "Don't come home. Stay with that mystic you're so in love with."

"His name is Hunter," I say. "Hunter Brooks."

"I know what his name is. I'm just choosing not to say it." Kyle sweeps his hand through his hair, then smiles. "You know there's a tracker on you, right?"

I find this comment incredibly strange. How could Kyle possibly know that I suspected the same thing—especially when Thomas was the one who tipped me off initially? "Incorrect," I say. "Hunter already checked for one."

"*Tsk, tsk,* Aria Rose," Kyle says. "Who do you think put it on you?"

"What are you saying, Kyle?"

"I'm *saying*"—he leans forward—"that you shouldn't trust that boyfriend of yours."

"And why not?"

Kyle shrugs. "I can't give you all the answers. If you don't want to do the right thing and come home with me, then you'll have to figure that out yourself." He opens his satchel and removes a small box. "Here."

He hands me the box, which is only slightly larger than my hand. The wood is stained a glossy black, the edges trimmed with gold leaf. Spread across the top, seven female figures are pressing palm to palm, each one outlined in a different color of the rainbow. I recognize them as smaller versions of the figures I saw back at the compound and in the mystic hideout. The Sisters.

"What is this?" I ask.

I try to open the box, but there are no hinges. The colors are so bright they nearly burst off the top. The blue is like a thousand crushed blueberries, the yellow like a pure drop of sun. I watch as a deep red swirls into an exotic orange on the far right of the box. *Mystic dye.*

"It was Davida's," Kyle says.

It can't be. "I've never seen this before."

He notes my confusion. "She kept it hidden. We found it underneath one of the floorboards in her bedroom. There was a note on it that said it was for you. Apparently, it has something to do with being a mystic and their heebie-jeebie religion. Dad was going to burn it, but I saved it. I know how much you liked her." He sighs. "Come home with me, Aria. This is the last time I'm going to ask."

I stare again at the female silhouettes. I still don't know what they stand for, and I've never seen seven of them linked together. I can't wait to ask Hunter what it means.

"No," I say. There's a stillness to Kyle's face that makes him impossible to read. Is he upset? Frustrated? Relieved? "But thank you."

"For what?"

"For this." I hold up the box. "And for not turning this meeting into an ambush."

"Oh, it's an ambush," Kyle says. He raises his fingers to his lips and emits a piercing whistle. "You thanked me too quickly."

"What?" I say.

And then all hell breaks loose.

Swiftly, a man rises from the mud behind Kyle. He must have been here this whole time. A towering figure, he shoots up from the ground with such force that mud splatters everywhere, covering my legs and part of Kyle's chest.

"Ugh!" Kyle says, wiping his lapel. "My suit!"

Now dozens of men rise from their camouflaged positions, strings of hulking soldiers bursting from the earth. Even though they're covered with muck, I can see that they're all holding guns.

I turn to run back to the gondola, but the men form a circle around me, making escape impossible. Mud flies everywhere, and the soldiers' grunts fill the air.

"Just surrender," Kyle says to me. "It'll be easier that way."

I stare at the wall of soldiers. There's nowhere to go.

All of a sudden, a familiar voice shouts, "Aria!" It's coming from Belvedere Castle. Turk's head peeks out one of the damaged windows.

Kyle sees him, too.

"Down!" Turk shouts, then points to the water a few feet away. "Swim!"

There's no time to think about what he means. I simply react.

I run as fast as I can, then shoot through one soldier's open legs, breaking the circle.

"Get her!" Kyle shouts. "And you up there, rush to the castle and get me that mystic!"

My clothes feel a hundred times heavier now that the mud is clinging to them. All I can think about is getting into the water, where the gondolier has tied up his boat. I spy him in the distance—he clearly sees us and is frantically turning himself around, trying to escape the Block. I hardly blame him.

"Wait!" I call out, but he's already off.

There's a splash. I look down and realize I've reached a canal.

Okay, I think. *Down I go.*

I take a deep breath and plunge into the filthy water. Davida's box is tucked tightly under my arm, which limits my speed, but I move as quickly as I can, trying to reach the bottom of the canal.

I open my eyes, but I can't see anything—it's too murky—so I squeeze them shut again. I can't hear anything except the water. I have no idea whether the men are behind me, and I don't want to take the time to look back.

Holding my breath, I push myself to keep swimming. I open my eyes again, just for a second, and I see it: a loophole just like the one Hunter used on my balcony. A glowing green circle of mystic light, pulsing in the water. Beckoning to me. The energy flares toward me. *I'm coming,* I think. *I'm coming.*

My eyes begin to sting. I close them and reach out, hoping I can make it to the loophole. A hand grabs my ankle from behind, and I kick, breaking free.

But only for a second.

Fingers claw at my feet and I propel myself forward in the water, toward the burning green circle. I feel a whoosh of air as the loophole closes itself behind me, and then—

I fall onto a stretch of cobbled pavement, gasping for air.

I'm still for a moment; then I push myself up. I'm not even wet. There are only a few streaks of dried mud on my right leg. I've lost my cap, but Davida's box is still safe under my arm.

And then I hear more footsteps. A block away, I see my brother's men gathering at the opening to the Block, scanning the water for any sign of . . .

Me. They're looking for me.

I turn and sprint in the opposite direction, down a narrow sidewalk, over a rickety bridge to a more populated street—anywhere someone might be able to help me.

"There!" I hear the men shouting. A chill shoots up my spine. I've been spotted.

· XIII ·

I run until my lungs ache, then stop to catch my breath. At least for now, I don't hear any of Kyle's men.

I see the remains of a row of brownstones: a tattered blue-and-white awning, a broken door, faded old posters with pictures of Violet Brooks above the slogan VOTE FOR CHANGE. Some of them have been graffitied over, but I can still make out Violet's effervescent smile, which only saddens me.

I recognize the street: this is Columbus Avenue. Where Lyrica lives.

The last time I was here, I searched for her address—481 Columbus Avenue—only to discover that it didn't exist. Until she made her house visible to me the same way Turk made the rebel hideout appear out of thin air.

Does she know I'm here? That I need help? Why has the loophole brought me here—and how did it get there in the first place, in time to rescue me?

I find the gate that I remember was next door to Lyrica's orange stucco house, practically hidden in a heap of tumbled bricks. I look to my right, where there used to be a brick town house.

Now there's *half* of a brick town house, the inside torn open, exposing plumbing and wooden beams tangled into one large, messy knot. Not far away, I hear shouts—I can only assume they're coming from my brother and his men.

With the box Kyle gave me still tucked under my arm, I hurry to the side of the town house and run my fingertip along the rough, broken edge, just like I did the first time I came here.

That time, the two houses groaned open, revealing Lyrica's hidden abode, red candles flickering against the glass of the two front windows.

This time, I wait.

And wait.

Nothing.

"Come on, Lyrica!" I shout, hoping she can hear me. "I need help!" I pound on the bricks in frustration, bruising my hands, but I don't care.

Suddenly, one of the bricks falls to the street, making a noise.

I'm about to pick it up when I see a slip of yellow paper flutter from the hole where the brick was. I pick it up and unfold it.

Look around the corner. This is your key.

Go to the mail slot on post 520.

I rush to the end of the street. On my left is another row of brownstones, ravaged to the point that they no longer resemble their former selves. In fact, there's only one brownstone that looks remotely intact.

I stop directly in front of it.

The three-story building looks like it was hit by a wrecking ball—the entire right side is missing, the windows blasted out. All that's left is a mound of peeling brown paint and a faded number near the entryway: 520.

The mail slot, I think. Where is that?

I step over the broken pavement, moving toward the crumbled, gray concrete steps. I can hear shouting behind me; have I been spotted?

Carefully, I make my way up the steps to the door, which is hanging on its hinges and covered with a layer of grime. There's a thin slot that seems to yawn like a hungry mouth.

Here goes nothing. I slide the paper into the slot.

And wait.

Seconds go by and nothing happens.

"Hello?"

I crane my neck, trying to see inside the empty brownstone. "Lyrica?"

This is stupid, I think. I hear Kyle's men more clearly now, shouting "Find her!" and "She can't be far!"

I can't stay here any longer. I've already wasted too much time. I pound down the steps and back onto the street, searching for somewhere to hide. And as my feet touch the sidewalk, the ground beneath me begins to shake. It feels like the vibration that comes from a Plummet Party, when the ground opens up and a building from the Aeries collapses into nothingness.

Only now nothing is disappearing. Rather, something is coming into view.

My vision begins to blur. Invisible hands seem to be parting 520 and the brownstone on its left. It's strangely quiet—only a swish of wind and the hint of a groan as the buildings shift apart and Lyrica's house drops in.

It's immediately familiar, with the same orange stucco walls, the same flickering red candles in the windows.

I hear the soldiers' footsteps behind me now, pounding the pavement like a herd of elephants. Lyrica is standing in the doorway, breathing heavily. "Come on, child," she says, reaching out her hand. "We don't have all day."

I step inside. Lyrica closes the door behind me, and I feel the floorboards beneath my feet shake the same way the ground shook right before the house appeared.

"What's happening?" I ask.

"That's just us moving again," Lyrica says.

I notice that, aside from the location, nothing about the house has changed. There are still candles everywhere, their tiny lights dancing at my arrival, and the walls are still a cozy burnt sienna, covered with framed pictures. I notice one with swirls of color— bursts of bright red and yellow twisting together like flames—that move around a figure that I now recognize as one of the seven Sisters.

"What do you mean?" I ask. "Why is your house moving?"

Lyrica smiles at me. She's wearing a silk dress the color of a robin's egg that flows down to her ankles, making her look like some kind of water creature. The blue contrasts nicely with her toffee-colored skin and the ceramic beads threaded through her mass of gray hair. She looks older than I remember. Worn-out.

"Come," she says, steering me down the hallway, into the same sitting room she brought me to the last time I was here. It hasn't changed much: the same tapestries coloring the walls and tiny green and yellow Chinese paper lanterns strung across the ceiling, the same glass orb dangling in the center of the room like a light fixture, only there's no bulb and it seems more for decoration than anything else. I recognize some of the charcoal swirls and symbols sketched on the walls from the mystic compound.

"My home has always been protected from those who would hunt me," Lyrica says. "But it is not simply invisible. It can be transported." She glances toward a window, its shutters tightly closed. "I moved us to evade your brother's men. Right now, as a matter of fact, we are in Queens."

I gulp. "Queens? Where's that? I've lived in Manhattan all my life and never heard of it."

Lyrica shuffles toward the back of the room, toward a champagne-colored curtain. "Many haven't," she says. "It's across the East River from Manhattan. Tea?" She doesn't wait for me to answer. She disappears behind the curtain and emerges with two ceramic mugs—one white, one blue—and makes her way over to me.

"Sit, dear." She hands me the blue mug and sticks a finger inside. Not even a second passes before the liquid begins to steam. "There you go."

I take a seat on the low sofa and bring out the box Kyle gave me, resting it on one of the cushions. Lyrica sits in a wicker chair.

"I have something important to ask you," she says, sticking her finger into her own mug. Lyrica's powers extend far beyond heating a cup of tea, of course, but it comforts me to watch her doing something so simple when this much chaos is going on around us.

"What is it?" I say.

She studies me for a moment, then sips from her mug. "What in the Aeries did you do to your hair?"

I laugh, running a hand over my scalp. "I needed a change. It's good to see you, Lyrica." The tea soothes me as it rushes down my throat—I taste honey and peppermint and something fruity I can't identify. It's delicious.

I breathe a sigh of relief as I sink into the sofa, knowing that, for the moment, I can relax. I slip my TouchMe from my pocket and send a quick message to Turk. *I'm safe. See you back at the house.*

I glance up and see that Lyrica is examining the wooden box. "Ah," she says when our eyes meet. "A mystic reliquary. I haven't seen one of those in ages."

"What is it?" I ask.

"A place to keep something sacred. Decorated by the Sisters— our holy seven." Lyrica rests her mug on the narrow mahogany table at her side. "It is believed that they were the first mystics," she says, "given their powers directly by God himself."

"It was . . . Davida's," I say, and Lyrica's eyes light up. "My brother, Kyle, found it in our apartment, hidden in her room, and gave it to me."

"Interesting," she says.

"Yes," I say. "Only, how do you open it?"

Lyrica gives me a smile. "The reliquary will open when it's ready."

"How . . . convenient," I say. "And what will be inside? Her belongings? She barely had anything."

Lyrica's eyes seem to flicker. "One might put it that way. You see, Aria, the power a mystic wields in life is all concentrated in the heart." She taps her chest. "So when mystics die, their bodies typically explode—like supernovas—and the hearts are destroyed. *What comes from the earth returns to the earth.*" She motions to the reliquary. "A saying of the Sisters. But sometimes, when a mystic dies in unnatural ways—"

"Like Davida?"

"Yes," she says, "like Davida did, then their hearts live on. They are incredibly powerful, valuable things. Not flesh and blood, exactly, but something else—something that survives even once the flesh decays."

Davida has been dead for nearly a month. Her body lost to the water. The image of rotting flesh in the canal makes me nauseous.

"It is priceless, a mystic heart," Lyrica continues.

My family has earned its fortune for decades selling Stic on the black market, so I know that humans will pay thousands and thousands of dollars for even a drop of mystic energy. How much must be contained in a mystic heart?

Lyrica presses her lips together. "In the occasion that a mystic perishes as Davida did, and the body remains intact after death, everyone who loved the person joins hands over it and the power is dissipated into the group. That is how we bury our dead."

The smell of cinnamon drifts into the sitting room from the scented candles in the hall. I feel incredibly calm.

"How many people are present for that?" I ask, curious. Why hasn't Hunter ever mentioned this to me?

"The heart is super powerful," Lyrica says. "So usually it's a dozen or so. Did Davida specifically leave this reliquary to you?"

"Yes."

I think about Davida, who left her family in the Depths to live with us. How she would wake me up gently every morning, and we would talk about our lives as she brushed my hair and helped me get ready for the day. *Don't let your parents get to you,* she would tell me. *You can be whatever you want to be. Do whatever you want to do, Aria. You're smart. You're beautiful. You have the world at your fingertips.* She was my servant, yes—but she was also my friend.

It was only recently that I learned the truth: that she was a rebel mystic who carefully hid the fact that she wasn't drained. That she'd been betrothed to Hunter basically since she was born, but that he didn't love her. She'd been sent to my family as a spy, meant to report back on the Rose secrets. But she protected me. Covered for me with me my parents. She saved Hunter's life.

Now she's gone. All that's left of her are threads of memories that are woven into my mind, and into the minds of her family, I'm sure.

Threads of memories and a heart.

Lyrica reaches for her tea. "Well, that is a responsibility you are going to have to swallow whole."

"What do you mean?"

"Davida is trusting that you can take in the power that she's left for you," Lyrica says. "Her faith in you is something that you can't deny but must absorb within yourself."

Lyrica's stare is intense—*too* intense. It's making me nervous. I look at the box, at the intricate carving of the Sisters. "Is Davida's heart in this box?"

"No, dear." Lyrica clucks her tongue. "That would be impossible. She died in the water, did she not?"

I remember the scene of her death: how I thought it was Hunter who was being killed, but really it was Davida. Even for mystics, her talent—taking on someone else's image—was a rarity. My breathing grows shallow and my chest begins to ache. Davida was so brave, so selfless. Even after nearly a month, it's hard to believe she's actually gone.

Lyrica stands up, smoothing her dress with her hands. "If you want to honor Davida, you must find her heart, put it in this reliquary, and return it to her family. Good luck, Aria," she says in a tone that sounds like a warning. "If she died in the deeps, who knows what happened to her body? She could have been swept out to sea."

She collects my empty mug and disappears into the kitchen, returning with a small plate of cookies. "I like something sweet after my tea," she says. "You?"

I take one of the cookies and break it in half: peanut butter. I don't realize how hungry I am until I take a bite and my stomach growls for more.

"Tell me something else, Aria Rose," Lyrica says. "What is life like for you these days?"

I find myself telling Lyrica more than I'd planned: about the attack at the compound and Markus's death, how both Thomas and my brother are after me, how Turk rescued me and took me to a mystic hiding spot, how there might be a spy among us and maybe that's how Thomas found me at the compound. "We thought I had been tagged," I tell her, "but Hunter did a scan and there's no tracker on my body. So we don't really know how they manage to keep finding me—unless someone is feeding my family information from the inside."

Lyrica shakes her head, the beads in her hair making tiny clicks. "Sure you weren't tagged, Aria. Just like when your parents told you that you'd overdosed on stolen mystic energy, when really they had erased your memories. You're a good girl, Aria, but perhaps a bit naive?"

"This is different," I say, trying not to be insulted. "Hunter checked for a tracker and didn't find one."

Lyrica raises her eyebrows inquisitively. "Did he do a mystic scan?"

"I don't know. There was a machine and . . . I guess he did."

"Let me see." Lyrica pulls her chair over and faces me. She holds out her hands. "May I?"

I nod.

She tilts her head up, toward the empty glass orb that hangs overhead. Her palm explodes with green light and suddenly her entire right hand is encircled by a thick, bright green ring. A single ray of light shoots out from her index finger and connects with the orb, filling it with pulsating energy.

The mystic energy begins to swirl inside the orb, growing brighter until I have to look away. There's a soft hum as Lyrica chants under her breath, and then, gently, a coil of energy emerges from a hole in the globe that must be no wider than a grain of salt.

It fans out, sweeping across the room and casting a green glow on the walls.

Then another ray pops out, like a strand of spaghetti.

Then another.

And another.

Before I know it, Lyrica is standing, and dozens of minuscule rays of energy are extending from the pulsating orb. I feel the energy wash over me, bathing me in mystic light, heating my skin and making it tingle. The sensation grows stronger, as if every cell in my body is electrified.

Lyrica is practically on her toes, her arm reaching toward the ceiling, fingers extended. She stretches out her arm until—

She makes a fist and the connection between her and the orb is broken. There's a huge flash as the rays of energy fizzle and pop like burned-out lightbulbs.

And then she sinks to the floor.

"Lyrica!" I say. The strange connection between us is broken, and I no longer feel the effects of the mystic energy. "Are you all right?"

She stares up at me with glassy eyes. "Yes. Just . . . tired."

I help her to her feet and sit her back in her chair. Her face is ashen; she takes a few deep breaths, and I fetch her a glass of water. When I return from the kitchen, some of the color has returned to her cheeks.

"I'm not as young as I used to be," she says, drinking. "But you *have* been tagged, Aria."

"Hunter checked, though," I say again. I let my eyes wander over my arms, hands, legs. "Where is it?"

Lyrica lowers her eyes. "On your *spirit*, Aria."

"You mean my soul?"

She nods. "I am sorry to have to tell you. But at least now you know."

Thomas. He knew there was a tracker on me. Could he have done this? "Was it done by Thomas?"

"Who?" Lyrica asks.

"Thomas Foster. My ex-fiancé . . . He lives in the Aeries."

She considers this. "I can't imagine anyone except a mystic being able to do this. It is powerful, dark magic." She glances up at the orb hanging from the ceiling, then back at me. "Do you want me to get rid of it?"

"Yes," I say. "Please."

Lyrica cracks her knuckles. "Then I will. It may be useful, though. You should keep the trace. I can transfer it to an object." She points to the chain around my neck. "Your necklace. May I use it?"

I take the silvery heart out from beneath my shirt. "Seems fitting," I say, unclasping the locket and handing it to Lyrica.

Lyrica takes the necklace. "Close your eyes," she instructs.

I do.

She grips the necklace with one hand and my shoulder with the other. I expect to feel a burst of heat, of electricity—what it normally feels like when a mystic touches me—but instead I feel . . . *cool.* Like every inch of me is being rubbed with ice cubes. Suddenly there's a pain in my stomach, like something rotten is twisting inside me, trying to escape.

My lungs begin to burn.

It feels like something is being ripped from inside me.

My mouth opens instinctively. Lyrica removes her hand from my shoulder and I double over in pain. She presses one fingertip to my forehead and my body begins to heat up; the warmth starts in my toes and spreads up my legs, into my torso.

"All right." Lyrica removes her finger and stands back. "You can open your eyes."

I look around, and my body seems to return to normal. Lyrica hands me back the locket. It's freezing.

"This carries the trace now," she tells me. "Be careful." I slip the locket back around my neck, securing the clasp. It's warm to the touch, heating the skin just below my throat. "It is time for you to go now, Aria Rose."

"How do I get back?" I ask. I have no idea where Queens is or what it's like.

"You'll see," Lyrica says cryptically, leading me out of the sitting room and back to the front entrance of her house. She hands me a crumpled tote bag for the reliquary. I carefully place it inside and sling the bag over my shoulder.

"Thank you," I say. "For your help—all of it. You've been so incredibly kind to me."

Lyrica smiles at me, and I realize her eyes are wet. "Of course, child."

She pounds her foot loudly on the floor, and there's a shift like the one when I arrived. The house is moving.

I turn the doorknob. Fresh air rushes inside; I look out and see that we're no longer in Queens, wherever that is. We're near the area formerly known as Times Square, looking out onto a narrow street and a canal bustling with energy—I recognize it immediately. A few feet away I spot a dock where a handful of gondoliers are waiting for passengers. Luckily, I still have the half-empty pouch of coins in my pocket.

"Goodbye, Lyrica," I say as I head down the stairs to the street.

"Aria?"

"Yes?" I say, glancing back.

"Many of the men in your life want to use you," she says, shielding her eyes from the sun. "What do you *want*?"

Lyrica winks at me, and before I have time to answer, she closes the door, vanishing—along with her house—from sight.

· XIV ·

"Where have you been?" Ryah asks, dragging me up the stairs.

I glance down at my TouchMe. Still no response from Turk, and I tried calling *and* texting him. Thankfully, he's programmed all the numbers I might need into the contact list, so I was able to message Ryah to help me through the force field. She responded immediately.

"I woke up, and you were gone!" Ryah is wearing a tight white T-shirt and cutoff denim shorts with frayed edges. Her hair is as blue as ever, though it's lying flat across her head, parted at the side. She hasn't gelled and spiked it yet today. I sort of like it better this way.

It feels like an entire day has passed since Hunter brought my breakfast, but it's only been a few hours—it's just after ten a.m.

Ryah shuts the door behind her. "Shannon ate the rest of your bacon before she went off with Hunter."

Shannon went somewhere with Hunter? "That's fine," I say, slipping off my sneakers and leaving them in the foyer. It's much cooler in here than it is outside. "Where'd they go?"

"There was an . . . incident," Ryah says. "On the Lower East

Side. I don't know all the details—only that there was an attack at a grocery store by some of the Foster army. Seems like a few people were killed, but I know Hunter brought troops to assess the damage."

"Oh," I say. "That's horrible." The bag Lyrica gave me for Davida's reliquary is heavy on my shoulder.

"Landon and Jarek are out also—the location of one of the Foster army bases was leaked, so they went to confirm the lead before Hunter plans an attack."

"Why didn't you go with them?" I ask.

"I was waiting for you!" Ryah smiles. "Turk's here, too. He's upstairs. Showering."

She pauses in the foyer. "I still can't get used to you being bald. Well, practically bald. You do have a little peach fuzz." Ryah giggles. "Anyway, Shannon and I woke up and you were gone, and I was like, *Oh my gosh, Aria's been abducted!* But then I saw that you'd had breakfast, and then Shannon was like, *Maybe she ran away!* And I was all like, *No!* Anyway, I'm just so glad to see you!"

"Thanks," I say. I've never met anyone with quite as much energy as Ryah. I'm still not entirely sure how to act around her.

Ryah rests her hands on her slim hips. She gets a funny look on her face. "Are you going to tell me where you went?"

My stomach jumps. Does Ryah know I went to meet Kyle?

"Just . . . out," I say.

I feel bad being cryptic, but I can't risk her telling Hunter the truth. Then he'd *never* go to the peace summit.

"Well, the next time you leave, you should let someone know where you're going," Ryah suggests.

Turk knew where I was going, I think, but of course I can't say that. "Is this a prison?" I say. "I always assumed I could do whatever I wanted to."

Ryah bites her bottom lip. "No, of course it's not a prison, Aria. It's just that—we're trying to look out for you."

"And I appreciate that, but I don't need a babysitter," I say. "I'm going upstairs."

I don't wait for Ryah to respond. I know she means well, but it bothers me that she and the others think I need to be watched 24/7, that I can't go out on my own without a protector or even be alone here unless someone knows where I've gone.

I start up the wooden stairs, one hand on the thick banister. There's someone I have to speak with. Now.

I head straight for Turk's room. I'm relieved he made it out of the Block safely, though I wonder how. I assume he'll have some choice words for me—for trusting Kyle and endangering myself by meeting him.

I reach the fourth-floor landing and start down the hall. The bedroom door is open about halfway. I'm about to knock when I see someone moving inside—Turk.

He doesn't see me. He's wearing a pair of snug navy boxers, toweling off his head after his shower.

He's stunning.

His legs are incredibly well defined, especially his calves, dusted with light brown hair. His underwear clings to his butt and the backs of his legs like it's holding on for dear life. Beads of water cascade down his back, falling to the floor as he rubs the towel across his head and his chest.

Turk is lean, all muscle. His body is so perfect it doesn't even look real. Broad shoulders and a sculpted back that narrows to a thin waist and a V that disappears into his underwear. I have seen boys with good bodies before: Hunter, of course, and even Thomas, but Turk looks like he was painted by an artist or cut from marble. And where there isn't smooth, olive-colored skin, there's ink. Not just pictures, but symbols and words.

Most shocking is the image of the Sister.

The tattoo covers most of his back. Etched in black ink are the oval lines of her face, which is void, featureless. Her flowing, wavy hair is emerald green and ocean blue and glittering lavender. The figure's hands are extended to either side, as though she is waiting for her sisters to press their palms to hers, as they do on Davida's reliquary.

I'm so intrigued that I don't move when Turk turns around.

And catches me staring at him.

My skin feels hot, and I start to sweat. I'm so embarrassed.

"Like what you see?" Turk asks.

"No," I say. "I mean . . . no."

He laughs. "Whatever." He goes over to a dresser and pulls out a black T-shirt and a pair of jeans. "What happened to you?" he asks, slipping them on. "I looked everywhere—"

"I'm fine," I say. For a second, I debate telling Turk about Lyrica. About the mystic trace on my soul that she discovered. But no—I decide to keep this information to myself, at least for now. "I hid until it was safe for me to come back here."

Turk swipes a hand over his scalp, as if remembering that he's practically bald, too. "Safe. Ha. You could have gotten killed. If I hadn't planted that loophole for you—"

"But it worked," I say. "Thank you."

A trickle of water runs down Turk's cheek, resting at the tip of his chin before it drops to the floor. "A lot of things could have gone wrong," he says. "I planted it before you arrived. I had to guess which way you'd exit, that you'd be able to swim to it and find it. If you hadn't, then—"

"I did, though," I say. "I escaped."

"Barely," he says.

"How did *you* get out of there?" I ask.

Turk waggles one of his eyebrows. "No mud-covered soldiers are gonna do me in."

I give him a tight-lipped smile. "You haven't told Hunter about the ambush yet, have you?" I ask.

"No," Turk says. "Not yet. Why?"

I step toward him. "You can't say anything."

A sour expression crosses Turk's face. "You were practically kidnapped, Aria," he says. *"Again."* He takes a deep breath. "Do you think I'm always going to be there to save you? Kyle lied to you about this meeting—and I kept it from Hunter because I trusted you." He lowers his voice. "I was supposed to keep an eye on you."

"What do you mean?"

"Today," Turk says. "Hunter didn't bring me with him this morning because he wanted me to look out for you. I went against his wishes, disobeyed him and basically lied to him, and then *this* happened. If he knew you met up with Kyle . . ." Turk trails off, casting his gaze out one of the windows.

I can tell he doesn't like being dishonest with Hunter. Neither do I, of course, but *Hunter* has been lying to *me*. Now he's getting a taste of his own medicine. Surely Turk sees that. "I'm not a little girl," I say. "I don't need to be looked after like some kind of invalid."

"If I hadn't been there today, you would have been screwed," Turk says. "Just admit you don't know what you're doing all the time. You want to believe the best of people, and I get that—but your brother is an ass. I have to tell Hunter that talking to Kyle isn't safe," he continues. "That he can't be trusted."

No, I think. This can't happen. "If you tell him," I say, taking a step closer, "then Hunter will never agree to the peace summit. Convincing him to compromise with the Aeries is the only way to get this city back on track."

Turk looks away. His skin smells like apple-scented soap. I pick up his towel from the floor and fold it, hanging it over a chair.

"You don't have to do that," he says.

"Look," I say, ignoring his comment. "There are other people—from other cities—waiting to overthrow Manhattan."

Turk scoffs. "What's that supposed to mean?"

"Nobody except *us* wants the mystics to win," I say. "Because if they do, mystics in other cities are going to revolt. If it looks like that's actually about to happen, somebody somewhere is going to wage war against our city. If we're too busy fighting internally to defend ourselves against foreign enemies, we'll lose. 'United we stand, divided we fall,'" I quote. "I'm not sure who actually said that first, but . . . it makes sense."

Turk frowns. "Does it?

"Unless we figure this out," I say, "we could lose New York completely. Who's to say things won't be worse then?" I take another step; I'm close enough to touch him now. "Keep this secret from Hunter so that he'll go to the peace summit. *Please.*"

Turk clenches his jaw. "Fine. I don't like this, though, Aria."

"Thank you!" I let the bag with Davida's reliquary drop to the floor and wrap my arms around his waist. He tenses, ensuring that his energy doesn't hurt me. My skin begins to tingle and feel warm.

"I care about you so much," Turk whispers into my ear. "I don't want to see you get hurt."

"I know," I say. Aside from Ryah, Turk has been the only one who has really looked out for me since I've returned to Manhattan. "I care about you, too."

"Do you?" he asks. An electric buzz washes over me and my skin heats up even more. "Or do you just care about what I can do for you—how I can help you?"

I pull away from Turk. "What do you mean?"

"I'm not your servant, Aria," he says in a husky voice. "I don't have to do everything you ask me to."

"I never said you were . . . I don't think . . ."

"Never mind," Turk says. He presses his hand to his forehead like he has a headache. "Let's talk about something else."

"Okay." I sit on the edge of his bed. Have I been treating Turk like a servant? I thought we were friends, that he was helping me because he wanted to. "I'm sorry if you feel like I've been selfish."

"I don't," he says. "I'm just . . . tense. Seriously, let's talk about something else." His voice softens, and he peers at me with his light green eyes. "Anything on your mind, Aria Rose?"

"Well," I say. "Yes. There is one thing."

"Shoot."

"Remember what I told you about that old woman Frieda from the compound? How she mentioned Davida's heart?"

Turk nods and sits down next to me.

"I think maybe I should try to find it—the heart, I mean."

No answer from Turk, but he turns so his face is inches from mine. Our noses are practically touching. He tilts his head and leans forward. He's going to kiss me.

Just then, Hunter's face flashes before my eyes: a memory from a few weeks ago, in my bedroom at my parent's apartment. I had just swallowed the capture locket and recovered all my memories of how I'd met Hunter. Hunter held me in his arms and whispered, *You've come back to me.*

"Stop," I say, pushing Turk away. "We can't do this."

He looks deeply into my eyes. He's about to say something when I hear a sound from the doorway.

"Ahem," Shannon says, staring at us with her arms crossed. She's dressed in black training gear, her fiery red hair pulled back in a ponytail.

How much did she see?

"Yes?" Turk says, getting up from the bed and wiping his palms on his jeans.

"I just got back," Shannon says sharply. "Aria, training starts in five." Then she swivels and marches away.

The two-hour session with Shannon feels more like two days.

The basement training room is wide enough that you can practice without having to really interact with anyone if you don't want to. The back half of the room is partitioned off as a place for the mystics to hone their energies. The other half—where I'm standing—is covered with mats, and various targets are pinned to the walls. Some show the outline of a person in black, while others look like archery targets, with different-colored circles and a white bull's-eye in the center.

Shannon has me throw ninja stars at targets, and while my aim is all right, I can't seem to hit any of the bull's-eyes. I keep wondering how much she saw upstairs with Turk. Nothing happened, but does she know that?

I throw a star that wedges itself into the wall, between two posters. "Aria!" Shannon hollers. "What's wrong with you?"

Did nothing happen? I ask myself. Turk tried to kiss me. I pushed him away. But he tried. And that's not exactly nothing.

"I'm fine," I say. "The grocery store attack—was everyone okay?"

Shannon shakes her head. "No, Aria. Everyone wasn't okay."

"How many people died?" I ask.

"Does it matter?" she replies. "Concentrate on what you're doing right now."

"I just wanted to know—"

"You don't get to know everything!" Shannon yells furiously. Her forehead tenses and her eyes redden. "Aria, just, will you throw the star again?" Her voice is wobbly, and for a moment I worry she might cry. I've never seen Shannon show any emotion other than anger.

I grip one of the ninja stars and, without thinking, hurl it toward an archery target. One of the sharp points hits dead center.

Bull's-eye.

Standing a few feet behind me, Shannon shuffles her feet. "Five," she says suddenly.

"What?"

"Five people died in the attack. Two children."

"Oh," I say. "Well . . . thank you for telling me."

She clears her throat. "You're welcome." Then she turns around and heads upstairs.

After a shower, I head to the dining room. I'm not hungry, though; all I can think about is my meeting with Lyrica, her instructions that if I want to honor Davida's memory, I need to find her heart and place it in the reliquary.

Of course I *want* to honor Davida. To repay her for what she did for me and Hunter, yes, but also for what she did my entire life: took care of me, dressed me, nursed me when I was sick.

Landon and Jarek have returned, but they're in a dark mood. It turns out the information they were leaked about the Foster army was false, so they came back empty-handed.

"Do you really think the peace summit might work?" Ryah says over a meal of boiled chicken and rice. "It's happening so soon—on Thursday. That's only two days away! Imagine if they worked things out and the war ended?"

"How do you know about the summit?" I ask.

Ryah shrugs. "Is it a secret? I heard some of the guys talking about it in the library."

Shannon is silent the entire meal, but I can see her shooting me the occasional glance.

"*I* don't know anything about it," Landon says, turning and staring up at Jarek. "Do you?"

Jarek shakes his head. "Nope. I was with you all day."

"Hunter mentioned it to me," Shannon says, "and to some of his inner circle this morning. He's meeting with Aria's brother and Thomas Foster. At noon, on the top deck of the Empire State Building."

"Huh." Landon takes a gulp of water. "Well, I'm not exactly optimistic. Nobody's going to work anything out. Not without a fight."

"Then it's a fight we'll give 'em," says Turk. "Right?"

Suddenly, a memory flashes in my head: my mother's voice, yelling through the intercom in my bedroom. *Aria! Now! We're going to be late!*

"Coming!" I reply into the speaker. I'm sixteen. I turn to Davida and roll my eyes. "I don't want to go. I'd rather stay here with you. We could eat chocolates and watch an old movie. Something with Charlie Chaplin?"

She smiles at me with her hazel eyes, her dark hair pulled back into an impeccable bun. "Your mother would never let me eat chocolates in your room while she was here. Besides, there are far worse things than attending the Governor's Ball."

She motions to the gown I'm wearing: a soft yellow vintage Valentino from the sixties, sleeveless, with one white strap that runs over my right shoulder.

"I know," I say.

"Now stand still." I feel the soft touch of Davida's gloved hands as she does the clasp on the back of the gown. "Turn around."

I spin my bare heels on the carpeted floor.

"You look like a princess."

"No, I don't."

Davida nods. "You do, Aria. Are you ready?"

"Ugh." I plop down on the edge of my bed. "All those boring people. Boring conversations."

"Fine," Davida says in a light voice. "Don't go. What'll you tell your mother? You know she'll put up a good fight. So will your father—these things are important to them, Aria."

I shoot up from the bed and curl my hands into fists, jokingly. "If my parents want a fight, then it's a fight we'll give 'em! Right? We'll—"

"Aria?"

I shake myself from the memory. I'm back at the table with Turk, Shannon, and the others. "Hmm?"

"Whoa," Landon says. His bushy eyebrows are raised questioningly, his brown eyes wide and staring right at me. "You were totally just somewhere else."

"No, I was listening," I say, though I'm sure my face gives me away. I must look spooked.

Landon sits back, rolling up his sleeves slightly. "Oh? Then what'd I just say?"

I fumble for a response, but he holds up his hand. "Can't play a playah, Aria Rose. Can't play a playah."

"What does that even mean?"

Landon wags a tawny finger at me. "You'll figure it out. Jarek, was Aria listening to me?"

"Hmm?" Jarek says, looking up from his plate. He hasn't touched his food, and I wonder what's on his mind. "Sure," he says. "If you say so, Landon."

"Jeez," Landon says, looking back and forth between Jarek and me. "Pay attention to me! What is with you people?"

Ryah starts to laugh. "Not everything is about *you*, Landon."

He scratches his smooth chin, considering this. Then he sticks out his tongue. "That's where you're wrong, sweetheart."

Everyone laughs, and for a second, I relax. It feels nice.

After dinner, I call Hunter's TouchMe, but there's no answer. "Call me," I say, leaving a voice mail. "I miss you." He didn't return to the hideout with Shannon, and no one seems to know where he is. Breakfast in bed this morning feels so far away, like a memory played in black-and-white.

We all go to bed early, hoping to get a good night's sleep. It's only once I'm sure Ryah and Shannon have fallen asleep that I sneak out, into the Depths.

I can't believe I almost let Turk kiss me, I think as I hand a gondolier a few coins and step onto a dark street. We're in an area of the Depths on the Lower West Side, near where Davida was shot.

I've snuck out because I'm convinced I must find Davida's heart and place it in the reliquary. Davida died an honorable death defending Hunter and me, and I must do the right thing and make sure the mystic tradition is carried out properly. Maybe then she can rest in peace.

I tread carefully, as nothing in the Depths is properly lit.

Garbage and broken bottles are scattered across the street, while dirty children rush past me, running along the bridges that cover the canals. The old Aria might have judged them, assuming they were out stealing food or picking pockets. I hope I understand their plight better these days. Even though I've thrown in my lot with the mystics, I've never gone hungry.

A few of the intact buildings have candles on the windowsills, and I can see shadows moving inside. Some people must be home. Wet shirts flutter on droopy clotheslines, and somewhere in the distance I can hear a lazy saxophone.

"Pennies, miss? Pennies?" A homeless woman approaches me, sticking out her hand.

I drop a few coins into her palm. "Thank you," she says, then rushes into an alley. I walk along the street, peering into the canals and trying to find the spot where Davida's murder took place. I pass a few empty storefronts, their glass windows broken, until I come across a strip of stores that seem to be open. One of them has STORE written in thick black paint across the dirty awning.

I step inside.

It's longer than it is wide, and while it's not full of customers, there are more people here than I expected—ten or twelve. There are aisles and aisles of everything imaginable: shampoo, soap, razors, washcloths, towels, sheets, bottles of water and soda and beer. There's a refrigerator that holds meat and other perishables. There are T-shirts and pants and first-aid kits and mystic lightbulbs.

There are more-exotic goods, too, with hefty price tags: cooling patches like the one Kyle was wearing, mystic-infused decals in various designs that act like temporary tattoos, dresses and shirts made with mystic dyes that change color every hour, clothing lacquered with mystic energy so it can never get wet.

Toward the back is a glass case full of firearms, many of which seem mystically enhanced: guns with extra-long barrels, black ray guns, and a selection of knives with ivory- and jewel-encrusted handles.

Behind the counter is a man in his twenties, metal piercings through his nostrils and eyebrows. He's watching an overhead TV and drumming his hands on his knees.

I look up at the screen. It's me.

The station is running video footage of me having my head shaved at the triage center. I'm smiling, and all the people around me are chanting my name. The video is wobbly, as if someone had recorded it on a TouchMe.

"As you can see," a female newscaster is saying, "Aria Rose clearly supports the rebel movement. Here she is shaving her head in solidarity with those who've removed their hair to address vermin issues in the Depths."

Great. Just as Hunter suspected—shaving my head turned out to be a political move.

I spot an aisle with shelves of wigs of various colors, near the beauty products. I walk over and scan the collection: long and short hair, blond and brunette, curly and straight. This store has practically everything.

Feeling bold, I grab a platinum-blond wig that looks like it would come down to my chin. Then I stroll over to the counter.

"Anything else?" the guy behind the counter asks. He looks

at the TV, then at me. He doesn't say anything, but I can tell he recognizes me.

"Do you have any swim goggles?"

He points to a shelf behind him that has cigarettes, lighters, and tiny bottles of booze.

And goggles.

Weird.

"Take your pick," he says.

I point to a cheap-looking pair of black goggles, which he grabs and rings up for me. "That's it?"

"That's it," I say, reaching into my pocket for a few coins.

The cashier raises his eyebrows. "Not interested in getting wild?" he asks so that none of the other customers can hear. He flicks his tongue ring against his front teeth. "I've got Stic."

"No thanks," I say. I pay my bill and grab the goggles and the wig, shove them into my bag, and leave.

Outside, I stroll along a cobblestone street, looking for a familiar landmark. The canal is mere feet away, and I can hear the swishing of the water slapping against the concrete; the tangy smell of seaweed and garbage fills the air.

A few feet ahead stands a streetlamp I think I've seen before. The light has been broken, but I recognize the unusual design on the base. Is this where Davida was shot?

Everything from that night is a blur. Escaping my parents and fleeing to the Depths. Rain teeming down, lightning fracturing the sky, the heat, the soaring of the sirens. My father ordered police boats to search for me and Hunter, and though we didn't know it, there were gunmen not too far behind.

I close my eyes, and the memory comes to me:

A circle of gunmen surrounds us.

"Hunter!" I scream.

"Aria!" he calls back, but then his voice is muffled. A gag has been shoved into his mouth, and I see Stiggson and Klartino saying something to him. In the distance, I think I see Davida at the edge of the street, near one of the gondolas.

One of the men pulls a bag over Hunter's head and clamps his hands behind his back with a pair of silvery handcuffs. He is carried aboard one of the police gondolas that followed us, then tossed belowdecks like a piece of cargo.

Someone shuts the hatch, and the boat pulls away from the dock, heading off to deeper water. There's a crunch behind me, as if someone has just stepped on a branch or broken a piece of pavement.

I turn my head.

My father emerges from the shadows. "You're going to watch this. As a lesson."

I shake my head no and close my eyes.

"Open your eyes, Aria."

Grudgingly, I do.

The boat slows. My father calls out a few orders; the men get Hunter from the hold and wrestle him into a standing position. The bag is yanked off his head, and I see his face—that gorgeous, beautiful face—look for me in vain. One of the men presses his gun to the back of Hunter's head.

"You've led us on quite a chase," my father says, "but this is where it ends, with the death of your mystic boyfriend. You will marry Thomas, our family will unite with the Fosters, and Garland will win the election. That is how this story ends."

He raises his hand into the air—a signal.

There is a flare of light and the sharp report of a gunshot.

Hunter's body falls forward, hits the side of the gondola, then folds over and drops into the water with a sickening splash.

Only it wasn't Hunter's body—not really. Davida was there, and she'd snuck belowdecks. While Hunter was paralyzed by the quicksilver handcuffs, she used her mystic powers to take on his image. She hid him and the gunmen shot her instead of Hunter.

Davida's power was uniquely rare: she could take on the full appearance of another person just by touching him. I remember the first time she demonstrated this for me in my bedroom as clearly as if it happened only yesterday.

Hold out your hands, Davida had told me, *and close your eyes.* Her fingertips had brushed mine, and then my entire body began to buzz like a beehive—I felt a pull stronger than anything I'd ever felt. Like something was digging down deep inside me and drawing out everything in my body that made me *me.*

When I opened my eyes, I was staring at myself: at my wavy brown hair, my hazel eyes, my face and my teeth. *I can borrow someone's appearance,* she said. *Cast a disguising glamour on myself and others. That's my talent.*

The memory dissolves, and now I open my eyes for real. I'm back in lower Manhattan. In the streetlight, I recognize the blotchy red awning of a storefront, its glass cracked into an intricate spiderweb design. *Yes,* I think. *This is familiar.*

I rush to the corner of an alley, a tunnel of blackness. *This is where Hunter gave me back the capture locket.*

Across the street is an old-looking wooden dock where a fleet of gondolas is tied up for the night. I blink, and I can practically see Stiggson and Klartino gagging Hunter and pulling him away from me.

I rush toward the edge of the street—in my mind's eye I see the police gondola Hunter was taken aboard, the hatch he was tossed down.

Where Davida was hiding, waiting to save him.

This is it. I can sense it: the spot where she was killed.

I glance around. It's dark out; there's little risk of being seen. I debate whether to take off my clothes so they don't get wet, but the water in the canal is so gross-looking that I decide to leave them on.

I set my bag down on the edge of the street, in the shadows where I don't think it will be stolen. I tuck the wig inside and pull out the goggles I bought in the store, snapping them over my eyes. I remove my shoes and socks, and dip my feet into the water.

Holy Aeries, that's cold.

I give myself to the count of three. One, two, three—

Then I push off and dunk myself in the water.

I'm immediately grateful for the goggles. With my eyes protected, I can actually open them, though the salty water is so cloudy it's hard to see. I swim down, my hands scouring muck and dirt and bits of dead plants, but the canal doesn't seem to bottom out.

How am I supposed to find a heart?

I return to the surface and take a deep breath. Then I dive back down. My fingertips scrape something rough, like rock, and I figure this must be the bottom. But even if there is a heart down here, how will I find it? Will it be . . . whole? Or will it be goopy and falling apart? What if a fish or some other water animal pecked it to nothing?

Or will there only be Davida's skeleton, her heart washed away completely, like a stone or a piece of garbage?

I shiver at the sickening questions that run through my head. Maybe this wasn't such a great idea.

I come back up for air and make one more attempt, but the only thing I manage to grab is a pebble. Not much I can do with that.

I swim over to a dock where a handful of gondolas are tied up for the night and hoist myself onto the wooden deck. I squeeze my shirt and shorts, trying to get the water out. Thankfully, no one has taken my bag. I slip on my socks and sneakers; then I stuff the goggles back into my bag with the wig and the reliquary.

I stare at the canal, which ripples silently. If Davida's heart is still down there, I must find it. But how?

Most of the gondoliers are off duty, but I find one who lets me off in front of the empty space where the rebel hideout is concealed. It's the middle of the night; everyone inside must be sleeping. My initial plan was to call Turk and have him come out and get me, but now that I'm standing on the street corner, a thought has occurred to me.

I glance down at the chain around my neck. The trace that Lyrica removed from my spirit and placed in the locket is made of mystic energy.

The energy should allow me to cross through. Right?

I squint, trying to see where the mystic force field begins, but I can't. If I attempt to pass through and the locket *doesn't* work, will I be electrocuted?

Okay, Aria, I tell myself. *Just walk.*

I remove the locket from my neck and hold it out in front of me, so that it sticks out farther than my fingertips. I inhale and take a step forward. Then another.

Nothing.

I glance down at the locket. *Don't fail me.*

Another step. Then another, and suddenly I feel a whoosh of air and a firm pressure squeezing me. There's a pop and the feeling of a large, invisible hand gripping my body—and I'm through the force field.

Before me is the brownstone. I've made it.

I rush up the steps. Inside, I'm thankful for the cool air and my safe return. All the lights are out. The door closes behind me and I tiptoe through the foyer, about to head upstairs, when a lamp clicks on.

Hunter is standing in the living room with a look on his face that I can't read. "Care to tell me what you've been up to?"

· XV ·

I'm still wet from the canal, and I must look incredibly guilty. "Just swimming," I say.

Hunter gives me an incredulous look. "Swimming?"

"That's right." I rest a hand on the banister. "It's . . . part of my training with Shannon."

"No, it's not," Hunter says. He's wearing a gray T-shirt and faded jeans. It's the most relaxed I've seen him, actually. He almost looks like his old self. His blond hair is swept off his forehead. His blue eyes sparkle. "Why are you lying to me?"

I don't *want* to lie to Hunter. I want us to have an open, honest relationship. But he isn't open and honest with me.

"You don't trust me," I say. "You're just as bad as my father."

Hunter winces. It's a low blow, I know. My father is a terrible man, fueled by greed, not by love. But in a way, it's true. My father only wants one thing—power—and he does whatever he can to get it. Hunter is the same, even though he wants justice for his people, revenge for his mother. He doesn't see the damage he's doing along the way.

Hunter snarls at me. "How can you say that? After everything we've been through. I *love* you, Aria. More than anything in the world."

"But things are different now, Hunter." I shake my head. "I wish they weren't, but they are. You're different."

"What do you mean?" Hunter asks. "How am I different?"

"We barely speak," I say, "and when we do it's always about the revolution. And that's beside the fact that you used our video chats as ads without telling me, and you've been keeping me in this hideout like some sort of prisoner."

Hunter stares at me as though we're speaking different languages. He seems confused, hurt. "I've been trying to make sure you're safe," he says. "And I've already apologized about the videos. But the mystic cause is my priority right now, Aria. I thought you understood that."

I let go of the banister. "I want *us* to be your priority."

Hunter starts to respond, but I hold up my hand. "I gave up my life for you," I say, "my entire world . . . and now we don't even see each other. I could be by your side, helping you—but you don't include me in anything. I don't even know the names of the people you keep around you. Every move you make is secret."

Upstairs, I hear someone stir. I wouldn't be surprised if our voices have woken people up, but I don't care. Hunter and I have been like two ships passing in the night—we're finally speaking about what's important. We need to finish this conversation.

"I have to pick up where my mom left off," Hunter says. The lamplight casts a radiant glow on his face, making him look almost angelic. The light stubble that shades his cheeks, the sharp lines of his jaw, the faint scar just above his left eyebrow—even his slightly crooked nose. His features are so familiar I can see them when I close my eyes.

But now it's like he's a stranger. I love him so much. Why is he pushing me away?

"It's my duty," he continues. "It's what my grandfather did, and my mother . . . she *died* for me." Hunter curls his hands into fists. "How can you not understand this, Aria? How can you be so selfish?"

His words hit me like blows. "I *do* understand," I say, "or at least, I try to understand. I've been through—"

"What do you know about what I'm going through?" Hunter asks angrily. "You're a pretty, rich girl from the Aeries. What hardships have you ever experienced?" He points a finger at me. "Has one of your parents died? No. *Both* of mine are dead—so don't talk to me about what you gave up."

His words are searing. "How can you say that to me? I'm your girlfriend," I tell him. "I can help you if you'd just let me in, break down those walls you've put up—"

"I've had enough." Hunter holds up his hands in surrender. "I'm tired. And I don't want to talk about this anymore."

"We're not finished." I reach out to grab his arm but he shrugs me off.

"Don't," he says softly. He stares at me, hurt. Suddenly, he seems so fragile that I'm scared he might break.

"You can't do this on your own," I say. "You need help."

"Oh?" he says. "I do? Help from who?"

"From me," I say. Why is my voice soft? It feels like I can barely speak. "From everyone."

He snickers. "Everyone including your brother and Thomas Foster? Is that why you want me to meet with them—so they can help me? I'm some kind of pity case?"

"No," I say, "of course you're not. But you *should* meet with Kyle and Thomas, to figure out a plan for the city—"

"Oh, screw the damn peace summit, Aria!" Hunter snaps. "You want me to include you in my plans? Fine. Here you go: the only reason I agreed to that in the first place is because I'm going to surprise your brother and kill him."

What?

Hunter blinks, staring at me with bloodshot eyes.

"Tell me that isn't true," I say.

"It is true," Hunter says, lowering his voice slightly. A vein in his forehead is standing out, ready to pop. "My men have developed a bomb that's going to wipe out every human within a quarter-mile radius. It's something we've been working on since the start of the war. I wasn't sure we were going to use it, but . . . this is the perfect occasion." His voice sounds harsh, cruel. "Don't you think?"

I'm stunned into silence.

He shrugs. "Unfortunately, only mystics will be immune to its effects, and not the poor who also side with our cause, but that's the price we'll have to pay."

"Who else knows about this?" I ask. "Shannon? Turk?"

He shakes his head. "No. I couldn't risk them trying to stop me. Only a handful of my inner circle knows, the ones who were devoted to my mother. We've tried to do things the right way," Hunter says. His features are suddenly distorted with rage, his cheeks flushed. "With *elections*. Being nice and proper and all that . . . *crap*. And where has it gotten us?"

"But, Hunter," I say, "a bomb isn't the answer. You're basically re-creating the Conflagration, and that's what led to the mystics being drained in the first place. I know you think you're doing the right thing, but you're not. What are you trying to prove?"

His lips tighten into a thin red line. "That we're strong. That we're not to be messed with. That you can't just kill us, or drain us, or do whatever you want to us because you have a certain last name and live in the Aeries." Hunter sucks in a deep breath. "The people up there will see what we are capable of," he says. "And we will come out victorious."

"No," I say softly. "You'll come out a *murderer*. I love you, Hunter, but . . . I can't believe you think this is a good idea."

"It's not matter of good or bad anymore, Aria," Hunter says. His eyes have grown cold, icy. "Or even right and wrong. We have to do what we must to survive."

I shake my head. "I can't be a part of this."

Hunter's body tenses. "I'm not asking you to."

He moves to the side, and I see a bouquet of freshly plucked red roses resting on a wooden end table. "Here," he says. He picks up the bouquet and throws it at my feet. "These are for you. Don't even think about leaving this place until I come and get you."

He pushes past me, out the front door. "Hunter!" I call, following him. "Don't walk away from me!"

Hunter is down the flight of steps when he stops for a moment. There's a second when I think he's going to spin around and rush into my arms and tell me he was kidding, there is no bomb; we'll apologize to each other and promise that starting now, we act like a true couple. We'll figure things out together. He'll kiss me, and everything terrible will wash away, and we'll be left with a relationship that is fresh and new and wonderful.

But Hunter doesn't turn around. He picks up speed, and all I can see is his back as he walks away, into the force field, where he disappears from sight.

I stare at the flowers, numb. A few weeks ago I would have cried if Hunter had spoken to me that way.

But now I don't feel like crying.

I just feel angry.

The next morning I am red-eyed and exhausted.

If Hunter follows through with this plan, innocent people are going to die. How can I stop him? It was so easy for him to walk out on me. And just as easy for me to lie to him. He doesn't trust me—he certainly isn't going to take my advice on something this monumental.

I'm alone in the room—Ryah's and Shannon's beds are already made. I shower, then dry off and slip on a pair of Ryah's gray training pants, a freshly laundered cherry-colored V-neck shirt that hangs off my shoulders, and the sneakers I wore yesterday. With the silver locket securely around my neck, I slip my TouchMe into my pocket and make sure that the bag with Davida's reliquary, the goggles, and the wig is still hidden under my bed. The next time I leave the town house alone, the wig will be the perfect disguise.

Downstairs, I pour myself a cup of coffee and a bowl of cereal.

I pass through the kitchen and into the dining area, where my friends are eating breakfast. They're seated at the table closest to the wall, near the door to the deck.

"I just wish I were stronger," Ryah is saying, taking a bite of omelet. She's already spiked her hair, which seems extra blue this morning. She's wearing a white T-shirt and tight lavender shorts. She turns to Jarek. "You lifted, like, almost two hundred pounds downstairs in the training room. I can barely lift a twelve-pounder without getting sore." She pokes her bicep, frowning at it. "Get bigger!"

I look over at Turk, whose shirt is soaked with sweat, his brow sweaty and red. Apparently, there was a training session this morning that I wasn't invited to.

"I wouldn't say *two hundred*," Landon corrects her. He blows on his coffee, trying to cool it. "That's what I'd call an exaggeration. No offense, Jarek."

Jarek says something in response, but his mouth is full and I can't understand him. Sitting next to Landon, he looks like a giant—Jarek is wearing a black wifebeater that shows off his arms, each one practically as big as Landon's head.

"What did he say?" I ask Turk, sliding next to him on the bench.

"Aria!" Ryah says, looking happy to see me. "You're up! You looked like you needed your rest, so we let you sleep in."

"Thanks, I guess," I say.

Turk doesn't even look at me. He keeps his eyes fixed on his plate, and I wonder if he's upset about yesterday, about our almost-kiss.

"I said"—Jarek repeats loudly—"that I could lift *a thousand* pounds and I still wouldn't have an ounce of your power." He frowns at Ryah. "So I wouldn't go around being jealous of me."

"Jarek," Ryah says gently. "You're not being fair to yourself. Your powers are—"

"Weak," he says. "I can't do what you do. I'm no help to anyone." He stands up abruptly—the bench he's sitting on screeches across the floor, and he rushes out of the dining room.

"Poor guy," Ryah says softly.

"And he definitely can't lift a thousand pounds," Landon says, rolling his eyes and playing with the collar of his yellow polo shirt. "He is de-*lu*-sional."

"He needs to grow up," Shannon says.

Like me, Shannon doesn't seem like much of a morning person: her head is bent over her coffee, long strands of red hair covering her face, and there are some scrambled eggs on her plate that she doesn't seem to be eating. Her black training gear peeks out from underneath a zipped-up white hoodie.

"He's just upset," Ryah says. "Let him be."

Shannon doesn't reply, and Ryah turns her attention to me. "You don't look so hot, Aria."

"I didn't get much sleep."

Landon coughs. "Neither did I. With all the fighting going on downstairs last night." He shakes a fork at me. "Didn't anyone ever teach you to keep it down? Or do they just let you scream however loudly you want to in the Aeries?"

"I'm sorry," I say, embarrassed that he heard us all the way up on the fourth floor. I wonder what he heard—surely nothing about Hunter's plan to bomb the peace summit, or he would've mentioned it by now. Landon is not one to mince words.

"No, you're not," Shannon says to me.

"Of course I am."

"Girls," Turk interjects, then takes a gulp of orange juice. "Chill." He turns to Landon. "Landon, stop being mean."

Landon's jaw drops. "I'm *not* being mean. I just don't need my beauty rest disturbed by a lovers' scream-fest." He pushes away his plate. "Jeez. Is that too much to ask?"

"Yes," Ryah and Turk respond simultaneously.

"I'm sorry," I say. "It won't happen again." *Because Hunter doesn't even want to speak to me.*

Ryah waves her hand. "Don't worry, Aria. Everyone is on edge about the peace summit. Wondering what's going to happen."

There's silence at the table. It seems as if I'm the only one who knows Hunter is planning to detonate a bomb.

"I for one hope there will be *some* kind of resolution," Ryah says. "This war can't go on forever."

"Can't it?" Shannon jumps up from the table. "Nothing is going to get resolved at some stupid peace summit. The only way to win a war is to *fight*. With weapons."

She leaves the room, but her words linger.

Even after the others return to their breakfast, I wonder, do I tell Turk—or anyone—what Hunter is planning? I'm not sure. Do I warn Kyle and Thomas and risk betraying Hunter?

Kyle and Thomas have both said they would sooner see me dead than fighting with the rebels. But that doesn't mean that *not* telling them is the right thing to do. If I keep the bomb a secret, they'll be walking into their own deaths and a second Conflagration. But if I warn them, I'll be betraying the rebel cause and the summit I helped orchestrate.

It's a lose-lose situation.

Landon excuses himself, saying he's heading upstairs to shower. Ryah grabs the remaining plates and utensils to bring to the kitchen. "Shannon and I are going back down to train," she says. "Holler if you need anything." Then she heads out of the dining area, leaving me alone with Turk.

"You okay?" he asks.

"Sure. Why wouldn't I be?"

He shrugs.

"Are *you* okay?" I ask.

He shrugs again. "Sure." Then he winks at me. "Why wouldn't I be?"

"Did you overhear any of our fight last night?"

Turk shakes his head. "I'm a pretty deep sleeper. When I'm out, I'm out. I'm guessing it was intense?"

"You could say that," I say. "He left angry, and, well . . . I feel bad about the whole thing."

Turk raises an eyebrow. "Want help in taking your mind off it?"

"No," I say. "I just want to get out of here."

"And go where?" Turk asks. "You don't like to stay in one place very long, do you?"

"No," I say. "I suppose I don't. The thing is . . . Davida's heart."

Turk's eyes widen. "What about it?"

"Last night. I tried to find it at the spot where she died, but I couldn't."

"You snuck out of here last night?" Turk asks, shocked.

"Keep your voice down!" I say. "And . . . yes. That's what Hunter and I were fighting about. Well, that's what we *started* fighting about. . . . Anyway, I found the canal where she died, and I swam to the bottom. But it was dark, and I couldn't see anything. I think if I go during the day—"

"You thought her actual corpse would just be lying there at the bottom of the canal?" Turk asks. "Just, you know, looking at her watch, waiting for you to turn up?"

His voice is thick with sarcasm.

"Aside from the fact that her flesh would be rotted, there are currents and tides and all sorts of things that would have carried her bones away," he continues. "Her heart is the only thing that would have remained—a mystic heart is impervious to the elements. But you'll never find it without knowing the ways of the water. The trick is to know how the currents move and where they go. The sort of thing sailors used to know."

"So should I look it up on my TouchMe?" I ask, reaching for my pocket.

"No," Turk says. "You need an expert. These days, you'd probably have to find the oldest sailor alive to get an idea about that stuff."

"So let's go find him." I hurry past the dining tables, down the long hallway toward the front of the town house.

"You think we can just walk outside and find some ancient sailor?" Turk says. "Don't be ridiculous."

"Why not? There must be hundreds of gondoliers in the Depths. At least one of them must know how to trace the currents."

When I reach the foyer, I glance back at Turk. "Are you coming with me or not?"

He's standing still, hands stuffed into his pockets.

"Fine," I say angrily. "Have it your way." I open the door and step outside, onto the stoop.

At least, I *think* that's where I'm going.

Instead, I find myself reentering the town house through the back door in the dining room, where we've just had breakfast.

I stare at the empty wooden tables and the yellow walls. What just happened?

I rush back down the hallway and past the kitchen into the foyer, to find Turk standing where I left him. He looks like he knows something he's not telling me.

"Are you messing with me?" I ask him. "What's going on?"

Turk shrugs. "Not me. Hunter."

"He's done something with all the exits?"

Turk nods.

I yank open the curtains to one of the living room windows and press the touchpad on the wall. The glass slides open, and hot air filters into the room. I grab the edges of the window and stick my right leg through the open space, then watch as it disappears— but to where?

Damn him, I think. I draw my leg back in, then stick my head out the window.

"Aria, don't!" Turk calls, but I've already done it.

There's a whoosh of air and suddenly my head is coming through a *different* window in another room, where I can see the entryway to the hall. Unlike passing through the force field, which feels like being squeezed in a vise, this doesn't feel like anything is happening.

What has Hunter done?

I pull my head inside, and I'm back in the living room, in front of the window. "This is insane," I say to Turk. "What's the deal?"

"He came back early this morning and looped all the doors and the windows," Turk says. "Every exit has a partner. If you open one, the other opens, too, and if you try to leave through any of them, you'll only end up back inside the house. None of us can leave until he breaks the loops."

I have to give it to Hunter—he's smart. Irritatingly so.

"So everyone knows about this and just decided not to tell me?"

Turk gives me a sheepish look.

Pushing past Turk, I rush up the stairs to my bedroom on the third floor. I hear him pounding up the steps behind me.

There are five windows in the bedroom—three on the wall next to my bed, and two on the adjoining wall that look out onto the street.

I head over to the closest window and press the touchpad to open it. I stick my head out—

And find myself staring into the window of the second-floor library. It's empty, with papers and leftover cups of coffee scattered along the conference table.

"Argh!" I scream again, pulling my head back inside. I turn, and Turk is right behind me. "So every floor—every possible exit—is blocked?" I ask.

"Yes," he says. "Which is exactly what I told you downstairs."

"This is so unfair," I say. "How could Hunter do this to me? You have to help me get out of here. Please, Turk."

He averts his gaze. "I can't. I promised Hunter I wouldn't."

"What about what you promised me?" I say.

Turk shakes his head. "You've gotten into too much trouble, Aria. You don't like to play by the rules, which I get, but I don't want to be responsible for you getting kidnapped—or worse. I'm sorry."

He gives me a tight-lipped smile, then turns and heads out of the bedroom.

In some small corner of my mind, I know this isn't Turk's fault. If anything, he's sympathetic, but I don't want to think about that now. It's easier to be angry with him.

"Fine," I yell. "Go!" I slam the door shut. I hope he feels awful.

What am I going to do? Wait until Hunter shows up and decides he's not mad at me anymore? Now that I know he's planning to set off a bomb, is there any chance he'll let me leave the hideout before the peace summit?

Not likely. Hunter was the one who freed me, who saved me from my parents. But ever since then, he's kept me cooped up, first in the mystic compound, and now here.

He's not the boy I fell in love with. And I'm not the girl he fell in love with. Have we changed too much to stay together?

Maybe our love wasn't meant to last a lifetime.

Just then, a head pops through one of the open windows in the bedroom.

It's Jarek, his impossibly broad shoulders filling the window frame.

"Shh." He holds a finger to his lips, motioning for me to be silent. "I can help you."

· XVI ·

I have no idea why Jarek is offering to help me, but I don't want to give him time to change his mind.

"Come on," he says. He grabs the ledge and pulls himself into the room, careful not to make any noise. No one can know what we're up to.

Quickly, I take off my locket and slip it into the pocket of a ratty-looking sweatshirt in the closet. Since the rebel hideout is untraceable, if I leave the locket here, then whoever is tracking me won't realize I'm gone.

And since it's probably Hunter who put the trace on me in the first place, well, he'll think I'm still here. His pretty songbird in a cage.

"Aria, seriously," Jarek says, looking nervous. "Let's go."

I pull out the bag I stuffed under my bed last night, removing the blond wig I purchased in the Depths; it came with a cap, which I stretch over my skull. Then on goes the wig.

The reliquary and the goggles are still tucked safely inside the bag. I grab another pouch of coins from the cabinet in the wall and toss the bag over my shoulder.

"Whoa." Jarek lets out a low whistle. "You look . . ."

"Strange," I say, glancing at myself in the mirror, seeing a girl with my features and bright platinum-blond hair staring back at me. I am instantly reminded of my mother and her friends, who love nothing more than going to the salon and having their hair infused with mystic dyes and sculpted into pieces of art.

I've never been one to focus much on my looks. The most my father ever said to me about my style was that I looked *respectable,* and that was on the night of my engagement party to Thomas. Kiki was the one who loved mystic-enhanced skin and hair, and she could spend thousands of dollars on one outfit. She tried to get me to highlight my hair once, and I refused. We got into a fight and didn't speak for three days.

"I was gonna say intense," Jarek says.

I look back at the mirror. Why didn't I choose a more demure wig? The shiny blond hair is almost white, with an asymmetrical cut shooting from the nape of my neck to just below my chin.

"Ready?" Jarek asks. "We've gotta leave now, before people start looking for us. The others are showering or training, and Diamond and Roderick are gone, so the place is pretty empty."

"Who?" I ask.

"You know," Jarek says, swiping his hair back behind his ears, "those older dudes who never speak to us."

Oh—those guys. Hunter's henchmen. "So where should we go?" I ask. "All the windows and doors are looped. That's what Turk told me, at least."

"At the core of the building, sure," Jarek says. "And we can't go up because there's a force field closing us in from the outside, and

Hunter surely wired that as well to make sure you didn't jump off the building or whatever."

I stare up at Jarek, confused. It's obvious he's figured out a plan.

He tilts his head down at me. Even if I stood on my tiptoes, I wouldn't reach his chin. "Why am I helping you?" he says.

"Hmm?"

"That's what you're thinking," he says. "Why am I helping you?"

"I appreciate it, but . . . yeah. That *is* what I was thinking."

He lets out a long breath. "What Hunter did, it's not cool. You should only be here if you want to. Not because anybody says you need to be."

"Thank you," I say. "I appreciate that. And I thought you didn't even like me."

His face is still. "I don't."

"Oh," I say, feeling my heart race. "Well—"

"I'm just kidding, Aria," Jarek says, rolling his eyes.

"Ha, ha," I say, letting my arms relax at my sides. "So . . . you're helping me, which is wonderful, but we can't go out and we can't go up. What's left?"

Jarek gives me a crooked smile. "Down, of course."

We sneak down the stairs to the first floor and pass the kitchen and the armory. The door to the basement is open, and I can hear Shannon yelling. "Blast him like it hurts, Ryah!"

Jarek peers down the steps, making sure no one is coming up, then waves me past him. The door to the infirmary is closed, then we're in the dining area. The long tables are empty.

"Where are we going?" I whisper.

"Here." Jarek strides over to a table that's against the far wall and moves it a few inches. He drops to his knees and runs his hands along the large stone tiles.

"What are you doing?" I whisper.

His fingers stop on a groove next to one of the tiles. He pushes down with his thumbs and the tile drops into the floor, creating a space wide enough for one person.

Jarek glances over his shoulder. "Emergency exit."

I peer into the darkness. "So we just . . . jump?"

He laughs. "Of course not. Are you crazy? The drop is over twenty feet." He reaches down and presses a button on the inside of the shaft. Suddenly, the vertical tunnel is full of light. "Ladies first," he says.

A metal ladder is fastened to one of the walls. "Are you sure this is safe?"

"Yes. Now go. We don't have much time."

I nod, stepping onto the ladder. I'm glad I'm not claustrophobic, because there's barely an inch on either side of me. I feel like I'm burrowing into some sort of cave.

Above me, Jarek begins to descend, and I hear a scratching noise as the tile above us slides back into place. Tiny circles embedded in the walls cast a pale green glow over the dark cement. There's a dripping noise coming from somewhere, and the air smells stale, as though it's been trapped in this passageway for years.

"You all right?" Jarek speaks quietly, but his voice echoes like we're inside some huge cavern.

"Yes," I reply. The rungs are a bit slippery. *Focus on your grip,* I tell myself.

"Almost there," Jarek says after what feels like a full ten minutes. "Should be, anyway."

My shirt is sticking to my back, and beads of perspiration line my forehead and drip down my cheeks. I reach my foot toward the next rung, and it lands on solid ground. "I'm at the bottom," I say, relieved. I step to the side to make room for Jarek, when—

"Watch it!"

Jarek grabs my arm just before I fall.

The ground is actually a cement platform, no wider than two or three feet. Below us is a sheet of water: a pool of black liquid that slaps lightly against the walls.

I nearly toppled right into it.

Jarek jumps down next to me and pulls me to the middle of the platform. There's barely room enough for both of us, and he slides his hand around my waist to balance us.

"What *is* this?" I ask.

"A sub-sub-subbasement," he says. "We're way underneath the training room right now. This was built as an escape route in case the hideout is ever raided. It shouldn't loop, because this is the only exit in the entire house below water level, and that's the extent of the force field." Jarek grips me tighter. "There's a loophole down there somewhere. All you have to do is swim through it."

I stare into the water. I see something shimmer and I think I can make out the green loophole beneath the surface, but then I look again and the water simply looks black. "Though in all honesty," Jarek says, "I have no idea where it lets out."

If I weren't worried about falling, I'd smack him. "So basically what you're saying is that you have no idea whether this will work," I say. "There may be a loophole down there, but if there is there's no saying it won't (a) *not* let me out of here or (b) let me out of here but dump me, say, right into my parents' apartment?"

"I don't think it will let you out into your parents' apartment." Jarek cracks a smile. "That would be pretty dumb of whoever made it."

"Is it safe?"

I can feel Jarek shrug. "Probably not. But is that going to stop you?"

Good point. I have no idea where this loophole will take me, but if it was meant to safeguard the mystics, then I'll have to trust that, wherever I end up, it won't be *too* dangerous.

"Are you coming with me?"

He shakes his head. "I'll soften the blow when everyone realizes you're gone. I can't hold 'em off for long, but I'll try to buy you some extra time."

"Okay," I say. "Thanks."

I remove the wig, stuffing it back inside the bag, but leave the cap on my head. I take out the goggles and snap them on.

Jarek gives my hand a squeeze. "Don't think too hard or you'll chicken out."

"I'm not a chicken," I say.

"Then jump," he says.

So I do.

I step off the landing and plunge into the water below. It's surprisingly warm, like bathwater. Swimming downward, I see the loophole immediately, a perfect circle of blazing green mystic energy in the murk. I kick out my legs, splashing water behind me and reaching, reaching—

Until I break the surface, gasping for air.

I toss back my head; my face is hit by rays of sunlight and the familiar, overwhelming heat.

Opening my eyes, I look around: I am in the middle of a canal in the Depths.

"Look!" says a young girl sitting on a gondola with her mother. "Someone is swimming!"

I tread water, spitting out a mouthful of brown.

"Get out of there!" a gondolier hollers at me from a few feet away. I glance to the side; a cluster of gondoliers are standing up in their boats shouting at me and waving their arms, cigarette smoke curling in tiny spirals. "What are you doing, girlie?"

This canal runs along a fairly busy street; people are hustling to and fro. The buildings, though covered with dirt, seem mostly intact. Where am I?

A few feet down, two children are sitting with their feet dangling into the water, next to a narrow stone bridge. I swim toward them, moving out of the way of whizzing gondoliers and water taxis.

"Why are you all wet?" the little boy asks me as I approach the canal's edge.

"Silly," the girl sitting next to him says to me. She's missing her front baby teeth, and both she and the boy are wearing dirty clothes—ripped shirts, pants with holes and stains. Their faces are smudged, and they have the same chocolate-brown eyes. "We're not allowed to swim in the canals. Everybody knows that."

"Mind helping me?" I say.

They nod excitedly. I grab the edge of the canal and hoist myself up, and the children help pull me onto the cobblestone street.

I lie there for a second, catching my breath. The boy and the girl stand over me, staring down. Their heads block the sun, and for a second I feel cool. I close my eyes.

"Are you dead?" the little boy asks.

"Of course she's not dead," the girl says. "I can see her breathing."

"Doesn't seem like she's breathing to me," the boy says. "Not one bit."

I open my eyes and the boy screams.

"I'm alive," I say, pushing myself into a seated position. "Don't you worry about me."

The girl pats the boy on his shoulder. "He gets scared easily."

"Do not!" the boy shouts.

They're cute. For a second, they remind me of Kyle and me when we were younger. "Thank you for your help," I say to them. I remove the wig from my bag—it's wet but not soaked. I take off my goggles, then place the wig over the cap that's still covering my scalp.

"Wow," the little girl says. "I like your fake hair."

"Thanks," I say. "Do you mind telling me where I am?"

"West Side," the girl says. "Just south of Houston Street."

"Thanks," I say, surprised at how far downtown this loophole dropped me. "You two take care of yourselves, you hear?"

They nod again, and I stand, wiping my hands on Ryah's pants. The way the sun is beating down, I should be dry in no time.

I walk away from the canal and the gondoliers, who are still staring at me. I check to make sure the reliquary and the coins are still in my bag—they are—and toss the goggles in as well. Inside my sneakers, water squishes between my toes. Thankfully, no one on the street seems to notice a wet, uber-blond girl strolling over the broken pavement.

I take a few quick turns to distance myself from the scene and spot another canal not too far away. I make my way toward it. It's time to begin my search for someone who can help me track down Davida's heart.

· XVII ·

I hurry west along the hot streets of SoHo.

A few gondolas churn the water as they pass. I see a row of brownstones that look like they've been covered with black paint—actually layers and layers of accumulated dirt. A few of the windows have shutters, which might be charming if the paint weren't peeling and the wooden slats broken.

Besides the brownstones, there are various mystic-enhanced buildings throughout the area. Some were built from scratch by mystics, while others have shiny modern additions of Damascus steel on top of older buildings. In those cases, though the steel has survived the bombings intact, the lower stories haven't, leaving transcendent Aeries skyscrapers resting on poles that seem far too thin to support their weight.

I crane my neck and stare into the sky: I can see the faint outline of the bridges that crisscross the Aeries, glistening in the sun like silvery spiderwebs. I wonder if anyone up there comprehends the fragility of the structures they inhabit; it would be easy for the rebels to break the reinforcements, causing thousands of buildings to plummet.

But how many Aeries dwellers have ever set foot in the Depths? This is a class of people who've been raised to think that buildings crashing into the water below is cause for celebration: Plummet Parties. They never think about the devastation left in the Depths—the dirt and debris and falling metal.

The destruction of the past month has been different, though. Has the war *really* affected people in the Aeries? Are they less enthusiastic about my family and the Fosters? And if they are, how can I help them understand that mystics and the humans who live in the Depths must be granted equal rights? Would people like Kiki and Bennie ever see that?

As I make my way along the canal, I spot a half-dozen wooden posts sticking out of the water near a rickety-looking dock. Gondolas are crowded around the posts, waiting for passengers. The gondoliers stand in the back of their boats, swaying with the water as they chat and smoke thin cigarettes. A few of the younger ones are splayed out on the dock with their shoes off, dipping their toes into the water for a brief respite from the heat.

I approach them first—they're most likely to talk to me.

"Hello?" I take one step onto the dock and jump back when a board snaps under my feet.

One of the boys laughs. "Fancy a ride, miss? Where to?"

I tug on the back of my blond wig, making sure it's secure. Thankfully, no one recognizes me.

"I'll give you a ride," an older boy says, cocking his head at me.

"Don't listen to him," another gondolier says. This one has a sweet-looking, if dirty, face and sweaty blond hair plastered to his forehead. "I'll make sure you get where you need to go." He motions to a dingy black gondola tied to the dock, its nose rising out of the filthy water. "C'mon."

I hold up my hand. "Thanks, but I don't need a ride." The boys all laugh. "I mean, I don't need to go anywhere. I need information."

"Whatcha wanna know?" a little boy asks me. He's sitting cross-legged on the dock, staring up with saucer-shaped eyes beneath a gray cap.

"Well," I say, not sure how to phrase my question. "I need to know about tides. And currents."

The boys look at me as if I'm speaking a foreign language.

"You know, how to navigate the waters."

They glance at each other. The sweaty blond boy steps forward and shoves his hands into his pockets. "So . . . you *don't* want a ride?"

I shake my head. "No."

A few of them curse under their breath, then turn their attention back to the water.

"Sorry, miss," the blond one says. "But we need to eat. And the only way we eat is if we get paid."

I have some coins in my pocket, but not enough for all of them—and I need to save some to pay a sailor who can help me track Davida's heart.

"I understand." I nod toward the older gondoliers. "Could any of them help me?"

The blond boy rubs his forehead. "Lemme ask my da."

He tramps down the dock, calling out to his father. The older gondoliers stop their chattering, and one of them pushes forward in his boat, removing his weathered cap.

"This lady has a question for you," the boy says.

The gondoliers stare at me, no doubt wondering what I'm doing loitering around the docks. I'm certainly not dressed like a lady, with my platinum-blond hair and my super-tight clothes.

The boy's father sweeps back a mop of gray hair, then puts his cap back on. He takes a drag from his cigarette and blows the smoke toward me. "Well?"

Under my wig, my scalp has begun to sweat. "Do you know how things flow in the canals?"

The man scrunches his nose. "Huh?"

"I'm looking for something," I say, "that, um . . . fell into one of the canals. A few weeks ago. Do you know how I would go about finding it?"

The man narrows his eyes at me.

And then he laughs.

"You're a funny one," he says, smacking his knee. He turns to a man in the boat adjacent to his. "Ya hear that? She lost something in the canals. Wants to find it!" He laughs so hard that he nearly doubles over.

The other gondolier chuckles. "Good luck, sweets." Then he smiles at me—he's missing two front teeth, and his gums are practically black.

I turn away from the sound of their laughter and head farther down the canal. At the first chance, I step onto a stone bridge that arches over the water, taking me to the other side. Its sides are pocked where stones have fallen off, exposing the gray concrete underneath.

Below me, the water doesn't look as dirty as usual; sunlight has cast a greenish-blue sheen over everything, and I can see reflections from the surrounding buildings playing off the water's surface.

On this side of the street, skyscrapers stretch into the Aeries, their bottoms eroding and stained with watermarks. Exposed pipes climb the sides like fat arteries, and rusty grates cover the windows on the lower floors.

A few feet down, another small group of gondoliers is idling, their boats tied to mossy posts. I call to them, waving a hand in the air.

When they look up, I cut to the chase. "Do any of you know how to navigate these waters in search of something I lost in the canals? I have money." I tap my pocket. "I can pay you once I find what I'm looking for."

The men don't laugh at me, but they do shake their heads. "We don't have time for that sort of game," one of them says, flicking his wrist at me. "Go on."

So I do.

I walk until my feet ache and I'm so hot that I would do anything for a mystic cooling patch—or even a spot of shade. But there's none of that, just crumbling buildings and the relentless sun. There is no shortage of gondoliers, but no one wants to help me. Either they laugh at me or they don't answer me at all.

I'm not sure which is more frustrating.

By the time I've crossed three different canals and covered nearly thirty city blocks, I feel like giving up. I stop at a tiny stand and buy a bottle of water. It's practically boiling hot, but I drink it anyway.

I adjust my wig and sit at the edge of the nearest canal, letting my feet hang over the side. The inner wall of the canal is lined with green algae so thick it looks like animal fur.

I blink, trying to hold back tears. I'm never going to find Davida's heart.

This is when I see him.

A gondolier wearing a blue-and-white-striped shirt is steering down the canal. He spots me and slows his boat. I grab the pointed tip as he approaches, helping him line up the gondola along the side of the canal.

"Need a ride?" he asks.

"Actually," I say, "I need help."

"Hmm." The man takes a cigarette out of his front pocket, then strikes a match. "Go on."

"I lost something in the canals. I need someone to help me find it—to pinpoint where it might have drifted. Someone who has knowledge of the tides and the way the water moves." I steady my voice, trying to sound confident. "It's very important. And I can pay."

The gondolier doesn't laugh at me. He takes a drag of his cigarette and then another, holding the smoke deep in his chest before exhaling.

Eventually, he drops the cigarette into the water and looks up at me. "Donaldio."

"Is that your name?" I ask.

He shakes his head.

"Okay," I say. "Well . . . is that another person's name?"

He nods.

Not much of a talker, I think. "A person you know?"

He nods again.

"And he can help me?"

The gondolier shrugs. "If anyone can, it's Donaldio. He's the oldest sailor I know." He motions to the gondola. "He still pilots one of these, though not often. Mostly keeps to himself." The gondolier grips the boat's wheel with one hand. "I'll take you to him."

I sit at the front of the boat as we navigate the Depths, drifting past brownstones and half-destroyed buildings with boarded-up windows and doors, down narrow waterways and underneath bridges, until I'm no longer sure where we are.

The water smells salty and dank. The gondolier stands behind me, making no sound. Finally, we turn onto a tight canal wide enough for maybe two boats to pass through at once. Metal doors open directly onto the water from dilapidated brownstones. The canal is so narrow and the buildings so tall that the sun is mostly blocked out, and the water is bathed in shadows.

The gondolier stops in front of a blue door. "Knock twice," he says. "Go on."

I stand up in the boat, careful not to topple over. Who is this Donaldio? Can I trust him? I lean forward and rap my knuckles on the door.

Too late to worry about it now.

I'm still touching the door when it swings open. "Will you wait for me?" I ask the gondolier.

He wipes his forehead. "No."

"Name your price," I say. "Please wait."

He thinks for a moment. "Five," he says, holding up his open hand.

I have twice that in my bag. "Two now, three later."

"Deal." I give the gondolier some money and he helps me out of the boat and into the open doorway. I take a deep breath and step inside.

"Hello?" I call, but there's no answer.

I can't see much—just a darkened hallway. I reach out, feeling along the walls to make sure I don't trip. "Hello? My name is Aria. . . . I was told to look for Donaldio."

Stupid, I think immediately. I shouldn't have used my real name. "Hello?"

I take a few more steps; then the walls on either side of me end. I still can't see anything, but I can sense an open space before me. "Hello?"

No answer.

"It's just that, well . . . I really need your help."

Nothing. He must not be here. Great. Just my luck.

I'm about to turn around when a bulb in the center of the ceiling clicks on. The room is washed in jaundiced light. Directly underneath the bulb is a tiny, shriveled man who looks like a peanut.

I presume this is Donaldio.

He's the size of a child, puckered like a raisin, as though he's been in the bath for days. A blanket is draped around his shoulders—something blue and red, woven with pictures that look like hieroglyphics. His irises are an inky black, his skin so thin that I can see the blue veins running down his forehead and cheeks.

Behind him, wooden beams stretch up the windowless walls; there's a mattress on the floor, and clothes are strewn everywhere, alongside stacks of papers and topographical maps that tower almost to the ceiling.

"Donaldio?" I say.

The man nods. "Aria, did you say?" His voice is high-pitched and faint.

Now it is my turn to nod. "Yes," I say. "I was given your name—someone said you might help me."

The man blinks. "That depends," he says, "on what you need help with."

I find myself wishing for the comfort of Lyrica's home. "I lost something in one of the canals," I tell him. "I'm trying to find it, and I'm hoping you can help me figure out where it might have drifted to. I'll pay you."

I feel myself wince after I say this last part. I hope I have enough coins left.

"And what is it that you lost?" Donaldio asks.

I can't reveal the truth—that I'm searching for a mystic heart. It sounds crazy, and if Donaldio is a mystic himself, surely he wouldn't approve of someone like me going after such a sacred thing. "Does it matter?"

"Of course it matters," he says. "The circumference of the object, its weight . . . those things will affect my mapping."

I have no idea how much a mystic heart weighs.

Donaldio stares at me, expressionless. "If you want my help," he says, "tell me what you are looking for." He raises a thin arm and points down the hall. "Otherwise, leave."

I bite my bottom lip. I have no choice but to spill the truth—all of it. "A friend of mine died a few weeks ago," I say. "Her body fell into the water."

"So you're looking for the body?" Donaldio shakes his head. "The water would have decomposed it, I believe."

We're both silent.

"Well," I say, "that's not all."

"Oh?"

"My friend was a mystic. I'm looking for her heart."

Donaldio's eyes widen.

"I've never seen one before," I say, "and I have no idea what they look like. But I need to find it. It's important to me. She died protecting me, and I need to do this for her. For her family—to set things right."

Donaldio presses his hands to his mouth for a moment. "Do not worry," he says. "I know the size and weight of a mystic heart."

I step closer. "Are you a mystic?"

"No," he says. "But I have had many close dealings with them, and I support their cause. They are the reason I am still here."

"They protect you?" I ask.

"How old do you think I am?" Donaldio lets his hands drop to his lap; I study his face, trying to guess.

"One hundred or so?"

He laughs—a high-pitched squeal. "You flatter me. You see, Miss Aria, I have extended my life via donations from mystics who value me and my knowledge."

"Donations like Stic?" I ask.

"Nothing like that," Donaldio says, his voice growing serious.

"Come." He pats the floor next to him, which is covered in papers. I move them away and sit. He seems even tinier up close.

"Mystics have inhabited Manhattan since the Second World War, but I have been around for much longer. Many consulted with me when they first arrived, new immigrants from all over Europe, before Ellis Island closed its doors in 1954. New arrivals *still* consult with me—and for that, they pay me with tiny bits of their life force."

"Back to my friend's heart," I say, uncomfortable with this knowledge.

He nods. "Many things control the currents in the canals," he says. "And there are many different kinds of currents. Perhaps you have learned of ocean currents, directed by the winds."

"Not really," I say.

"No matter." He reaches for a long sheet of golden paper, unrolling it and stretching it out across the stained wooden floor. It looks like a map of Manhattan.

Donaldio removes a charcoal pencil from underneath his blanket, then begins to mark arrows along the map. "An ocean current is a continuous movement of water manipulated by the elements. Things have changed over the years. Oceans have bled together, lands have been enveloped, the temperature has risen—all of this affects the flow of water."

"So . . . how can you figure out where my friend's heart might have gone?"

Donaldio ignores my question. "A mystic heart is quite a dangerous thing," he says. "You've heard of Stic, it seems."

I nod.

"That is nothing compared to the power of a pure mystic heart. Most humans will never see one in their entire lives."

"But you have," I say.

"Yes." He pauses. "But I have lived many lives. I have known Manhattan before the Conflagration, before mystics were quarantined and drained. When they were valued for the work they did to enhance the city. I have seen Manhattan when it was one level."

"No!" I gasp. It seems so long ago it's like a fairy tale: Manhattan before global warming took hold, before the water broke up the city and mystics helped build it upward. "How old *are* you?"

"Where did her body fall, would you say?" Donaldio asks, ignoring my question.

I lean over him and point to a spot on the map. He continues to make calculations on the side of the paper with tiny scratch marks, following the paths of the canals with his fingertips.

"And how long ago?"

"Just over a month," I reply.

Eventually, he looks up. "You have a sweet soul, Miss Aria."

"Oh," I say. "How can you tell?"

"You are not trying to find the heart for power or for greed. You are trying to find it for *good*. And because of that, I will tell you how to do so."

"Thank you," I say, feeling a flood of relief.

Donaldio scribbles something on the side of the map, then carefully rips the paper until he has a tiny square in his hand with some markings. "Here." He hands it to me. "Free of charge."

I grasp the paper. "You're too kind." I stare down at the markings—latitude and longitude, I believe:

40.7406891128

−73.9859676361

"I'm not sure what to do with this," I say.

Donaldio frowns. "What do they teach in school these days? Use a compass, of course."

Outside, the gondolier is waiting for me, smoking another cigarette.

"Was he any help?" He flicks ash into the canal.

"Yes," I say. "He was."

"Where to?"

I stare down at the paper. Then I take out my TouchMe. There's a text from Turk: *Where are you?!?!*

I ignore it and click through to find a compass app. I punch in the numbers, and it starts spitting out directions. "A left up here," I say, pointing to where the canal veers into a Y. "Then the first right."

"Fine." The gondolier starts the engine and the boat begins to move, wobbling as it picks up speed. *Here I come, Davida,* I think. *Here I come.*

"And a right here," I say as we turn down a canal that will bring us to the spot Donaldio indicated. We're on the East Side, near an area of the Depths called Gramercy.

"Uh, miss?"

I glance up from my TouchMe as the boat begins to slow. "What's going on?" I say.

Stripes of yellow tape run across the canal a few hundred feet ahead of us, blocking entry. From where I'm sitting, some sort of temporary walls have been inserted into the canal. A long, thick tube runs from the canal to the street, where dozens of men are working.

"Looks like the canal has been drained over there," the gondolier says. "We'll have to turn around."

"No!" I say. "I mean, can you let me off?" I point to the side, where a bunch of gondoliers have gathered to watch.

I pay the gondolier and hop off the boat, scurrying down the dock. A crane is pulling rock from the bottom of the canal and dumping it onto the sidewalk. There are tons of onlookers.

Pushing through the crowd, I try to get as close to the edge of the canal as possible, holding out my TouchMe to see where Davida's heart should be located.

A few feet away, as I'm wedged between a mother with two children and a couple of teenage boys standing on their tiptoes, my TouchMe beeps.

It says Davida's heart should be exactly where the canal is being excavated.

"Excuse me." I turn to the mother. "Do you know what's going on?"

"Beats me," the woman says. "Something having to do with the Roses. Kyle Rose made an announcement about an hour ago"— she points to a JumboTron—"that the canal was being drained to ensure that the water was clean, but everyone knows the canals are anything but clean. And no one has seemed to care much before. Maybe they're looking for gold or something." She laughs and grips her daughter's hand. "Though they certainly wouldn't share it if they found it."

I thank the woman and snake my way through the crowd. It's too much of a coincidence that my family would be draining this canal. But how would they know to look for Davida's heart? What importance would it have for them? And—most importantly—have they beaten me to it?

I'm at the front of the group of spectators, so close I can see the grimy bottom of the empty canal, full of crud and dead fish and tangles of weeds and plants. I scan it, looking for something, anything, that might be a mystic heart.

Someone grabs my elbow. I cry out in pain and stare up at a familiar, slimy face.

It's Klartino, one of my father's men.

He snarls. "And what is your business here?"

· XVIII ·

I'm speechless.

It's only when he asks me a second time that I realize he doesn't recognize me. Thank God for the blond wig.

"Uh, well . . ." I fumble for words, trying to think of an excuse. My father must have learned of the heart. Has he already found it?

"Sister!" I hear someone shout behind me. "That's my sister!"

I turn around, half expecting to see Kyle.

It's Jarek. His dark hair is loose, parted in the center and falling over his face. He's thrown a lightweight button-down shirt over his wifebeater and is wearing a pair of tan shorts.

"*Susie*. There you are." Jarek grabs my other elbow as Klartino furrows his brow, looking at us with a confused expression. "I'm so sorry," Jarek continues. "My little sister is . . ." He taps his head with his hand. "*Slow.*"

Klartino grunts. "Pay attention to your brother," the thug says, letting go of my arm. It hurts where his fingers dug into my skin. "Get outta here."

"Don't say a word," Jarek whispers in my ear. "Thank you!" he says to Klartino, then hurries me away, back into the crowd and through to the other side of the street. We turn a corner onto an alley behind a group of empty stores, and there's Turk, standing next to his motorcycle, arms crossed over his chest.

He looks furious.

"Are you insane?" Jarek says to me. "Talking to one of your father's bodyguards? He could have recognized you!"

"But he didn't," I say. "Besides, I didn't have a choice; he—"

"But he *could have*," Turk repeats. "Dammit, Aria. I can't believe you." He lets out a low growl. "You have to come back with us. Now. Hunter knows you're out here, and he's pissed."

I stomp away down the alley. "I don't care. I'm not leaving until I find what I came for." I turn back to Jarek and Turk. "How'd you find me, anyway?"

Turk clenches his fists. "I made Jarek tell me—and before you get mad at him, you're lucky he told *me* and not the others. We've been looking for you for the past half hour, and thank *freaking* God we found you. If something happened to you . . ."

"You would have been upset?" I ask.

"Hunter would kill me," he answers through gritted teeth. "What could possibly be so important that you'd risk getting killed for?"

I glance back and forth between the boys. I'm not sure I can trust either of them, but what choice do I have? Jarek did help me escape the hideout, and Turk's been pretty decent to me. More than decent, actually.

"Davida's heart," I say.

Turk and Jarek immediately stop moving.

"What did you say?" Jarek whispers. His expression is one of pure shock.

"I've found her heart," I say. "Well—I've found where it should have drifted to."

Turk looks stupefied. "But the currents . . . Who—"

"It doesn't matter. Someone helped me, and Davida's heart should be right out there." I point back toward the empty canal. "Only my father's beaten us to it."

Jarek seems upset. "This is awful. A mystic heart is so rare, so valuable. . . ." His eyes light up. "Do you know how much power is in a mystic heart? And *Davida's* heart?" He blinks rapidly, seeming almost entranced. "That would be incredibly valuable."

"Wait," Turk says. "What makes you think that your father, or Kyle, would know about the heart?"

"It's too much of a coincidence for them to be here," I say. "Kyle was the one who gave me the reliquary—maybe he knew what it was for and didn't let on."

"Why would he do that?" Turk asks.

"I'm not sure. But we already suspect that someone in the hide-out has been feeding information to my family—"

"You what?" Jarek says, shocked. This obviously is news to him.

"It's a long story," I say, not wanting to get into the mystic tag, especially since I'm still not clear on who, exactly, is tracking me. "But we were talking about Davida's heart the other night," I say to Turk. "Maybe someone overheard us?"

He shakes his head. "I don't know. But whoever is excavating for the heart—your father, or Kyle, maybe—they haven't found it yet. If they had, they'd have already packed up and gone home. Right? So either they're *about* to find it, in which case there's nothing we can do to stop them, or someone else has already found it and removed it. And if that's the case . . . the trick is to figure out where it might be now that it's gone."

I hold up the slip of paper with the latitude and longitude coordinates for Turk to read, but he pushes it away.

"Let's be optimistic and assume that someone else got to it first—before your family had the canal dredged," Turk says. "Though I'm not sure who would even know it existed. If it were another mystic, he would have returned it to Davida's family already."

"Unless it's a mystic who just wanted the money," Jarek suggests. "Or more power."

Turk bites his lower lip. "True. It's possible that the heart has already been . . . *used*. But let's say it hasn't. Then some mystic, or some Depthshod, must be trying to sell it for a high price." He turns to Jarek. "And where would you go to sell something illegal for a lotta dough?"

"The black market," Jarek replies.

"*What* black market?" I ask.

Jarek shakes his head. "You've got a lot to learn, Aria Rose."

"Come on." Turk unties the sweatshirt that's around his waist and hands it to me. "It's yours—Jarek brought it for you. You'll need it if you're going to the market."

I take the sweatshirt and slip it on. I'm already too warm, but

Turk is right—I don't want to be recognized. The wig has worked so far, but I don't want to take any chances, especially if we're going somewhere dangerous. "Pull up the hood."

As soon as Turk hands over the sweatshirt, I gulp. It's the one I hid the locket in back in my room. The locket that now carries the mystic trace.

Which means that I can be tracked.

I fish inside the pocket, but the locket isn't there. I scan the ground, thinking it must have fallen out, but I don't see it anywhere.

"Come on," Turk repeats, taking my hand. "We don't have any time to waste."

"There doesn't seem to be anything sinister here," I say. "It looks like a regular open-air market." Not that I've ever been to one before. Turk parks his bike and hides it behind a pile of rubble, covering it with a ratty sheet he finds on the ground.

We're in Greenwich Village now, and Turk and Jarek lead me through a maze of stands and booths. There are women selling bruised fruits and vegetables and greens for ten cents a pound—celery and peppers and watercress and cabbages. It seems incredibly cheap to me, but then, I've never purchased my own groceries.

In the Aeries, I never saw any food being delivered to our apartment. Deliveries were made through the service elevator in the kitchen, and the servants dealt with them.

But I suppose this is how people in the Depths do their shopping. The market reminds me of the mystic carnival Hunter took me to in the Magnificent Block, minus the sense of wonder and excitement. Before the block was destroyed and his mother was killed. Before the rebellion.

"The black market is part of the regular market," Turk says.

We pass a booth full of copper-colored earrings and costume jewelry. "Pretty, yes?" the woman behind the stand calls out to me.

"You just have to know what to say and who to ask," Jarek adds, lumbering forward. The streets are full of people bargaining for food, swarming to stands like bees to honey.

At one point, as we're walking, a man with garlic breath sneaks up behind me and tries to steal my TouchMe out of my pocket. "Get away!" I shout. "Thief!"

Turk pulls me closer to him. "Stay by me," he says. To our right, children are surrounding a man selling strips of dried beef. Directly next to him, a woman is peddling multicolored scarves. "Anyone?" she's asking as people pass her by in droves. "Anyone?"

Turk approaches the man selling the beef, parting the sea of children and holding out a sack of coins. "How much?" the man asks, motioning to the pounds of meat that hang above the smokers.

"None," Turk says. He lowers his voice to a whisper. "I'm looking for a heart."

The man shakes his head rapidly. "No, no. Not here."

We back away and continue walking. Jarek and I watch in awe as Turk slips from stand to stand, slippery as a fish, trying to lure out whoever is selling the heart—that is, assuming someone is actually selling it and my father's men haven't found it already.

"Shouldn't we be going to the stands with meat?" I ask. "Wouldn't that be the logical place for it?"

Jarek shrugs, wiping sweat from his face. "Because a heart is meat?" He grimaces. "Anyone dealing in illegal goods will want a place to sell that isn't too crowded. So they'll likely have a stand that doesn't seem all that appealing at first glance."

This makes sense.

"Aria. Look."

I turn my head at the sound of Jarek's voice, but I can't tell where he's gone. "Jarek?" I call out.

"Here," he says.

But where is here?

I walk past a stall with dozens of wooden matryoshka dolls lining the shelves, each wearing a different outfit, stern expressions painted onto white-and-black faces. "Jarek?" I repeat.

"You like?" a woman at the front of the stand says to me. "I give you a good deal."

"No thanks." I turn back to the wall of dolls. "I'm just looking for my friend."

I stare at the dozens of dolls and one of them blinks at me.

Or rather, two eyes blink at me.

A figure steps forward from the wall. It's Jarek, only his clothing and skin have taken on the coloring of the dolls he's standing in front of, so he's blended in with them.

"Wow," I say. "You really *are* good at camouflage."

Jarek steps into the aisle and his regular coloring returns. "If you don't know I'm there, then yeah, I blend in pretty well." He laughs. "A lot of good it does me."

"You never know," I say. "Maybe one day you'll put your talent to good use."

He sighs. "Maybe. But I wish I had a power like Ryah's. Or

Landon's. I've trained as hard as I can . . . days and nights spent practicing mystic combat . . . but nothing I do seems to work. My energy is too weak."

Jarek's face is filled with sadness, his lips turned down at the corners. It must be terrible to be a mystic—a member of a group known for wild displays of power—and never be able to live up to that potential. Especially for someone like Jarek, who *looks* so powerful. But I know all too well that looks can be deceiving.

"I'm sorry," I tell him. "But there's more to life than power, you know."

"If I'd had power," he says, "*real* power, I would have been able to save my parents the day their hideout was raided. Instead, they were killed." He rubs his forehead. "And I'm still here."

I had no idea this was how Jarek's parents had died. That he witnessed it happening. "That wasn't your fault," I say, placing a hand on his shoulder. "I'm so sorry you had to go through that. But power or no power, you're a good guy, Jarek. Your parents would be proud of how you've turned out."

He shakes his head. "No, I'm not a good guy. Not really." Then, all of a sudden, his frown stretches into a wide smile. "Anyway," he says, brushing his hair back behind his ears. "Let's keep walking."

Turk is being turned away from stand after stand selling everything from socks and shoes to cheap electronics to sandwiches and soft drinks. As Jarek pointed out, Turk tends to stray from the more populated stands, focusing on the nearly empty ones. But we've been looking for nearly an hour and nothing has turned up.

"Maybe it's not here," I suggest.

"Oh, it's here," Turk says. "We need to find someone who's selling Stic. Then we'll find the heart."

Jarek and I buy a sandwich to split and a bottle of water from a cooler. Eventually, we find a butcher who is smoking meat. The woman in the stall next to him is selling clothing. Behind her is a makeshift wall display of dresses made of different fabrics and colors, all handmade, with intricate stitching and glittering beads and patterns. They're a little old-fashioned for my taste, but they *are* beautiful.

As I'm studying them, a round man with a long, scraggly salt-and-pepper beard emerges from an opening in the wall. He approaches the woman, waddling as he walks, and whispers in her ear.

"Turk," I say, waving him over.

"Yes?"

"This sandwich is good," Jarek says between bites. "Like, really good."

Turk raises an eyebrow. "That's what you wanted to tell me?"

"No." I point to the booth and to the man. "Maybe you should ask *him*."

Turk nods. "Okay." He steps forward. "Excuse me," he says.

The man stops speaking to the woman and stares at us. He has a blunt nose and fat lips. "You're excused," he says.

Turk clears his throat. "I'm looking for something very specific."

The man shifts his gaze to us, then back to Turk. "And what would that be?"

"A heart."

There's a spark in the man's eyes. "Something like that would cost a lot."

"Yes." Turk nods to Jarek and me. "We've got it."

"Watch the stand," the man says to the woman. He motions for us to follow him, parting the row of scarves and leading us into the back part of the stall.

The space is dark, and the man clicks on a lamp. There's an uncomfortable-looking cot with a deflated pillow, and stacks of dresses in plastic wrapping. So much for their being handmade. There aren't any walls, really, only sheets of stained fabric hanging down to the ground, blocking us off from the stands on either side. The same fabric—navy blue—covers the top of the stand, creating a tiny room.

The man scratches his beard, then bends over and reaches underneath the cot. His shirt rides up, exposing the spotted skin on his back. Two rolls of fat seep over his pants, and it doesn't seem like he's wearing any underwear.

Gross.

He fishes out a small metal cooler, then approaches the three of us. "We've already harvested it," he tells Turk. "And that cost us two lives, so it's not cheap." He squints. "But it's also not safe unless you know what you're doing. And I don't want this traced back to me."

"I understand," Turk says. He straightens his spine. "And I have ample experience with these. It will be in good hands."

The man nods, pressing a finger to the side of the cooler. The lid slides back and a burst of silver light pierces the space, illumi-nating everything.

"It's perfect," the man says. "In ideal condition."

Turk reaches into the cooler and removes a glass box no bigger than his hands. I can't see what is inside—only that the glass is lined with quicksilver, like the glass tubes in the mystic draining room in my father's office.

The bearded man lifts the box from Turk's hands, placing it back in the cooler and snapping it shut. The silvery light disappears.

"So where's the money?" he asks.

Turk glances at me.

"I . . . need to transfer it to you," I say, making something up on the fly. "I don't have that much on me." I take out my TouchMe, stalling for time. Before I can ask the man how much he wants for it, there's a whoosh of air and a blast of sunlight from above as the roof of the stand falls in.

"Aria!" Turk calls.

"What's happening?" the man cries out. "You lied to me! You tricked me! Help!"

Two men burst into the hidden room from the street. The Rose family crest is sewn onto their black uniforms in blood red, just above their hearts.

They point their guns at me.

"Attack us and we'll kill her," one of them says to Turk, who has put up his fists, about to fight.

"Careful," Turk says to Jarek. "Get in front of Aria."

Jarek goes to step in front of me and one of the soldiers points a gun at his head. "Don't move a muscle. Give us the girl and no one gets hurt."

"Over my dead body," Turk says, spitting on the ground.

A loud whirring fills the air above us. I glance up and see a gray helicopter, just as its door slides open and two more men drop into the stall. The old man is crouching down, whimpering. There's no sign of the woman, his partner. I wonder if she escaped.

Turk raises his hand and a jet of green light bursts from his palm, striking one of the men directly in the chest. He topples to the ground and writhes in pain, injured but not dead.

"That wasn't very nice," the soldier standing next to him says. Then he shoots off a round at Turk and Jarek, who deftly dodge the bullets.

I whip around as yet another soldier breaks into the room and smacks me with the butt of his gun. The sounds of the helicopter grow louder. Circles of light dance in front of my eyes, and as I pass out, all I can think is *The heart, the heart, the heart.*

· XIX ·

I wake up in a small, sterile room.

My arms are in front of me, cuffed at the wrists. A thin cord stretches across my chest. From what I can tell, it seems to be tied behind the chair I'm sitting on.

Against the other wall, Turk is strapped to a metal chair, his face beaten to a pulp and purpled underneath the eyes. A huge gash marks his forehead, and a scary cut runs straight down his lips. Both are bleeding.

Everything from the cool, sterile air to the seamless way the touchpads are integrated into the walls tells me I am in the Aeries.

Plus the fact that my brother, Kyle, is standing in front of me.

"Well," he says to me. "We meet again, little sister."

He's wearing a black suit with a crisp blue dress shirt underneath, open at the neck. No tie. His wheat-colored hair is perfectly parted. "You sound like a comic-book villain," I say. "Cut it out."

"Me?" he says, pointing to my wig. "You're the one who looks ridiculous."

I meet Turk's eyes. *Don't worry,* he mouths, but his words don't make me feel any better. The only consolation I have is that Jarek isn't here—I hope he's gotten away safely.

To my left, near the door, two of my father's men stand at attention, silver pistols in their grips.

A cooler rests in the center of the room. Behind it, on a metal table next to Turk's chair, are two vials full of liquid mercury—quicksilver—that shimmer underneath the fluorescent lights. Next to them is a plastic bag that holds three empty syringes.

"How did you find us?" I ask my brother, struggling against the cord that's keeping me tied to the chair.

"You've been tagged, Aria. I already told you."

Kyle looks at me inquisitively. He doesn't know I've had the trace removed, that it's now on the locket. And since I'm not wearing it, and the locket wasn't in the sweatshirt, how could Kyle have found me? Where's the locket now?

Clearly, Hunter didn't put the trace on me after all. But then . . . who did? The only person I can think of to blame is Kyle, since he keeps finding me, or Thomas, but Lyrica said the trace was too intricate for anyone but a powerful mystic to perform.

"You're not really going to keep us here like this, are you?" I ask. "How will this help your cause?"

Kyle shakes his head. "How will it help *your* cause is the real question."

"What are you talking about?"

He steps toward the cooler. "That." He bends down, running a finger over the top of the container. "The heart." He presses the side of the cooler and the lid slides open. Silver light bursts forth. "How do you use it?"

"Use it? What do you mean?"

His face reddens. "You know exactly what I mean. The heart—how do you *use* it?"

I'm silent. There's no way Kyle knows, or cares, about the ritual for the heart of a lost mystic; he only wants to extract its power. He must suppose that it's too delicate for him to dissect without knowing the proper way to do so.

But I don't know the first thing about that.

"It was Davida's," I say. There's no use in lying. "It's all that remains of her body. I was going to return it to her family."

Kyle snorts. "I know exactly what it is."

"You do?" I ask. "How could you possibly?"

"Elissa," Kyle tells me. "I didn't realize what Davida's box was until I'd already given it to you. I mentioned it to Elissa afterward and she went hysterical. She said it must have been a reliquary and that I was an idiot to have given it away. No matter, though. I'm not one for lacquered boxes. The real prize is here."

He looks at the silver light radiating from the cooler. "Elissa explained all about the mystic heart—how it holds all your power." Kyle sneers at Turk. "I realized then that we had to go back, to see if Davida's heart was still intact."

Kyle whips his head toward where I'm seated, glaring at me. "It was difficult to find, as you well know. Turns out it wasn't where it should have been. I have no idea how someone beat us to it, but"—he glances at the open cooler—"at least I have it now." He gives me a fake smile. "Thanks for leading us right to it."

"You'll always be a Stic junkie in one form or another," I say.

"And you'll always be a little mystic tramp," Kyle says, turning his attention to Turk. "You. Mystic. How do you use this heart?" He takes a few steps in Turk's direction, then leans down and stares into his eyes. "Tell me."

Turk raises his shoulders and looks innocently at Kyle. "I haven't the slightest idea."

Kyle backhands Turk against the cheek, and I jump in my chair. "Don't lie to me, mystic. I've put those quicksilver cuffs on you for a reason—so you can't use your powers. Now talk to me, man to man."

Turk remains silent.

"Not feeling chatty?" Kyle says. "Maybe this will change your mind." He motions to the guards. The one on the right comes forward and sets down his pistol. He removes a syringe from the plastic bag, then uncorks one of the quicksilver vials, draws the liquid into the syringe, and replaces the cork.

Needle in the air, the guard approaches Turk.

"Quicksilver is the only liquid that can contain mystic energy," Kyle says to me. "Did you know that, Aria?" He doesn't wait for me to answer. "I'm sure you do. But perhaps what you *didn't* know is that quicksilver is a volatile, deadly element in its own right. And no one has studied the effects of liquid mercury being inserted into a live mystic."

Kyle gestures to Turk, who is rocking back and forth in his chair. His eyes are enormous, eyebrows arched in fear.

"Until now," Kyle says. "Our very own guinea pig."

"Get away from me!" Turk screams. "Back off!"

"Silence him, please," Kyle says calmly to the other guard, who removes a long piece of cloth from his pocket and inserts it into Turk's mouth. Turk thrashes his head left and right, hollering, but the guard manages to secure the cloth around his face and tie it behind his head.

Suddenly, his screams are muted.

"Let's begin," Kyle says. He snaps his fingers and the guard with the syringe tests it, letting a jet of quicksilver into the air. Then he presses the tip of the needle into Turk's forearm.

"If you decide to tell me how to use the heart, we'll stop," Kyle instructs him.

Turk simply shakes his head.

I watch as the guard empties the syringe into Turk's arm. The skin on the inside of his elbow, where the needle is inserted, begins to shimmer. I can actually *see* the mercury traveling up his arm, turning his skin a silvery blue.

And then Turk convulses.

His entire body shakes as though he is going through a draining. His eyes roll back in his head and he foams at the mouth, drool seeping down his chin and onto his shirt.

"Stop!" I cry out. "That's enough!"

Kyle snaps his fingers again and the first guard removes the syringe. It's half empty.

The other guard unties the cloth around Turk's mouth.

For a second, it looks like Turk is dead. Then he sputters up a bunch of mucus and begins to cough.

"Are you ready to tell me how to use the heart now?" Kyle asks, seeming entirely unconcerned that Turk could have just died.

Turk groans softly. "Yes."

"Good," Kyle says, rubbing his hands together.

"The answer is simple," Turk manages to get out. "You suck."

Kyle makes a strange face. "What?"

"You. Suck," Turk says. And then he sticks out his tongue.

I suppress a laugh. Only Turk would make fun of my brother at a time like this.

"All right, then," Kyle says stiffly. "If that's how you want to be." The cloth is placed back around Turk's mouth, and Kyle motions for the guard to inject him again.

Once again, the silvery liquid shoots up Turk's bicep, turning his entire arm a pearly silver. He convulses wildly. The skin of his arm looks as though it's hardening—as if he is turning to stone right before my eyes.

This can't be good.

"Just tell him!" I shout to Turk, hoping he's conscious enough to hear me. "Kyle, stop—you're hurting him!"

"That's the point, Aria," Kyle says, watching as green energy seeps from Turk's pores, turning a sickly yellow as it hits the air, running like egg yolk down his arms and legs—as though the mercury is pushing out his powers. His body writhes.

"Stop!" I repeat. "Just get Elissa to tell you!"

Kyle waves his hand and the guard pulls the empty syringe from Turk's arm. "I don't want *Elissa* to tell me, because then I'll have to share the heart with her." The cloth is untied, and I watch as Turk takes a few shallow breaths. At least he's still alive.

"So you're not only a junkie, you're greedy, too."

"Oh, stop your wailing, Aria," Kyle says, pointing at Turk. "How do you use the heart, mystic? How do you extract its power?" He's shouting now, and the veins in his neck look like they might burst.

"Well," Turk says in a weak voice, just above a whisper. "First you open the box."

Kyle looks on eagerly. "And then?"

"And then . . . you . . ." The words come slowly, painfully from Turk's cracked lips. ". . . suck it."

"Damn you!" Kyle raises a fist and punches Turk in the side of the head. His neck whips to the side and I hear something snap.

I squirm in my chair again, trying to loosen the cord enough to slide out from underneath. Kyle isn't paying any attention to me— he's busy muttering to the guards, instructing them to fill another syringe with quicksilver.

I look over my shoulder and realize there's an IV stand behind me, as well as an open bag of medical tools. The stand is tall and thin; for some reason it reminds me of the kendo stick Shannon used to train me back at the compound.

Which is when I get an idea.

"Inject him again," Kyle says. "Let's see if the third time is the charm."

He and the two bodyguards have their backs to me now, their focus on Turk. I watch as the quicksilver crawls up his neck and spreads across his skin like a terrible rash.

I use the sound he is making—the *thwomp*ing of his back against the chair and the scratching of the chair's metal legs across the floor—to mask the sounds of my own chair as I wobble back and forth, attempting to crawl closer to the IV stand. At the same time, I heave my chest out, then in, trying to loosen the cord. With every move I make, I can feel more slack.

"Arrrggh!" Turk begins to scream.

Come on, I urge myself. *He's in agony. Just a little closer.*

"Are you ready to tell me now?" Kyle hollers at him. "Come on, mystic!"

I keep shifting my weight back and forth. For a second, Turk's screaming stops and I hear the tiniest whisper: *"Suck it."*

"This is it, mystic," Kyle says. "I'm guessing that once the quicksilver reaches your heart, you're done. Dead."

I can't let that happen.

I shift my weight and feel the cord come undone and fall to the floor.

I try to remember some of the moves Shannon showed me, but my mind is a blur. I am so scared that Turk is going to die.

So I strike.

My hands still cuffed in the front, I bring the IV stand out in front of me and swipe it through the air, connecting with the head of the guard who is holding the syringe. The metal pole pierces his temple and he crashes to the floor, sending the syringe flying.

Kyle turns his head. "Aria?"

But I'm too fast for him.

I jump onto my right foot, slamming the pole into the other guard's face. Blood bursts out of his nostrils, and I bring my right knee up and kick him directly in the groin. The soldier collapses, and I give him one more quick blow to the back of the head. He's out cold.

I sense someone behind me. It's the first guard, stumbling to his feet and clicking off the safety of his pistol.

He shoots. A bullet whizzes past my head, scraping the skin off my temple.

I spin in the air, letting the pole guide me. Then I smack the gun out of the guard's hand. It clatters to the ground.

He looks at me with a frightened expression.

I tighten my grip on the pole, tilting my left hand up and my right hand down. The pole shifts diagonally in the air.

I step forward and, with one clean motion, drive the end of the pole into the guard's chin.

His head snaps back and he flies against the wall, hitting it with a smack and crumpling to the floor like an abandoned puppet.

I spin again and face my brother, who is standing still. Shocked.

"Where did you learn to fight like that?" he asks.

I shrug. "Around." I take a step forward.

"Come on now, Aria," Kyle says, holding up his hands. Next to him, Turk is breathing heavily, the cotton tie still secured around his mouth. His arms are lumpy with congealed quicksilver.

"It's me. Your brother." Kyle takes a step backward. "Put that down. You're not going to hurt me." He gives me a nervous smile.

I don't respond with words.

Instead, I raise the pole and whack him into unconsciousness.

Then I drop the IV stand and rush over to Turk. I remove the cloth from around his mouth, staring down at his cuffs. "Turk? Can you hear me? Everything is going to be all right." I scan the room for a key.

"Aria," Turk whispers. "Good job."

"Keep breathing," I say frantically. "Don't you dare stop breathing! I'm going to get you out of here."

One of the guards is on the floor right next to me. Still handcuffed, I reach down and unhook the key ring from his belt, then try the keys on the cuffs. The second one fits, and I rip the handcuffs from Turk's wrists. I don't risk taking the time to undo my own.

"Come on," I say, moving in front of him. Nearly half of his body is silver, and his face looks still—immobilized. "What should I do?" I say, trembling.

Only Turk's eyes move. "Cut me," he manages to say. "Open me up."

"What do you mean?"

But then his eyelids close. His face grows more and more silver by the second, and bubbles begin to form underneath the skin on his neck and shoulders.

I stare down at the set of keys that I'm holding. *Open me up.* Could he mean . . . ?

There's no time to think. Only to act.

I drag the sharp end of one of the keys down Turk's arm, starting from just under his shoulder all the way to his elbow, digging deep into the flesh until his skin tears open. I expect him to start bleeding, but it's not blood that pours out of him.

It's liquid mercury.

The silvery goop leaks out of him, trickling down his arms and dripping onto the floor, forming a large quicksilver puddle.

Carefully, I drag the same key across Turk's other arm, making another long wound. He groans.

Then I wait.

Sure enough, the silvery sheen on his skin begins to dissipate as the poison flushes out of his body. The pools of quicksilver on the floor grow larger and larger. His eyelids flicker open, and I watch as the color returns to his face and his skin begins to soften back to its normal state.

"Turk? Can you hear me?"

"Aria," he says, flexing his fingertips. "Thank you."

A few minutes pass and the silver leaking out of his wounds turns red with blood. Weakly, Turk stands up and presses his fingertip to one of the jagged cuts. It glows green, and he runs it along the incision, healing his own wound with his energy. He repeats this on the other arm. There are still dozens of cuts all over him that he's too weak to heal.

His shirt is soaked with quicksilver and his own expelled energy. He pulls it over his head. "Come on," Turk says, motioning to Kyle and the guards, who are sprawled across the floor. "We've gotta get out of here before they wake up."

Glancing down, Turk sees that I'm still cuffed—he presses a fingertip to the metal links that join my hands; there's a sizzling sound as the metal liquefies and my hands break apart. The silver cuffs dangle on my wrists like bracelets.

Turk grabs my hand and presses the touchpad on the wall. The door slides open to reveal a long, dark corridor. "Follow me."

I pick up the cooler with the heart inside, close it, and together, Turk and I leave the room.

We tread softly around corners and past closed doors, on the lookout for more of Kyle's men. Eventually, we reach a large door at the end of a hallway. I press the touchpad next to it, and it opens onto a silvery bridge.

Aside from when Thomas kidnapped me, it's the first time I've been back in the Aeries for over a month. The hot air hits us as we cross the bridge, keeping our eyes out for the triangular POD elevator that will take us down to the Depths. It's night now, and the sky is black save for white lights from the surrounding buildings, the skyscrapers illuminated like majestic metal beasts.

I feel like an outcast, a stranger in the place where I grew up. Turk and I rush along the network of bridges that connects the skyscrapers, allowing people to travel to and from their homes and school or work. From the looks of it, there has been no real damage in this area: the skyscrapers are magnificent, offering no hint of the wreckage that lies below. The only real signs of change are the emptied mystic spires, no longer pulsing and glowing with stored mystic energy.

Cables and wires glisten in the night, and we run as fast as our legs can carry us. In the distance, I can see the white glow of a POD. We're safe.

"Hurry," Turk says. "Not too long now."

We're over one bridge, then another.

And then, a few yards away, I see a line of soldiers, the Rose insignia gleaming against their black uniforms, their guns pointed.

At us.

My heart begins to race. "How did they—"

Turk pulls us to a stop as a figure appears, staggering toward us from behind, followed by another gang of soldiers.

"What do we do?" I whisper to Turk, my breath short.

"You've got nowhere to go!" someone shouts behind us.

Kyle.

I glance back at my older brother. He's limping toward us, a silver pistol in his hand. Behind him, soldiers are marching steadily. Up ahead, more soldiers have created a wall that neither Turk nor I will be able to break.

I look to the side. The fragile railings of the bridge—metal beams that seem to float in midair—would be easy enough to jump over, but then what?

We would fall, swiftly and desperately, into the Depths.

For a second, I see something shimmering in the air nearby. Something that looks an awful lot like a face.

Flanked by his soldiers, Kyle approaches. "This is the end of the road, Aria."

I stare again at the dark blue sky.

Inhale deeply.

"Trust me." I squeeze Turk's hand. "Just follow me, okay?"

"What?" he says. "Aria, what are you—"

Making sure the cooler is still securely tucked under my arm, I take a running start straight for the railing of the bridge.

"Aria, no!" my brother screams.

I jump.

The breath is sucked out of me as I tumble toward the dirty canals hundreds of stories below.

To my death.

PART THREE

The way is not in the sky. The way is in the heart.

—Buddha

· XX ·

It's funny how your mind empties when you're about to die.

Gone is all my anger toward Hunter, my disappointment that our relationship didn't work out. All I'm left with are slivers of memories: falling in love, stolen kisses, the time he made a dachshund appear in the sky and wag its tail. Laughter.

Gone is my hatred for my parents. I don't think about being a prisoner in my own home, unwillingly depleted of my memories to serve their political cause. I think of being a little girl, holding my father's hand. I remember when I was sick as a child and my mother would watch over me, dabbing my forehead with a wet cloth and waiting for my fever to go down.

I think of Kyle when he was younger and sweeter, and of the friends I am lucky enough to have, like Kiki and Bennie and now Ryah and Jarek, and maybe even Landon and Shannon. I think of Davida, who I miss seeing each morning and each night, who protected and took care of me unconditionally until she drew her last breath.

And Turk. I see him differently now: the tattooed boy with the silver motorcycle turned out to be quite wonderful.

The silver motorcycle . . .

There it is. A flash of chrome, a familiar wheel. Was I right?

The wind wraps itself around me as I fall into black nothingness, sucking the air out of my lungs as I drop farther and farther toward the Depths—

Until a flash of green pierces the air like lightning.

Rays of mystic energy shoot out underneath me, stretching across the sky like pulled taffy. I count ten of the long green beams of light and suddenly I'm no longer falling but lying flat across the rays as they support me, buoying me in midair, the cooler with the heart firmly in my grip.

Saved.

The green energy pulses, and I glance to the side.

There's Ryah, a look of intense concentration on her face. Her arms are extended, mystic rays shooting from her fingertips, keeping me afloat. Each one is as thick as my wrist, and double my height in length.

She shifts one of her hands, turning her fingers slightly inward, and five of the rays sweep underneath the others, weaving together like threads on a loom until I am floating on a secure net of light.

"Got her," Ryah says triumphantly.

But who is she talking to?

Ryah looks like she's hanging from an invisible string bobbing in midair. I squint and see bits of silver against the black-blue sky. It's hard to see through the wisps of smog scattered across the night like cotton candy, but then I see another pair of eyes.

"Ryah? How are you—"

"Be quiet, Aria," whispers a masculine voice. "Or you'll give us away."

Jarek.

Jarek is riding Turk's motorcycle.

He's hovering in the sky, halfway between the Aeries and the Depths, camouflaging himself to blend into the dark night. Now that I know what I'm looking for, I can make out his arms gripping the handlebars, his jaw clenched, his eyes focused. Ryah is seated beside him in a chrome sidecar I've never seen before.

Dozens of voices are screaming from the bridge above, and I watch as a figure hurls itself toward us. They must be wondering where the mystic energy is coming from.

"I don't know much longer I can hold this," says the almost-invisible Jarek. "I've never camouflaged anything this big."

"Let's hope this is Turk," Ryah says, staring up at the figure, who is growing larger by the second. "Otherwise, we've got a very unwelcome visitor."

And then there's Turk, bouncing onto the grid of light beside me.

He's staring at me with wild eyes. "How did you know they were here? That Ryah would catch you?"

I reach out and touch his arm. "I took a chance."

Turk smiles. He still looks weak from the quicksilver, but at least he's alive.

We're both alive.

"Come on, guys," Ryah says. "Before those soldiers jump down here as well."

She raises her arms in the air as if she's holding a large serving platter. The rays of energy beneath us flatten out and begin to incline.

All of a sudden, I can feel myself falling forward; the energy rays are angled so that we can slide down them, onto the bike. Turk plops into the sidecar with Ryah, and I slip behind Jarek, grabbing his sides for support.

"Here," I say, reaching around him and placing the cooler between his thighs. "Don't lose that. It's important."

"Gotcha." Jarek grunts, then twists back one of the handlebars. The bike roars forward, blasting green fuel out of its exhaust pipe and into the sky.

Ryah curls her fingertips into her hands and the green rays disappear. "You guys are heavy," she says.

Just then, a soldier falls past us. He must have jumped off the bridge after Turk. His arms and legs flail as he realizes the web of light we fell onto has disappeared.

His screams echo into the night.

Turk reaches out and squeezes my hand. "I'm glad you're all right."

"Me too," I say. "I'm glad we both are."

"Where'd you guys rush off to?" Shannon says the moment we burst through the door to the hideout. She's in black training gear, and she shoots me a fierce glare. "Hunter blocked the exits for a reason, Aria. You weren't supposed to leave. You're lucky we were able to break the loop, that we—"

"Stop!" I say. Turk is leaning on my shoulder, and I'm helping him walk. Jarek is behind us with the cooler. "We have bigger concerns right now. If you want to help us, then great. Otherwise, go away, Shannon."

She's about to tell me off when Ryah says, "Seriously, Shannon. Just chill for a minute. Or twenty."

Shannon turns her attention to Turk. As she realizes how injured he is, she looks aghast. "Turk?" She rushes to his side. "Are you okay?"

"I will be," he manages.

Landon comes rushing down the stairs. His dark, delicate features are full of concern. "Turk, you look *terrible!*" he says, fanning himself with one hand. "I mean, like . . . really bad."

"Thanks," Turk says.

"Are you okay?" Landon says.

"I'll survive," Turk says, groaning.

Together, Shannon and I drag Turk into the sitting room and gently deposit him on one of the leather sofas. He relaxes into the cushions and takes a few labored breaths. The olive color has mostly come back to his skin, and the gashes across his face are beginning to smooth over into new skin. I remember how quickly Turk recovered when Elissa Genevieve shot him—surely he can come back from this as good as new.

"Where's Jarek?" Landon asks. "Is he all right?"

"He's parking Turk's bike," Ryah says, jittery with nervous energy.

"Sit back," Shannon says to Turk. She tucks her fiery hair behind her ears, then extends one of her hands to Turk's face. Her fingertips begin to glow, and she runs her index finger along Turk's remaining wounds.

Turk sucks in a long gulp of air as the strength seems to return to his body. His eyes light with their familiar glitter, his lips moisten, and the cuts on his arms where I sliced him open heal completely.

"There," Shannon says. She leans forward and gives Turk a gentle kiss on his forehead. I look away. Where's Jarek with the cooler?

"Let me get you some water. You need to rest." Shannon motions for Landon and Ryah to follow her into the kitchen, leaving me alone with Turk.

"Are you all right?" I ask, taking a seat next to him on the couch.

"Yeah." Turk stares at me. "Are you?"

I nod. "What Kyle did to you was—"

"Don't." He presses a finger to my lips; the energy from his touch makes my mouth tingle. "It doesn't matter. It's over now."

"But it *does* matter," I say. "I'm the reason you were hurt. I went looking for Davida's heart—"

"And you found it," Turk says. "I can't even begin to tell you how much that will mean to her family. How much it means to all of us." Turk runs his hand along my cheek. "Hunter was wrong to lock you in here. I'm sorry that I went along with it."

"That's okay. I understand."

"I was so worried that something was going to happen to you," Turk says softly. "I don't know what I'd do if you were hurt."

"Me? When they were torturing you, I thought I was going to die."

Turk gulps, glancing down at my wrists. The silver cuffs are still there, the metal links that joined them together dangling off each one. "Here." He sits up and holds out his hand. "Let me."

"You're still too weak," I say. "I'll ask Ryah or Shannon to—"

"I'm fine," Turk says. He gives me a half smile. "Really. Now hold out your arms."

I do as he says, stretching my hands out in front of me. Turk curls his hand into a fist, sticking out his index finger. There's a soft hum as his finger turns green—a bright, electric color. He touches the tip of it to the lock on the right cuff.

It snaps open.

Then the left.

The handcuffs clunk to the floor. I stare at the bloody red indentations that they've left on my skin, which suddenly throb with pain. Turk presses his finger to my right wrist, drawing the tip of it along my wound.

I feel a rush of heat fill my body, and my arm begins to tingle, as though something is stirring just beneath my skin.

"Is that better?" he asks.

"Yes," I whisper. I lean my head back and Turk heals my other wrist, the angry red marks disappearing beneath his gentle touch.

When he's done, he leans forward to kiss the inside of my wrist. His lips are soft, barely there at all, like the wings of a butterfly.

I crane my neck to stare into his eyes. He lifts his lips from my wrist to my neck, kissing up to my chin, approaching my lips. . . .

The sound of the front door slamming shut breaks us apart. I push away, toward the far end of the couch.

Ryah rushes into the sitting room, her blue hair even more on end than usual. "Um, guys?" she says.

Turk lets out a cough. "Yes?"

Ryah's left eye is twitching nervously. "Something's wrong," she says.

"What is it?" I ask.

"I went outside to see if Jarek wanted anything to eat," she says. "He was parking the motorcycle." She pauses. "But he's gone."

Turk lets go of my arm. "What do you mean, gone?"

"The bike isn't there," Ryah says.

Just as she says this, Shannon and Landon enter the room. "The bike's gone?" Landon repeats.

"And Jarek with it," says Ryah.

Landon looks stunned. "Where'd he go?"

"I don't know," Ryah says.

"It's not like he has any other friends," Landon mutters.

I do a quick scan around the room, then turn to Turk. "The cooler. Jarek was the last one to have it."

"What cooler?" Shannon asks.

Turk's cheeks flush. He rushes into the foyer and opens the front door of the hideout, searching for any sign of Jarek.

But there is none.

"The cooler with Davida's heart," Turk says, turning back to the four of us.

Ryah lets out a gasp. "*That's* what was in the cooler?"

I nod. A queasy feeling fills my stomach. "And now it's missing."

· XXI ·

"Where do you think Jarek went?" Ryah asks.

She perches on the edge of the ottoman, and Landon drapes himself over the arm of the sofa. "This is so shady of him," he says with a sigh. He looks tired, and I can't blame him. It's been a long day for everyone—and it's about to get even longer.

"Let's not jump to any harsh conclusions," Ryah says. But the shakiness of her voice gives her away. "I'm sure there's a logical explanation for this."

"For what?" I say. "Running off with Turk's bike and Davida's heart?"

"You don't know that he did that." Ryah runs a hand through her hair. "Maybe he just . . . you know. Went to run an errand."

"Yeah." Landon guffaws. "I'm sure that's it. I bet Jarek was all like, 'Gee, I know everyone is waiting for me inside, but I, like, really need a smoothie, so I'll just go do that and come right back.' Get real, Ryah." Landon sits up and keys something into his TouchMe, presses Send with his thumb. "I just messaged him. Let's see if he responds."

Turk is pacing the room, head down. "And what if he doesn't?"

I say. "I think we need to head out of here. Start a search party. Maybe we should—"

"Maybe you should shut your trap, Aria Rose," Shannon says. She crouches down and shoves her face right in mine. "Your dumb ideas are what's gotten us into trouble in the first place."

"Me?" I say.

"*You*," Shannon says. She crosses her arms over her chest. "You think you're better than everyone else. That you don't have to play by the rules. Well, let me tell you something—rules were made for people like you. What were you thinking, escaping, when Hunter wanted you to stay here?"

"It wasn't fair—"

"All you ever think about is yourself." Shannon's face is pulled into a tight knot of frustration. "What if Ryah or someone else had been hurt trying to rescue you? What then? Turk almost died."

"But I didn't." Turk steps between us, pushing us apart. "So let's move on."

I try to calm down, but I can't. Just looking at Shannon makes me see red. Why is she always so obnoxious to me?

"What's the point of imagining terrible things that *didn't* happen?" I say. "If my brother, or a mystic like Elissa Genevieve—or *both*—had gotten their hands on Davida's heart, the consequences would be . . . tragic."

"I don't even want to think about it," Ryah chimes in.

"Stop accusing *me* when your friend Jarek turns out to be a sneaky thief!" I say to Shannon. "He's the one with the heart. He betrayed us."

Shannon clenches her jaw; I know she wants to tell me off, but she's worried I'm right.

"It must be a mistake," Ryah says, shaking her head in disbelief. "Jarek would never."

"We need to find him," I say. "Quickly."

"Aria's right," Landon says. He claps his hands together, then rolls up the sleeves of his purple T-shirt. "As much as it pains me to say it, Jarek is a rat."

A rat. Landon's words echo in my ears. Does Jarek have something to do with the mystic trace that was put on me? Is he somehow working with Kyle? Why else would he run off with the heart?

"But the timing is shitty," Landon says. He glances down at his TouchMe, then back at the group. "It's practically two a.m. First of all, I'm exhausted. Not to mention that the peace summit is at noon . . . which is basically today, in ten hours. Aren't we going to help Hunter prepare? And shouldn't we call him now to tell him about Jarek?"

"No," I say.

Everyone turns to me and stares.

"Hunter has a different agenda," I say. "He's going to ambush my brother and Thomas and set off a bomb that will wipe out every nonmystic in the vicinity."

Turk shakes his head. "No way, Aria. Are you nuts?"

"It's true," I say. "I know it's hard to believe, but he told me."

Landon and Ryah look astounded. "What . . . how . . . ," Ryah whispers.

Even Shannon looks like she's seen a ghost. Could it be that

Hunter really *didn't* fill her in on his plan? Or is she only pretending to be surprised?

"But we can't let that happen," I say. "Nobody hates Kyle more than I do." I get a flash of him instructing his solider to inject Turk with quicksilver. "But he's agreed to meet with Hunter, and so has Thomas. If Hunter goes ahead with his plan and we betray Thomas and Kyle, we'll be no better than my family. The only thing people in Manhattan will ever associate mystics with is death."

There's silence for a moment. Then Shannon says, "*Us?* Since when are you one of us?"

"Since she abandoned her family to support our cause," Turk says, frowning. "Shame on you for questioning her, Shannon." He glances at Landon and Ryah. "Are you with us?"

Landon lets out a low whistle. "I can't believe I'm saying this, but . . . yes, Aria. We can't give the people of this city any reason to doubt our motives. We want peace. No more destruction." He puts his hand over his heart. "No more death."

"I agree," Ryah says. Her lower lip is trembling, but I'm glad she's on board.

Which leaves Shannon.

"Well?" says Turk.

Ryah and Landon focus their stares on Shannon.

So does Turk.

So do I.

We stand like this for what feels like a long time. Waiting.

Until Shannon finally throws up her hands and says, "Fine. Just so long as nobody gets hurt."

Ryah beams and rushes over to hug Shannon. "I knew you'd come around."

Shannon rolls her eyes at me over Ryah's shoulder. "Just for the record, though, I still think you're a bitch."

"Whatever," I say.

"But how are we going to stop Hunter?" Ryah asks. "Everyone in Manhattan thinks the two of you are, you know, on the same page. All those clips they've been broadcasting around the city— whatever Hunter does, people will think you did it, too."

The video clips.

I think of all of the JumboTron TVs, how they played the edited footage that Hunter put together of me from our video chat sessions, of me shaving my head. All that had such a great effect on the morale down here.

What if I could use that to my advantage? Instead of letting someone else create a message from me, what if I created one myself?

"I have an idea," I say.

"Oh joy," Shannon mutters. "Here we go."

"Turk," I say. "Do you have your TouchMe?"

He pulls the silver device out of his back pocket. "Yup. Why?"

"Can you set it up to film me?" I ask. "I want to record something and then have it leaked to the media. I bet you anything they'll play it everywhere."

"Great idea!" Ryah says. "But what are you going to say?"

"The truth," I reply.

"To the people of Manhattan:

"You've seen me on your television screens, but this is the first time you are truly hearing from me. Some of you may think what I've done is heroic, while others, I'm sure, believe I am a large part of the reason you have lost friends and family to this war.

"There are others in this city, including my parents, my brother, and the Foster family, who would gladly see many of you perish if it meant extending their hold on Manhattan once more.

"But I do not share their beliefs. Since I witnessed a mystic draining firsthand and spent time here in the Depths, I have not believed that mystics should be drained—any more than I or any other human should be drained against our will of our own blood. And while I have left my family and the Aeries to live in the Depths with Hunter Brooks, I can no longer stand by and watch as he continues to fight this war as aggressively as my family does.

"Hunter Brooks is a good man, but he is not perfect. His family has a long legacy of fighting for mystic equality here in Manhattan. He believes that what he is doing is for the best, and perhaps many of you agree with him.

"But I no longer support his course of action.

"Hunter Brooks and his followers are planning to detonate a bomb today near the Empire State Building. The bomb will affect every nonmystic within a quarter-mile radius—maybe more. I am going to attempt to stop him, but if you are watching this, please evacuate the area for your own safety."

I pause. "Hunter Brooks is desperate to end this war. We all are. I urge you all not to hold this against him once everything is resolved. I believe that things *will* be resolved, as peacefully and amicably as possible. I still believe we can reach a truce. And I hope you believe in me."

I give a tiny nod, and Turk stops recording.

"Wow," he says. "That was intense."

"Intense good or intense bad?"

"Good," he says. "Very good. And very brave."

"No." I wave him off. "I'm not brave. All I did was sit in front of a camera and speak. It's the people out there, in the Depths, living this war . . . those are the brave ones."

Turk pockets his TouchMe and tilts his head, staring directly at me. Warmth radiates from his eyes. One of the images tattooed on his left bicep—a fire-breathing woman—seems to dance.

"What?" I say.

"You're something else, Aria," he says.

I know he means this as a compliment, but I'm full of mixed emotions. Recording the message was the right thing to do. My father told me once that Manhattan is my city. Well, if that's true, I can't let innocent people get hurt here when there's something I can do to help. But there's no going back now. Hunter will never forgive me. Ever.

This message may save thousands of people in the Depths, but it will surely destroy *us*.

Do I care?

Of course I do. But what other option did I have?

"Ahem." Landon clears his throat. He, Ryah, and Shannon have been sitting on the leather sofa at the far end of the room this entire time. I practically forgot they're here. "What now?"

"It should only take me a few minutes to upload the footage,"

Turk says. "I know someone with contacts to the people who monitor the Grid—they should be able to link this to every JumboTron in the city."

"Good." I glance at the clock on the wall. It's around four a.m., and I feel like I've been up for the past twenty-four hours without any sleep. "The summit is in eight hours."

"So before then," Shannon says, "we have to track down Jarek. And the heart."

"Exactly," I say.

Shannon stands and heads past the kitchen, toward the armory room. "Well, what's everybody waiting for?"

"A nap?" Landon says, rolling back his head.

"No time for napping." Shannon opens the door to the armory and grabs a pistol off the nearest shelf. "We'll sleep when we're dead."

· XXII ·

We're huddled inside the armory.

I stare at the weapons, hundreds of them in a room no larger than our bedroom upstairs.

Suited up, I'm carrying a collapsible wire kendo stick and have a loaded pistol strapped to my waist. Not that I really know how to use it. Shannon's training hasn't included firearms. I'm wearing the platinum-blond wig for good luck.

"You look ridiculous in that," Shannon says, zipping a lightweight silver jacket halfway up her chest. She passes a pistol to Landon, who straps it to his thigh, and another to Ryah.

"Well, you look ridiculous in general," I say.

"Grow up, Aria," Shannon says, turning away from me and tucking a knife into her belt.

"So, not to be a total downer," Ryah says, "but *how* are we going to track down Jarek?" She grabs a knife from one of the shelves and a ninja star with a serrated edge, tucking them both into a leather sheath.

"Easy," I say. "He has my locket."

Turk raises an eyebrow. "Hmm?"

"Jarek helped me figure a way out of the town house when Hunter looped the exits," I say to the group. "He came into my room after Turk refused to help me. . . . He must have seen me place the locket in the sweatshirt pocket."

Turk scratches his chin. "But why would he have taken your locket?" The black fabric of his fight gear is tight across his broad shoulders, accenting the muscles in his chest. He looks completely revived—you'd never know he was at death's door not even an hour ago.

"How is some old locket going to help us find Jarek?" Shannon twists her ponytail into a tight bun, pinning it back behind her head. "I don't get it."

"The locket has a mystic trace on it," I say.

"It does?" Turk says. "Why?"

"Because that mystic trace used to be on me."

"You had a trace on you?" Ryah says. "How could that be?"

Turk shakes his head. "Hunter checked you. He said you were clean."

"Well, he was wrong," I say. "I visited a mystic I know, and she discovered the trace. She removed it from me and transferred it to the locket. It was meant to keep me safe. Since the hideout is off the Grid, as long as the locket stayed inside . . . Supposedly, no one could find me."

"But somebody *did* find you," Landon says. He slips on his sneakers, which are bright purple and match his T-shirt. "At the black market."

"Exactly," I say. "My brother."

"So Kyle is the one who put the trace on you?" Ryah asks.

"When Jarek handed me my sweatshirt in the Depths, the locket was missing," I say. "I didn't know what happened to it—I thought maybe it had fallen out or gotten lost somewhere, but Jarek could have found it and pocketed it. That's how Kyle must've known where we were."

"But if Jarek knew there was a trace on the locket, why would he have kept it?" Landon asks. "That doesn't make any sense."

I think about this for a second. "He must not know, then. Maybe he just thought the locket was worth money, something he could sell. . . . Who cares? The point is that more likely than not, he has it—and *we* can use the locket to find *him*."

I turn to Shannon. "You can do that, right?"

Shannon's purses her lips. "Your locket? I'm not sure I even know what it looks like."

"A tarnished silver heart," I say, placing my hand just beneath my collarbone. "I wore it every day."

"Yes," Shannon says, "but I can barely recall it seeing it. I don't have a strong enough connection to it." She shakes her head. "It's not going to work."

"You touched it once," I say. "Back at the compound."

A flicker of memory ignites in Shannon's eyes.

"Try," Ryah says. "Please, Shannon."

Shannon turns away from us. She glances at Turk, clearly wanting his encouragement. He gives her a nod. "Fine," she says. "But I make no guarantees."

Shannon steps out of the armory, into the hallway. "Describe the locket to me."

"Silver," I say. "Though nearly blackened now. Mostly smooth, with tiny grooves in a sort of swirling pattern. No hinge. It's completely solid."

We stand around her as she closes her eyes, pressing her hands to her breastbone. She is still for a moment, and then I hear a small vibration—a low buzz—coming from the center of her body.

Her hands begin to glow with the familiar green mystic energy, the color growing more intense with every passing second. Her fingertips begin to flutter, moving faster than hummingbird wings. The iridescent green rushes up her arms and seeps into her chest, illuminating her neck and cheeks with a radiant glow.

She tilts back her head, and out of her mouth flies a thin green ray of energy, looking surprisingly delicate coming from a warrior like Shannon. It shoots down the hallway and disappears from view.

Shannon is statue-still. Then she drops her arms to her sides and opens her eyes.

Her mouth is closed, but the line of energy projecting from it is still there, so thin it's barely visible.

"Are you all right?" Turk asks.

Shannon blinks. "Let's go," she says. "I have a hold on the locket. Who knows how long it will last."

We follow Shannon's lead, heading down from Harlem and across the Depths toward the West Side.

Since Jarek has stolen Turk's bike, we flag two gondolas: Ryah, Shannon, and Landon in the first, me and Turk in the second.

The bright green line of energy acts like a sort of mystic homing device; Shannon barks out orders to the gondolier, following the trail left and right, under stone bridges and down canals.

To our gondolier—a man with black shaggy hair and ragged tweed pants—Turk simply says, "Follow them."

Turk sits directly in front of the gondolier, staring past me at the city as we creep forward along the waterways. The boat is too narrow for us to sit side by side, so I crouch on the tiny wooden seat facing Turk, my knees pressed tightly together.

We approach a stone archway; a chipped gargoyle ornament stares down at us as we pass underneath. Turk's face is expressionless, his dark eyes focused on the canal. The fuzz on top of his head seems to have grown a bit thicker, though perhaps it's merely the shadows. The sun is trapped behind thick clouds, only a trickle of yellow light piercing the smog. Everything else is gray.

There's a light drizzle on my skin. I glance overhead at the swollen rain clouds. I hope it's not about to pour.

"What are you thinking?" I ask Turk. It's not like him to be so silent.

"I'm thinking," he says, "this ain't good."

"Of course it's not," I say. "We all liked Jarek. He was our friend—"

"No." Turk shakes his head. "I mean, it's not good that we're going this far west. We're way past Times Square, at least two canals over." I glance around—the area is growing more and more deserted.

There are few buildings here, and the ones that haven't been knocked down seem oversized and very industrial. "What do you think it means?" I ask.

Turk rubs his temples. "This is where your brother has taken up."

"Kyle?"

Turk nods. "I noticed last night that his interrogation room was extremely far west—practically right over the Hudson."

I hadn't noticed that at all.

"He wouldn't take up in an Aeries building unless he was also controlling the bottom of it," Turk continues, "in the Depths, which worries me."

"It means Jarek must be working for him," I say. "In some way."

Turk scrunches his forehead—he's clearly frustrated.

"Maybe we're wrong," I suggest.

His lips tighten into a frown. "Unfortunately, I don't believe we are."

"You can trust me," I say. "I promise."

"I know," Turk says. He holds out his pinky finger. "And you can trust me. No matter what."

I link my pinky with his. "Deal," I say.

"Duck!" Turk shouts, pushing my head down as the gondola shoots underneath a particularly low bridge.

The gondolier lets out a whistle. "Sorry." We turn left, onto a smaller canal, following Shannon and the others.

And then it starts to rain in earnest. The drops sprinkle across my nose and cheeks and wet my hair. In a way, it's a blessed relief from the blistering heat.

"We're close!" Ryah yells back to us from the other gondola. Ahead, I can see the green line of energy extending from Shannon's mouth into the darkness ahead.

The buildings thin out here. They're incredibly long, taking up whole city blocks, and they all look abandoned, as though no one has inhabited them in years.

The gondola in front weaves onto a narrow canal to the left, and suddenly we're in front of an old warehouse on the edge of the city. It's a wide, gigantic structure; empty, from the looks of it. The building itself is only a few stories high; it doesn't extend up to the Aeries. Nearly half of it has completely caved in.

The canal runs past the warehouse, filtering into the Hudson River. The gondolier pulls up to a rickety wooden dock and loops a rope around one of the poles sticking up out of the water. Turk pays him and we leave the boat, stepping onto land.

"Whoa," I say. From here, I can see partially behind the warehouse to a graveyard of old ships half swallowed by the water. There are gaping openings in the hulls, which are reddish brown with rust and spotted with algae and brown seaweed.

"What *is* this place?" I whisper.

"It's spooky, that's what," Turk says. He tugs on my sleeve. "Ready?"

I nod. "As ready as I'll ever be."

We meet up with Ryah and Landon, who are standing outside the warehouse a few steps behind Shannon. The wispy line of energy is still trailing from her mouth, snaking through an open window.

"Eew." Ryah turns up her nose. "This place stinks."

I have to agree. The salty water mixed with the stench of the Depths makes for a very unpleasant smell. I wonder if it will be any better inside.

"This way," Shannon says quietly, waving us forward. I grip the pistol that's strapped to my side—just in case.

It seems too obvious to enter the front of the warehouse, so we sneak around the back. Forming a single line, we press ourselves as close to the wall as possible, moving stealthily around the bits of crumbled stone and twisted metal scattered on the ground.

Shannon disappears around the corner, and Landon and Ryah quickly follow. Turk and I are next, and we see the three of them waiting for us in front of a hole twice my height. It's jagged around the edges, like it was made by a wrecking ball.

"Come on," Landon says. "Quiet now."

I glance behind me at Turk, who gives me a thumbs-up, and we all follow Shannon through the hole. The inside of the building is pitch-black.

"Stop, please." Ryah creates a muted green light with her energy, holding her hand up near her head so we can see. It casts a chilling glow over us; I feel a jolt of nervous energy that makes me shiver even though the air is warm.

"Let's go," Ryah says.

I step carefully; there are unexpected breaches in the cement every five steps or so, and I don't want to accidentally twist my ankle—or worse.

I can't see much except Ryah and, in front of us, the line of energy emitting from Shannon's mouth. Shannon makes a sharp right. We follow her, and my foot sinks into something wet. There's about an inch of water covering the ground.

"Careful," Turk whispers. "If there's water here, then there must be a leak somewhere in the building."

We continue forward, the water growing deeper with each step. Shannon leads us left, then right. The water begins to taper off.

Ahead, something white pierces the darkness of the hallway. It looks like a tiny glowing ball that seems to be beckoning us. With each step, the ball glows brighter—until we reach a room filled with light.

Ryah shakes the energy from her hand, and I look around in awe.

It's a large loft space, two stories high. A set of metal stairs leads to a catwalk that lines all four walls and overlooks the room, extending halfway into the open space. The walls here are intact, made of gray cement. Exposed copper pipes run along the ceiling.

In the middle of the space is Jarek.

Bound and gagged.

His huge body hanging off a thick chain that dangles from a giant hook in the middle of the ceiling.

The ball of white light is coming from a fixture in the ceiling, illuminating the entire space.

When Jarek sees us, he begins to struggle, though he's wrapped in so many heavy chains that he can barely move a finger. His weight begins to swing the chain like a pendulum.

On the floor beneath his feet is the cooler.

Landon lets out an audible sigh. "What the—"

"Shh," Turk instructs, stepping out from behind me. I glance up at Jarek. His eyes are wide over the gag.

He's terrified.

The trail of energy from Shannon's mouth is wrapped around Jarek's ankle. She closes her lips and bites into the ray, severing her connection to it. It whips across the floor and untangles from Jarek's leg—then it bursts into nothingness.

Turk takes a step into the room.

Jarek shakes his head violently. Who tied him up like that? It must have taken someone powerful to subdue him. And is whoever did it still here?

There's a *zip* in the air and a burst of green light.

I look up on the catwalk.

Standing with her arms raised, energy pulsing from each of her fingertips, is Elissa Genevieve.

She looks more powerful than ever. When I knew her, she was masquerading as a drained mystic—covering her face with makeup to look so sallow and weak so no one would question her, when in reality she was healthy, a double agent who was working for my father.

Now there's no makeup to conceal who she really is.

Her blond hair is loose, her thick curls cascading down to her shoulders. This isn't the Elissa Genevieve I remember from my father's office. She has abandoned her corporate attire for a shimmering golden catsuit nearly as bright as the sun. She looks like a character out of a movie: the garment fits her like a second skin, so shiny there must be crushed crystals in the threads. Her knee-high black boots look painfully pointy.

"She's certainly dressed for the occasion," Landon mutters.

Turk starts forward, but I hold him back.

"Aria Rose!" Elissa cries out.

Our eyes meet and she spreads her arms, sending the bright green energy exploding from her fingertips across the room.

"Oh!" she says, her voice filling the vast space. "A reunion." She smiles a dazzling white smile. Her lips are painted a deep red. "Me. You. Davida—or rather, the only part of her I care about."

Elissa squeezes her right hand tightly, as though there's something delicate in her palm that she wants to destroy. The five individual rays of energy braid themselves together into one thick, powerful ray.

Elissa's energy looks almost black. Lethal. A darker green than I've ever seen from any mystic.

She sweeps her arm across the room and the ray shoots forward, stopping directly in front of the cooler holding Davida's heart.

· XXIII ·

Elissa closes her eyes.

She murmurs something and her entire body shudders, nearly launching her off the catwalk.

And then the energy from her hand begins to spin in midair.

The ray narrows itself to a fierce point, making a noise as loud as an electric drill. It spins so quickly that it almost looks like it isn't moving at all, darkening with every passing second.

Then Elissa drags the fierce green beam across the cement floor, just parallel to the cooler. The ray burns a charcoal mark into the cement with a sharp hiss as she moves the beam along the edge of the cooler.

"What is she doing?" I whisper to Turk.

As she maneuvers the narrow beam, a sheer greenish-blue wall rises from the mark she's made in the floor. The wall is approximately three feet high, extending well past the top of the cooler.

Then she draws another line.

And another, until the cooler is surrounded by a force field of semitranslucent energy. She completes the force field with a lid over the cooler, sealing it off completely. When she's finished, Elissa retracts her rays with a sound like the bursting of a hundred balloons.

The force field remains intact, shimmering incandescently. It's so beautiful that I almost want to reach out and touch it.

"One can never be too careful," Elissa says, her voice echoing off the walls. She focuses her attention on me. "You tend to have greedy little fingers, if I remember correctly." She motions to the force field and the cooler inside it. "And I want *this* all for myself."

Ryah and Landon stare at Elissa in silent awe. She looks terribly impressive standing atop the catwalk, the golden collar of her bodysuit flipped up against her neck, her blond hair glistening in the light. I once thought Elissa was my friend, my confidante.

I was wrong.

She is responsible for so many deaths: Violet Brooks's, for one, as well as many of those killed in the Conflagration twenty-odd years ago, not to mention in this year's war.

Elissa is the reason—one of them, at least—that the people of Manhattan are starving and fighting and killing. Anger begins to swirl inside me like boiling water.

Jarek makes a noise, but his cry is muffled by the gag in his mouth.

"Ah," Elissa says from the catwalk. "Silenced screams." She moves directly above where Jarek is hanging, staring down as if he's a museum exhibit. "Reminds me of home."

"Is this it?" Landon shouts from behind me. "You lured us here so we could watch Jarek hang from the ceiling?"

"Landon!" Ryah says. Her left hand is twitching nervously, her fingers hovering just above the gun strapped to her waist.

Elissa blinks at us. "*Lured* you here? You stumbled into this room of your own accord." She points directly at me. "I was looking for *you.*"

"My parents and brother aren't enough?" I say. "What do you want with me?"

Elissa stares at me with keen interest. "Your family has proved a helpful alliance, it's true. But I've decided to go out on my own. Roses need dirt to grow, Aria. But me—I need nothing but air."

"What does that even mean?" Ryah whispers to me.

Landon puffs out his chest. "What are you talking about, Elissa? You brought Jarek here. Why?"

"Jarek. Is that his name? Silly boy," Elissa says. She reaches for the chain that Jarek is hanging from, giving it a gentle push so that his body swings back and forth. "I'd hardly say I *brought* him here." Elissa catches the rope, steadying it. "It was an unexpected turn of events, really." She touches something hanging from her neck. I squint and realize she's wearing a locket.

My locket.

"Look familiar, Aria?" she asks.

"How'd she get your locket?" Turk asks. "I thought Jarek had it."

"So did I . . . ," I say, and then I realize what must have happened—why didn't I think of this before? Neither Hunter nor Kyle put the mystic trace on me. I stare up at Elissa. "*You.* You're the one who tagged me."

"You figured it out," she says. "Took you long enough. At first I thought you were *pretending* to be simple. But no. You're just daft."

Turk steps forward. "Hey—"

"Take one more step, boy"—Elissa holds up a hand suffused with her particular dark green mystic energy—"and I will annihilate you."

He glances back at me, and I shake my head. Elissa is too dangerous. I won't let him get hurt because of me.

"And why am I simple?" I ask. Maybe if I can keep Elissa talking, one of us will come up with a plan to stop her.

Elissa sighs. "I tagged you when we were with that one"—she points to Turk—"about to enter the underground. Right before the battle where poor little Hunter lost his mommy. I thought it would be handy, a way to keep tabs on you. You never felt a thing.

"As part of my arrangement with your father, I've been keeping him apprised of your whereabouts. I even told Thomas Foster you were at that compound upstate—just in case things ever went south with good old Johnny Rose. It's always good to have a backup plan." Her voice is as exactly as I remember it—steely and calm.

"But this war is *draaaagging on*," Elissa continues, "and I've decided to take things into my own hands. I followed the tag tonight, thinking I would find you. My plan was to ransom you off to the highest bidder, to use you to gain control over your parents *and* the Fosters."

She glances over at Jarek with disgust. "How was I supposed to know you had it transferred to your locket? A smart trick, so obviously you didn't think of it yourself."

Elissa removes the locket from around her neck and dangles it above Jarek's head. "Then this little thief shows up. I was about to kill him outright when I realized that he had a surprise with him:

a mystic heart. And not just any mystic's heart—your old servant, Davida's. Jarek here was going to use the heart for himself, isn't that right?"

Jarek says something, but it's muffled by the gag.

Elissa cups her hand to her ear. "I'm sorry, what did you say?"

He repeats himself, but his words are still incomprehensible.

"Poor thing." Elissa reaches forward and pulls the gag out of Jarek's mouth, letting it rest on his chin.

"I'm sorry!" he cries, gasping for air. "I just wanted to be powerful." He closes his eyes. "I didn't know . . . I didn't think . . ."

"But you *do* have power," I say to Jarek. "You saved me and Turk in the Aeries. We wouldn't be here now if it weren't for you."

"It's not the same," Jarek says rapidly. "I was going to ingest the energy myself and then sell the heart to Kyle when it was worthless. Would've served him right."

"So you're working with him?" I ask. "That's why you came here?"

"No," Jarek says. "I just thought he'd pay a hefty amount of money for the heart, and by the time he figured out that I'd already drained the energy, I'd be far gone. I came here to find him. I didn't know that she—" He looks at Elissa and holds back whatever he was about to say.

"And the locket . . . ," Jarek says, "I didn't even realize it was yours, Aria. I saw it on the ground back when Turk and I found you at the excavated canal. I figured somebody dropped it, that it was something I could pawn. But I was wr—"

"Enough." Elissa stuffs the gag back in his mouth. "I liked him better when he talked less."

So Jarek *isn't* working with my brother. He just wanted more power, and he saw Davida's heart as an opportunity. And he wasn't the one who ratted us out to Kyle—in fact, there was no rat. This entire time, it was Elissa working behind the scenes. It was just an unfortunate coincidence that Jarek brought along the sweatshirt that I'd hidden my locket in.

"I suppose your friend Davida never imagined that her heart would be serving me when she died," Elissa says.

Once again, she extends her fingertips and rays of dark-green energy burst from them like deadly streamers. She brings her hands in front of her, weaving the rays of light together the way Ryah did on Turk's motorcycle. They form a threaded platform extending from the catwalk to the floor near us.

With a flick of her fingers, Elissa blends the rays together into a single sheet of green; tiny ripples run across the surface, and the sheet begins to indent in various places, revealing itself as a set of stairs.

Elissa climbs over the railing, first one leg, then the other, slowly descending. There's a soft clink as she steps onto the cement floor.

"Show-off," Landon says, pointing to the metal ladder at the far side of the room. "You could have just used that."

Elissa laughs. "And how is that any fun?"

She fans out her arms and the sheet of green energy oscillates and separates into individual rays of light.

"You're going down, traitor." Landon snarls, then extends his own rays. They're a softer green than Elissa's, and shorter.

"Careful, Landon," I say, but he ignores me and steps forward. "She's dangerous."

"I would listen to Aria Rose," Elissa says, curling her lips upward. Her eyes burn with the same emerald color as her energy. "One wrong move and your friend Jarek here could just . . . die."

Elissa whips one of her hands into the air.

A jolt of energy blasts Jarek right in the stomach. His entire body swings on the hook, and he lets out muffled cries of pain.

"Aria," Elissa says calmly. "Tell your friend to retract his claws."

I turn to Landon. He's seething with anger, though he must know he's not a match for her.

Then again, there are five of us and only one of her. I wish we could communicate without Elissa's hearing, to plan an attack against her. Shannon and Ryah have their eyes trained on Elissa, perhaps thinking the same thing I am. Turk is staring at me; he raises his eyebrows, but if he's trying to send me a message, I have no idea what it is.

"Back off," I say to Landon. "For now. Let's hear her out."

"Fine," Landon says in a deep voice. The light from his hands disappears. "But I'm not happy about this."

"None of us are." I turn back to Elissa. "What do you want?"

She laughs. "Power, of course. I thought you knew me well enough by now to realize that." She closes her fists and the rays of light disappear from her fingertips, leaving both of her hands a scorching green; she's ready to attack at any moment.

"And now I'm going to have it. *Loads* of it," Elissa continues. "Once I transfer the power from Davida's heart into my body, I will be the most powerful mystic there has even been—as powerful as a Sister." She stares longingly at the cooler. "Intact mystic hearts are so rare, and one as special as Davida's . . ."

"I still don't understand what you want with Jarek," Shannon says, a slight quaver in her voice. "Let him go."

"I don't give two shakes about *Jarek*," Elissa barks. "He could die in an instant and the world would keep on spinning." She shifts her gaze around the room and steps around Jarek's hanging body.

"You've been a pretty little fool, Aria Rose. You had it all, and you sacrificed it for true love. And where did that get you?" Elissa motions to the rest of our group. "I don't see your dearly beloved here. Trouble in paradise?"

"At least I'm not a liar," I say. "Or a murderer."

Elissa shakes back her hair. "Call me whatever you want, Aria. I know what I want and I *take* it. You don't know what you want, so you let others make decisions for you. You're a nuisance, and if it were up to me, you'd be in the ground already."

Elissa creeps closer to me. I can smell her crisp, barely-there perfume—a mixture of white lilies and pear. "But you still seem to be important to your parents, and to the revolution. So you're going to come with me."

She reaches out to grab my wrist, but Landon pushes me out of the way. "Aria!" he shouts. "The heart!"

There's a burst of green light as Elissa punches her arms in front of her. The sickening sound of mystic energy against bare skin fills the room as Landon is thrown backward against the wall and crumples to the floor.

Elissa shouts something, but I can't hear what it is. The windows are beginning to shake. I whip my head back to see Ryah crouched on the floor, her blue hair in sharp contrast to the energy swirling around her, which is throwing dust from the floor into the air.

Ryah's energy flickers like the start of a fire: she knots her electric green rays into a tangle that grows brighter by the second. The knot begins to lengthen and spin in tiny circles, widening as it extends into the air.

Hints of red and orange shimmer in the green of Ryah's energy as the rays burst upward into a full-blown miniature cyclone that hisses and sputters.

Jarek continues to thrash in the middle of the room as Shannon blasts Elissa in the stomach. Elissa uses her energy like a shield, reflecting the burst of energy back at Shannon, who ducks in time to see her own ray double back and shatter a hole in the wall behind her. Meanwhile, Landon is pushing himself to his feet.

Sweat pours down Ryah's forehead as her cyclone of energy bursts into flames that roar as they expand, licking the high ceiling. The cyclone continues to spin, gaining speed. Ryah stands and pushes her arms away from her. The tip of the cyclone, closest to her fingers, tilts forward, changing the direction of the fire so that it's spinning out toward Elissa. Yellow and orange flames mix together, and smoke begins to fill the room.

Ryah makes a circle with her right arm. She pushes the tip of the cyclone toward the center of the swirling mass of flames. The cyclone collapses inward, becoming more focused. The flames grow angrier.

From my spot on the floor, I watch as Ryah makes a pinching motion with two fingers, and the cyclone, which now looks like a long funnel, begins spewing forth tiny balls of fire.

The first burst of flames is no bigger than my fist. Ablaze with mystic energy, the fireball soars directly toward Elissa.

Elissa's eyes widen. She's impressed. A flicker of fear crosses her face.

But then she springs into action.

Ryah's projectile sails straight for Elissa, followed by another, then another in quick succession. Just as the flames are about to kiss her forehead, Elissa bends backward, pressing her hands to her chest.

Green energy shoots up her skin, flooding her face with light. Her entire head glows green, her cheeks and lips and nose turning a dark olive.

She exhales, and energy flares from her mouth.

The fireballs suddenly stop their trajectory toward Elissa, coming together in a mass of green, yellow, and red flames that burns so brightly I'm scared the entire room will explode like a supernova.

The flames bounce back toward Ryah, who freezes, terrified.

"Move!" Turk calls.

Landon, now on his feet, hollers, "Watch out!"

But it's too late.

Elissa's energy meets the cyclone, which turns against Ryah and circles the flames back at her. They catch her clothes and hair and skin, consuming her in a magic show of light and energy. She screams in horror and pain, and I smell burning flesh.

"Ryah!" Shannon and Landon shout, rushing over to her.

Gray smoke fills the air, seeping into my lungs and making me cough. I duck low and crawl toward the cooler. Just behind the wavering walls of green energy lies Davida's heart.

I can't let Elissa have it.

Staring at the cooler, I realize there is no way around the force field—not even from above.

Quivering in fear, I thrust my arm right through it.

A shock of energy runs through me, frying my skin as if I'd poked my finger into an electric socket. I'm thrown backward, and my head slams on the cement. My hand throbs with pain. I glance down: my fingers are blackened.

"Turk!" I call, but he can't hear me—because Elissa is attacking him, shooting rays of energy that curl around Turk's legs like hungry snakes.

He fires off rays of his own, but it's no good. Elissa's beams crawl up Turk's limbs, covering his torso in what looks like emerald-green wiring. They travel down his arms, encase his hands, and wrap around his chest like some sort of mystic straightjacket, so quickly that Turk barely has time to react before he is immobilized.

In the center of the room, Jarek is shifting his weight, apparently trying to break the chain off the ceiling hook.

I cradle my burned hand against my chest. Shannon and Landon are still trying to douse the fire around Ryah, who's gone silent.

With Turk encased in mystic light, Elissa pivots on her heels, heading straight for Shannon.

"Watch out!" I cry.

Shannon hears me, turning just in time to duck Elissa's rays of energy. She rolls out of the way, and the energy pierces the wall behind her, making another hole. This time, it's so big that the wall begins to crumble, and the space behind it is exposed—a labyrinth of rusty pipes that explode on contact. Water gushes into the room, covering the concrete.

Water, I think. *That can put out the fire.*

Thankfully, I'm not the only one who realizes this.

Landon immediately goes into action, sucking in a breath of smoky air and stretching out his arms. His energy rays connect with the water, casting a green sheen over the rusty liquid spewing from the broken pipes.

Then he yanks back the rays, pulling the water with him so that it gushes into the room. There's a slap as the water hits the concrete with the speed of a waterfall, crashing over Ryah, encircling her.

The fire dies with an anguished hiss.

Landon lowers his arms and the swirls of water break away.

Ryah lies on the ground, unmoving. She's unrecognizable—even her hair is gone, the fine blue strands burned to a crisp. I can't tell whether she's dead or alive.

"Finally," Elissa says to me. "You're all mine."

But before she reaches me, I hear the sound of water again.

To my side, Landon is crouched near the floor, concentrating so hard his entire body is shaking. His lithe arms seem suddenly tremendous to me, full of strength.

The water on the ground begins to bubble, as though Landon is heating it with his energy. The bubbles swell and begin to rise.

Elissa shakes her head in disbelief. "What the—"

The bubbles begin to erupt, spurting jets of water into the air. They jump across the room, spreading out until nearly half the space is covered with liquid.

Landon brings his arms together and stands, manipulating the water upward into a swirling bluish wall. It foams and churns as its center begins to spin toward Elissa, morphing into a pointed cone. It keeps extending, growing thinner and longer as Landon continues to draw in water from the swamped hallways of the warehouse.

When the swirling water resembles a sharp spear, Landon attacks, throwing his arms forward so swiftly they seem like they might fly off his body. The water-spear moves toward Elissa and begins to freeze midair.

The liquid turns to ice, crystallizing with a thousand tiny crackles. The ice glistens, shiny as silver, sharp as a sword.

Elissa looks around frantically for somewhere to hide, but her feet seem glued to the ground.

The frozen missile launches right into the center of Elissa's chest like an ice pick.

She glances down in disbelief.

For a second, her face softens. She looks calm. Peaceful.

And then an explosion of green light fills the room, shattering the windows and twisting the catwalk into a hunk of metal that clatters to the ground.

Landon cries out in agony; pure white light pours out of every inch of his body, illuminating him like some sort of angelic being.

The ice melts in a split second. Water pours over everything.

I am thrown backward onto the concrete. A beautiful shattering of energy fills the room like a shower of stars, spilling over everything—gorgeous reds and blues and greens, and then, like the aftermath of fireworks, nothing but black.

· XXIV ·

The room is calm when I wake. It's the sort of quiet that's a sound itself—as powerful as any shout or cry or thunderstorm.

I open my eyes.

Pain spikes up my side and through my blackened hand. I try to move my arm, but it feels like the entire right side of me is broken.

Smoke lingers in the room, filling my nostrils. My lungs are still burning, and the back of my head throbs where I smacked it against the concrete.

With my left arm, I push myself to a seated position and then stand. I'm wobbly, but I make it.

Everyone else is on the floor.

Elissa is buried under a heap of tarnished metal from the fallen catwalk, her legs twisted at an unnatural angle. Blood trails from underneath the metal into a dark pool.

On the other side of the room, Ryah is burned beyond recognition. Next to her, Shannon is stirring, brushing strands of red hair from her face. A few feet away from her, Turk is unconscious.

I hobble toward him. *Please be okay,* I think. *Please be okay.*

He looks so peaceful that if I didn't know any better, I'd think he was taking a nap. His eyes are closed, his face only slightly dirtied from the smoke. I wipe a bit of grease from his forehead with my good hand.

"Turk," I whisper, giving his shoulder a gentle shake. "Are you okay?" I run my hand over his head, feeling the soft fuzz. "Can you hear me?"

His eyelids flicker open. "Aria?" he says groggily.

"You're alive," I say.

"Of course I'm alive." He draws in a sharp breath. "What about Elissa?"

I sit up straight. "She's dead. Or badly hurt—either way, she's out of commission."

Turk shakes himself into consciousness. The color begins to seep back into his cheeks. He stares at my bad hand. "Let me help you."

"No, save your energy for Ryah."

Shannon is awake, bent over Ryah's limp body. "It's bad," she says.

Every inch of Ryah's skin is black and bloodied, the flesh ravaged so terribly that I can see hints of white bone in places. It's so gory that I have to look away.

Turk gulps. "Is she—"

"Dead?" Shannon shakes her head. "She's breathing. Barely."

"Thank God," I say.

"I'm scared to touch her," Shannon adds. "I don't want to end up hurting her more."

Turk closes his eyes; there's a soft hum as his hands glow green, and he lays them gently on Ryah's legs.

We look on, hopeful, but nothing seems to happen. Turk opens his eyes and stands up, shaking his head. "This is beyond what I can do. We need to get her to an experienced healer. Fast."

Shannon nods. "You're right." She looks around the room, spotting Jarek. The chain has fallen from the ceiling, and he's stretched across the floor like some sort of knotted-up caterpillar.

"Where's Landon?" I ask. I don't see him anywhere.

Turk closes his eyes, saying something underneath his breath, his hands clasped in front of his chest. Shannon does the same thing. Neither of them answers me.

Turk sways back and forth gently. After a few seconds, he opens his eyes, with an expression of sadness and frustration on his face. "Landon's gone."

"Gone?" This doesn't make any sense to me. "Where did he go?"

"Sometimes a mystic uses too much energy," Shannon says, without the usual harshness in her voice. "He just . . . exploded."

I remember the white light around Landon. How strange and brilliant it was. I thought it was beautiful . . . but that was him dying? "That can't be," I say. "You must be wrong."

Turk rests a hand on my shoulder. "I'm sorry, Aria. It's how most mystics hope to die, actually: burning up in a blast of light." He bites his lower lip. "He died for a good cause. We will honor him once this is over."

A rush of gratitude surges through me—if Landon hadn't fought Elissa, we might all be dead. He saved us, like Davida did. And like Davida, he was too young to die.

Turk is gazing at Elissa's body. "I'm going to finish her off."

"No." Shannon grabs his arm. "Leave her." Her hair is matted with sweat, her eyes red from the smoke. "She's probably dead. And even if she's not"—she looks down at Ryah—"we have to help Ry. Now. She doesn't have much time left."

"You're right," Turk says. He goes to Jarek and breaks his bonds. Jarek begins to speak, but Turk gives him a firm smack that shuts him up. "Not now. Don't say a word. Just help me with Ryah. Careful."

Together, they let loose mystic rays from their fingertips, weaving them into a makeshift stretcher. We all help move Ryah onto the rays; then Turk and Jarek lift her off the ground.

"Come." Turk motions for Shannon and me to follow. I take one last look around the space, at the overwhelming amount of destruction—the collapsing walls, the remaining water pooled across the floor.

Then my eyes catch it: the cooler.

Elissa's force field has vanished, and the white cooler is perfectly intact. I pick it up and tuck it under my arm. Then I rush to catch up with the others.

Outside the warehouse, Turk and Jarek rest Ryah on the ground near the canal. Turk shakes away the rays of energy and takes his TouchMe out of his back pocket, keying in a message. "Someone will be here momentarily," he says to Shannon.

"Okay," she says. "Don't wait with me." She glances down at her TouchMe. "The summit! You don't have much time. It'll be starting soon."

Even though it's morning, it doesn't look—or feel—like it. The sun is hidden behind dusty clouds that are reflected in the gray water. I'm feeling weary from everything that has happened plus the lack of sleep.

"We'll take care of it," I say. "Just get Ryah some help."

Shannon grabs my good hand and squeezes. "I will. And, Aria?"

"Yes?"

Her brown eyes seem full of concern—more concern than I've ever seen from her. "Make sure everyone comes home in one piece."

"I will," I reply. "I promise."

Moments later, a gondola shows up. Its driver is an older mystic, thin as a string bean, with a dark mustache and wavy brown hair.

He helps Shannon carry Ryah onto the gondola. Shannon climbs on board, and Turk, Jarek, and I watch as it moves away until it's only a black dot against a sea of twisting canals and tattered buildings.

Jarek shifts his gaze from me to Turk. "Guys," he says nervously, "I just want to say—"

Once more, Turk smacks him upside the head. "Not now, Jarek." He turns toward the graveyard of rusting boats. "Where's my bike?"

Jarek shows us Turk's motorcycle, hidden under a tarp. The bike looks as good as new, the sharp chrome wheels and stark white paint spotless.

Turk glances at his TouchMe. "Hunter, Thomas, and your brother are meeting in less than an hour. Who knows when this bomb is going to go off? We've gotta get moving."

Jarek brushes his hair back. "Should I just head back to the hideout? You guys probably don't want me around."

"You're right," Turk says. "You're the last person I want to see right now." He points to the back of the cycle, then smacks Jarek's backside. "Which is exactly why I'm not letting you out of my sight. Aria, you take the sidecar. And don't forget to put your helmet on."

We mount the bike; then Turk pulls back on the handlebars and the motorcycle soars away from the wrecked warehouse, picking up speed as we glide into the murky sky, heading away from the Hudson River. The water below us shimmers, as if bits of glass are hidden within the waves.

I breathe a sigh of relief when I see the bag I left in the sidecar, the one that holds Davida's reliquary. Huddled here as we drive the car, the cooler sandwiched between my legs, I'm not comfortable, but at least none of this—the battle, Landon's death—has been in vain. We still have the heart *and* the reliquary.

Now we just have to stop Hunter before it's too late.

My burned hand has taken on a life of its own: it's oozing some sort of clear fluid, and a large chunk of flesh just below my wrist looks charred. It almost doesn't hurt at all anymore, which worries me.

I remove the reliquary from the bag with my good hand, tracing the design of the Seven Sisters. Who were they? How did they get their powers? Did any of them have to make sacrifices like Davida and Landon did? I'm running my fingers absentmindedly over the smooth wood when suddenly I feel the box *pulling* me.

Right toward the cooler.

It's almost as if there's a magnet embedded in the fine wood-work. The box heaves forward and connects with the cooler.

I hear a click from the reliquary.

Could it be?

The middle of the lid has parted, the two sides sliding in opposite directions. Fresh cedar and a hint of cinnamon fill the air. Inside, the name *Davida Kane* is etched in gold leaf. A thin black border runs along each side of the box.

Then it hits me: Davida's heart.

Somehow, the reliquary must have sensed the proximity of her heart and opened, expecting the muscle to be deposited inside.

I glance over at Turk, who's navigating through the sea of tow-ering skyscrapers toward the very top of the Empire State Building. Gray fog off the river mixes with city smog, making it difficult to see. Jarek's eyes are tightly shut; fierce wind whips his hair over his face.

Nobody is watching me.

I duck even farther into the sidecar, opening the reliquary com-pletely. There are more mystic symbols etched inside, and in the very center of the box is a note, folded over.

My name is written on it.

I sneak another look at Turk and Jarek, then open the note:

Aria,

*Don't consign my heart to a box. By now you know what to do
with it.*

$$—D$$

Even before I see her initial, I recognize the handwriting as
Davida's. I read the note a second time. *By now you know what to do
with it.*

I have no idea what to do with a mystic heart other than par-
ticipate in the ceremony Lyrica mentioned. But that doesn't seem to
be what Davida is referring to here—and why would she suggest
anything else?

The only heart *I've* ever even seen is . . .

A million pictures flash before my eyes, fitting together like
puzzle pieces: Frieda, the old woman back at the compound, questioning what had happened to Davida's heart. Lyrica's cryptic
advice about how I must absorb Davida's faith within myself. And,
of course, the heart-shaped capture locket that I wore around my
neck, where Patrick Benedict stored the memories of Hunter that
my parents extracted from my brain.

The only way to open the locket was to swallow it. And when
I did, all my memories returned to me.

My eyes travel past my knees to the cooler between my legs.
Inside is Davida's heart. She must have written this note before
she snuck out of the apartment to follow Hunter and me into the
Depths. She knew there was a good chance that she would die, so
she left this note, instructing me what to do.

Davida doesn't want me to give her heart back to her family.

She wants me to eat it.

I think back to when I swallowed the capture locket. *Not again.*

Is it dangerous? Could I die? What will Hunter and the others think? There are a million reasons to talk myself out of following Davida's wishes.

But this is what she wanted.

I reach down and open the cooler. The lid retracts and the sidecar is filled with silver light.

The heart is encased in a glass box lined with liquid mercury. The quicksilver is trapped between two layers of glass; when I pick up the box and rotate it, the silver rushes around like blood—only deadlier.

I slide open the lid and there it is:

The heart.

It's smaller than I expected. No bigger than a fat strawberry, a meaty thing that fits neatly in the palm of my hand. And it's blue—the bluest thing I've ever seen in my life, cobalt at the top and lighter toward the bottom, swirled with slivers of white fat and indigo arteries.

Davida's life force—her essence.

An image of her flashes in my mind: us sitting together on my bed. *"Do you love him?"* she asked me of Hunter. I told her I did. *"Then I will protect you both. For as long as I can."*

Davida has always watched out for me—even after her death, it seems. I glance at her heart and feel myself start to cry.

"Aria?" Turk calls over his shoulder. I turn away from him, blinking back tears. He looks at me quizzically; I don't know how much he can see. "What's going on?"

I cringe, staring down at the organ. I can't bear to bite into it. The thought of chewing it . . .

I hold back a wave of nausea.

Now, I think. *Do it now.*

I close my eyes and open my mouth as tears run down my cheeks; then I push the heart into my mouth, letting it rest for a second on my tongue.

It's weightless. I don't feel a thing.

Suddenly, my taste buds burst with sweetness, as though the inside of my cheeks have been doused with syrup. *Remarkable,* I think, and then I swallow Davida's heart whole.

· XXV ·

I feel everything and nothing. The colors around me seem brighter. More exact.

My vision is more precise: I watch my reflection in the plate-glass façades of the skyscrapers as we climb higher into the sky, heading toward the peace summit.

The warm air smells salty, almost putrid. Smog covers my tongue; I can actually *taste* the *air:* a mixture of dirt and dust and oil. My breath grows shorter as we soar.

Every pore in my skin seems to have expanded, tingling with a sense of urgency and delight. I feel alive. Awake. The burn on my hand has begun to heal itself: my blackened fingertips have turned pink, the new skin as smooth as a baby's, spreading down to the rest of my hand. I open and close my fingers. The pain has been extinguished.

I am calm. I can actually hear my heart thumping as it pumps blood and oxygen and nourishment through my body.

I open my mouth but my lips are sticky, like they're covered in peanut butter. I pull myself to a normal seated position in the sidecar. Turk is glancing at me as he navigates the cycle, shooting me a concerned look.

"Aria? What's going on? You look sick."

Sick? I feel *wonderful*.

Turk levels out the motorcycle and we speed along the rooftops of the Depths. The sun is shining through the smog, a bright, hot yellow—as if nothing is wrong, as if nothing tragic is about to happen.

For the middle of the day, there aren't many people in sight, which is good: they must have seen my video and evacuated. At least, I hope they did.

"Almost there," Turk says.

The inside of my mouth is a jumble of flavors, the intense sweetness now bitter and sour, as though I have just eaten a lemon.

How much time do we have? I think. *How much time, how much time?*

My thoughts are jumping on a miniature trampoline inside my skull. My nose feels stuffed; I sneeze and bloody mucus sprays from my nostrils.

"Bless you," Turk says. I wipe the blood with my sleeve.

Turk's concerned eyes multiply from two to four, then six: they start at his hairline, then continue down to his chin. They all blink at me simultaneously. "Aria?" His voice echoes. "Aria?"

I shake my head and look at him again—now he only has two eyes. Strange.

"What did you do?" Turk says. His gaze travels from my face down to the open reliquary, the open cooler. "Open your mouth," he instructs.

I shake my head.

Turk swerves the bike to avoid colliding with one of the triangular PODs that run from the Depths to the Aeries. "Aria, open your mouth!"

He stops the bike midair and we hover over a canal. "Take the handles," Turk says to Jarek. Then he leans over and pries open my jaw. "Stick out your tongue," he says.

I shake my head and try to bite down on his fingers, but he's too swift for me—he gives my tongue a gentle pull and tilts back my head.

"Your tongue is blue," he says. He stares down at the empty cooler. "Aria, you didn't. Tell me you didn't—"

"Guys." Jarek cuts him off. He nods ahead, in the distance.

The Empire State Building. The perfect meeting ground, halfway between the Depths and the Aeries, one of the few buildings that remain practically unchanged over time. Before the expansion upward, the Empire State Building was one of the tallest skyscrapers in Manhattan, reaching almost fifteen hundred feet into the sky. A famous landmark, it was left intact as the Aeries were built above it: a relic of old Manhattan before the city was ushered into a new era. The pointed tip of the broadcast tower points toward the Aeries, practically shouting *Look up!*

I expect the area surrounding the building to be deserted—evacuated.

But in fact, it's quite the opposite: it's full of people.

Thousands of them.

Men, women, and children line the streets of the Depths,

packed together like sardines. Mystics and humans both are standing in gondolas in the water, sitting atop one another's shoulders on the sidewalks, poking their heads out of windows.

The bridges and raised walkways are flooded with people holding up multicolored signs and shouting so many different things that it's impossible to decipher a clear message.

Above us, I can see people crowding the silvery bridges in the Aeries, leaning forward and participating in the biggest rally I have ever seen. The Empire State Building is swarmed.

My mind clears for a moment, and I feel a surge of pride for my city.

Instead of heeding my webcast prompting them to flee, hundreds upon hundreds of Depths *and* Aeries dwellers have flocked here. Ignoring their own safety, they are chanting, and at last I understand their words: *Peace! Peace! Peace!*

"Whoa," Turk says. "This is intense."

The lines of people snake through the canals and streets. From our view in the air, they look like ants—thousands and thousands of them clamoring to show their support for their city, for restoring Manhattan to its former glory.

Before the mystic drainings. Before the war.

Before the Conflagration.

There's no way Hunter can set off this bomb.

This is a good thing.

This is the thing that might save us.

Turk grips the handlebars tightly as we zip up to the observation deck at the top of the Empire State Building, where the summit is to take place. We pass the main deck on the eighty-sixth floor and zoom to the very top, the deck just below the needle. Somehow, a camera captures us on Turk's bike; our image is streamed live on all the JumboTrons in the area.

I stare at an oversized screen on the side of a building on Fifth Avenue and catch a glimpse of myself: My eyes are darting everywhere, glazed over like I'm high. My cheeks have turned bright pink; I look sweaty and disoriented. My wig is blonder than I remember, poking out from underneath my helmet.

My mouth has gone dry, my jaw slack. I'm parched, craving water, soda—anything to wet my lips. My nostrils are full of the scents of the city; fog coats my skin like a slick moisturizer, and every hair follicle on my body seems to be tingling. My hand is nearly healed; only a speck of black remains in the center of my palm. I flex my fingers—they feel stronger than ever before, full of power.

Something about the moment makes me think of Patrick Benedict, the mystic who saved my memories and turned out to be one of my greatest allies, before he lost his life at the hands of Elissa Genevieve. I wonder if he would be proud of me.

The cycle exhales a burst of fire as we descend. A metal railing lines the observation deck like a fence—presumably so that tourists don't fall over the edge as they're snapping pictures.

We land behind a wall that extends onto the deck, so we're hidden from view. Turk silences the bike and extends the kickstand, then helps me out of the sidecar. "Aria," he says as I take off my helmet, "I don't even know what to say to you right now. You shouldn't be here. What you did was dangerous."

Turk gazes at me with a concerned expression. "You could die," he says softly. "Ingesting so much mystic energy . . . Your body is on overload. I'm a healer, but even I can't help you, Aria. You need someone older, more powerful than me."

"Later," I say. I feel pins and needles in my legs. I try to walk but can't keep my balance. Turk catches me before I hit the ground.

"Brrr!" I say. "It's cold, isn't it?"

Turk blinks. "It's sweltering hot, Aria."

"It is?" It feels like someone is rubbing dozens of ice cubes all over my body. I'm so cold my teeth begin to chatter.

"Stay here," Turk says to Jarek. "With the bike. I'm trusting you."

Turk and I peer around the wall. Light from the sun and the surrounding city brightens the observation deck. The view looking down is full of windows and metal and water and people, all covered in a thick white haze.

"Who's there?" someone calls. Thomas—I recognize his voice.

"Me," I say, holding up my hands. For a second, they blaze green; then the color disappears. No one but Turk sees—I hope. I look around for Hunter. Is he already standing out there with Thomas and Kyle?

Turk glances at me. "Keep quiet about what you've done," he says. "For your own sake."

We step out past the wall, so we're in full view. I check my belt, feeling for my kendo stick and my gun—just in case.

Immediately, I see Hunter, Thomas, and Kyle standing together.

"Aria?" It's Hunter. His dirty-blond hair is messy over his forehead, and he's wearing his all-black fighting gear: long pants and sleeves with a fitted metal-plated vest. "What are you doing here?"

So many words rush to my tongue that none of them come out. I stand there, speechless.

"Nice video," Thomas says suddenly. I'm not sure what he was expecting at the summit, but he's dressed as though he's about to attend a fancy dinner party: a sleek black tuxedo, with a thin tie, a stark white dress shirt, and a cream-colored vest half hidden beneath his jacket. His dark hair is combed nearly and parted on the side. Even his shoes are freshly shined. "It deserves an award. Maybe . . . Most Desperate Newcomer?"

"This is hardly a time for jokes," Kyle says angrily. He has two black eyes and a purplish bruise on the side of his face, likely from when I smacked him with the IV stand. He's wearing the Rose family officer's uniform, the crest above his heart gleaming in the light.

He motions to the throngs of people in the buildings above and below us. "I've been working so hard to get control—you shave your head and send one little crybaby message and suddenly everyone loves you." He purses his lips. "I hate you."

I hate you, I hate you, I hate you. The words repeat themselves on loop in my head; I picture my mother, my father, and Kyle standing next to me on the roof. In one swoop, I mentally push them over the edge, and they fall to their deaths.

Hunter peers out at the city, at all the people who now know of his plan. He gestures into the air. "This is all your fault, Aria. I had everything under control, I was picking up where my mom left off, I was taking care of things—and then you go and cause *this.*"

"Calm down, Hunter," Turk says.

"Stay out of this, mystic," Kyle sneers. He cocks his head at Hunter. "You measly little prick. A bomb? What's the matter? Too scared to fight us like a man?"

I'm no longer cold. Now my skin feels like it's crawling with insects; I want to scratch them off. "What are you going to do?" I say to Hunter. "Kill all these people? Are you going to kill me?"

He looks torn, as though he's actually considering going forward with his plan.

Thomas chuckles. "I love it when you get self-righteous, Aria. But what exactly are you talking about? Your little boyfriend isn't going to do anything. Not after the stunt you pulled. Why do you think your brother and I still bothered to show up?"

I glare at Hunter. Where are the rebels? Where is the bomb?

Kyle looks at Thomas, then at Hunter. We all hear the shouting of the people surrounding the building. *"Peace! Peace! Peace!"*

"What do we do now?" Kyle says. "I don't trust you, Foster. And I certainly don't trust you"—he points to Hunter—"but we've got to a figure out a plan. And fast."

Hunter shakes his head. "I'm not working with either of you."

Thomas snorts. "Very mature, mystic. It's not as if any of us is eager to work with the others. Shall we all just walk away?"

There's a tap on my back. Turk. He pushes me forward. "Go on," he says.

I turn to my brother. "Kyle, if you call a truce with Hunter, the Fosters will follow. There are ways for both sides of this war to come out ahead."

Kyle stares at me. "You actually want me to call a truce with that mystic? Mom and Dad will never go for that. Neither will our supporters in the Aeries. Not everyone thinks like you do, Aria."

"Really?" I say, looking upward. Kyle raises his chin and stares into the Aeries, where the silvery bridges are lined with people holding the railings and chanting for peace, calling out my name.

"Kyle, if you don't negotiate a peace, if you keep fighting, there's a strong chance that the mystics will win. And then we could very well be overtaken by another city anyway," I say.

Thomas's eyes seem to blaze with recognition that these are more or less his words, that I remember what he told me. "Everyone needs to give *something*," he says to the group.

This is it, the moment of truth. Either the three of them will shake hands and everyone will leave this rooftop alive, or . . .

I shake my head. Can't think about the alternative. I feel myself warming up, as though I've just been stuck in an oven. I have to keep talking, keep them listening to me.

"We know that the Conflagration wasn't caused by a group of mystics rebelling against the city," I say. "It was caused by *one* mystic: Elissa Genevieve. She admitted this to me personally. The rest of the population shouldn't be punished for the evildoing of an individual."

Thomas narrows his eyes. "But—"

"There are no buts," I say firmly. I'm sweating now. I see dozens of bright white circles before me. I blink and they're gone. "Mystics must be recognized as citizens of New York, with the same rights as everyone else. They cannot be quarantined and drained against their will."

"That's all fine and good," Kyle says, "but you're forgetting one thing—Manhattan runs on mystic energy. The light-rail, the PODs, our electricity . . . everything depends on it. We've only been able to function these past few weeks because of the extra energy we had stored. But that will run out eventually, Aria, and if the mystics aren't drained, how will the city function?"

"The mystics have been *over*drained for years," I say. "The amount of energy the city needs is minuscule compared to what has been taken by our families to sell on the black market." Tabitha was the first one to tell me about this, back at Java River, and I haven't forgotten it. "We have enough stored energy to run the city for at least the next few months, I imagine, and we can open up discussions on how to safely harvest small amounts of mystic energy in a nonpainful, humane way." I look at Hunter, waiting for him to speak. His jaw is tightly clenched. "Does that seem fair?"

"Fair?" He growls. "That my people have been oppressed for decades, that you're asking me to compromise with the demons who killed my mother?" He glares at me with stone-cold eyes. "I'd hardly say that's fair."

I take another step toward him. I want to rest my hands on his cheek and feel his arms around me, but he'll only push me away.

"What happened to your mother was a terrible thing," I say. "But she would want this sort of compromise. I didn't know her well . . . or really at all . . . but judging from her values and the way she raised you, I believe it's true."

Hunter's head is down, so I can't see his expression. I turn my attention to Thomas and my brother. "There should be no more Aeries and Depths," I say. "Everyone should live together."

"Ha!" Thomas throws his hands up in the air. "You've gone mad!"

I ignore him. "The mystics will be allowed to use their powers—"

"So they can kill us?" Kyle says, cutting me off. "Great idea, Aria."

"No," I say. "They can use them within reason—the city can establish laws and rules they will have to follow. There will be no more Roses and Fosters running Manhattan. We can let the people choose a new mayor, one with no ties to either of our families."

There it is. The big compromise. It could work, I think—if I can convince Hunter that it's the right move before he blows us all up.

Cheers and screams from above and below blend into a cacophony of sound. "Hunter," I say. I'm about to go to him when my head pounds with pain.

I stumble forward, pressing my hands to my temples. Then I feel a vibration in my feet. My stomach lurches, and I double over in agony.

"Aria?" Turk says worriedly. "Are you okay?"

"What's wrong with her?" Kyle asks. He points his gun at Turk. "What did you do to her, mystic?"

Hunter spins around and rushes toward me. I feel his hands on my back, pulling me into his body. "Just breathe," he tells me. My blood calms, and I can see straight again. The throbbing in my head begins to dull.

I bury my head in his chest and let him hold me the way I've been longing for since I got back to Manhattan. He smells like sweat and smoke, but I don't care. Once I'm in his arms, I remember how right it feels for us to be together, how our bodies are made for each other.

Tenderly, he leans forward and kisses me on the forehead, then presses his lips to each of my eyelids—faint ghostlike kisses that send chills down my spine and make my toes curl.

The chanting around us grows louder, more urgent. Hunter sucks in a breath, then says, "You're right."

I open my eyes and stare up at his face. He is the most gorgeous man I've ever seen.

"I was wrong," he says. "All these people came to support you because they believe in what you've said. I should have listened to you from the start. But my mom . . ." His eyes well up with tears that spill over onto his cheeks. I wipe them away with my fingers. "She wouldn't have wanted this. She wouldn't have wanted war, and she wouldn't approve of my plan."

He takes a step back from me and turns to Kyle and Thomas. Then he raises his hands in surrender. "We rebels lay down our arms. There will be no bomb—today or ever." Hunter looks at me and smiles—the first genuine smile I've seen from him in a long, long time. "As the mystic representative, I accept the terms of Aria's proposition. I am truly sorry for my actions."

"Well, I certainly hope you're sorry," Thomas says. "A bomb?" He sighs. "I should have known never to trust a mystic."

I grab Hunter's hand. I'm proud of him, and relieved for the people of Manhattan.

Kyle, however, doesn't seem satisfied. He lets out a guttural laugh. In the blink of an eye, he raises a pistol—where did it come from?—and aims at Hunter. "Goodbye, mystic."

Then he shoots.

The silver bullet spirals out from the cylinder.

Without thinking, I jump in front of Hunter, shielding him with my body.

I stifle a cry as the metal pierces my chest.

· XXVI ·

For a moment, everything is still.

The air around me seems to freeze, and I view the world in slow motion.

I attempt to drag my hands to my chest, but they're terribly heavy, as though each one is weighted with a dozen bricks.

Kyle stands with his arm in the air, the gun still pointed at me. There's an incredulous look on his face, his blond hair flapping in the wind.

Next to him, Thomas is saying something—or trying to say something, only his lips are moving so slowly that I can't make out any words. The sounds coming from his mouth remind me of when Kiki and I used to record ourselves speaking and play the conversations back on our TouchMes, slowing down the speed so that we sounded like cartoon characters.

"Arriiiiiaaaaa," Thomas says. *"Arrrre yoooou ooookaaaay?"*

It takes every ounce of strength I can muster to turn back and look at Hunter, whose mouth has formed a wide O of shock.

Hunter is reaching for me, but his arms are moving as if they're smothered in marmalade. It feels like it will take him years to touch me. Next to him is Turk, who appears to be falling forward, arms outstretched. It's impossible to tell whether he or Hunter looks more upset.

Shouts from the surrounding buildings thin out, until I'm aware of a keen silence across the observatory deck, and nothing but white noise beyond that.

I stare down at my chest.

A dark plume has spread across the front of my shirt. It seeps into the material like a deadly flower opening its petals.

I can feel something tunneling inside me—the tiny bullet—spiraling its way through tendon and muscle and fat, navigating past my organs and the blood rushing through my veins.

It feels like a sparkler has gone off inside me. No pain—only sharp crackles and pops as the bullet tears through my chest.

The shot exits my back, ripping a hole the size of a dime through my flesh, dinging off a piece of the metal fencing along the edge of the observation deck.

The sound wakes me up, returning life to a normal speed.

The middle of my back, where the bullet exited, begins to itch. My entire body is covered with a prickly sensation. The blood that has been seeping out of my chest slows to a trickle. The ravaged skin around the bullet hole simmers; the wound expels a loud hiss as the skin heals itself.

I run my finger over the wound, but it's solid pink flesh. I feel my back: it's as if I've never been shot.

Hunter grabs my shoulders. "You're alive," he whispers into my ear. "How?"

Kyle is clearly shocked as well. "Aria. You're still . . . here."

"Yes," I say. "I am."

His pistol still trained on me, Kyle gives me a tight-lipped smile. "Impressive," he says.

Hunter steps out from behind me, extending an open hand to Kyle. "So, about Aria's plan?"

Kyle glances nervously from me to Hunter and Turk, then to Thomas. To my side, Jarek has emerged from his hiding place; he strides toward us with confidence, which only makes Kyle more nervous—he aims the gun every which way, until finally, he sighs and shoves his free hand into his pocket. He leaves Hunter's hand dangling and turns to me.

"I gave you plenty of chances to come around, Aria," Kyle says. "And you talk a good game—I'll give you that. But your view of the future isn't my view. And it's certainly not our father's." He removes something small and black from his pocket and clips it over the barrel of his pistol. "If you're not with me, Aria, then you're against me. And if you're against me, then you leave me no choice."

Kyle raises the gun in the air and fires off a shot. A burst of red billows in the sky, mixing with the smog and forming a layer of light pink clouds that hover over us.

"Is that your idea of a light show?" Turk asks sarcastically.

Kyle grimaces. "Guards!" he yells. "Attack!"

They come from everywhere.

Soldiers descend on us, dressed like Kyle, in black uniforms with my family crest sewn over their hearts.

They burst through the doorway, heavy rifles in their hands. They pull themselves over the fence along the edge of the observation deck. I look closely and see ropes knotted to various sections of the rail—how did I miss those before?—as soldiers climb up from the sides of the building and tumble onto the deck, spreading out to surround us, waiting for Kyle's commands.

They plunge down from the sky, dropping out of open windows and off the bridges in the Aeries and triggering parachutes that balloon open into crimson canopies that carry them down, toward us.

One of the soldiers presses his gun into the small of Turk's back.

Hunter raises his arms, about to blast him and start an all-out brawl, when Kyle makes a *tsk*ing noise. "I wouldn't do that if I were you. Look around." There must be nearly a hundred of my father's soldiers on the deck.

"Ninety-five men," Kyle says, as though he can tell what I'm thinking. "With two hundred more on backup." He points his gun at Jarek. "Aria, you must have ingested a ton of Stic to heal that quickly. Should we play a game and see if your friend here can do the same?"

"No," I say. "Don't hurt him, Kyle."

Kyle scratches his head with the tip of his pistol. "Oh, Aria. You love to play the patron saint of whininess. No more of that. Mom and Dad are on their way. They're going to collect you and bring you home. We'll deal with the fallout from all of this like rational human beings, instead of following your mystic everybody-is-equal mumbo-jumbo." He lets out a sharp breath. "Everybody is *not* equal."

"I'll second that," Thomas says. I'm surprised he hasn't been more vocal. That he's letting Kyle call the shots. No doubt he's considering his options, biding his time. Knowing Thomas, he has something up his sleeve . . . I'm just not sure what.

"I'm serious, Aria." Kyle sticks two fingers in his mouth and whistles—a piercing shriek. Every soldier on the deck steps forward menacingly, closing in. Kyle is actually grinning. I'm sure this is giving him quite the thrill.

The guard who has his gun in Turk's back throws him to the ground, and drags him over to Kyle. Two other guards cover Jarek, yanking his arms behind his back and pushing him headfirst to the stone floor.

"Aria," Hunter says. "What do you want to do?"

But I can barely hear him.

I feel even stronger now, like I could break an entire bridge in half with my bare hands.

My vision is sharper than ever. I can see every grain of dirt on the deck, every crevice and line, every thread in the Rose family crest on the uniforms. I can make out the faces of all the guards, the curve of their eyes and the slant of their noses, whether their lips are thin or thick, their pants wrinkled or crisp, their boots too tight.

I can see all the way down to the canals. I can even make out four men crowded into a gondola, hands cupped to their mouths, shouting, *"Peace! Now!"*

My arms and legs weigh nothing. I am made entirely of air, of energy.

Nothing inside me hurts. There is no longer a single bruise on my body. I could break a human skull with one fingertip. I could rip through a man's chest with two.

I have so much strength inside me that I don't know what to do with it.

I've got to let it out or I might explode.

"There's no escape," Hunter whispers into my ear. "I came alone—I didn't bring any of the rebels because I didn't think I'd be leaving here alive. But I didn't know you'd show up, Aria. I won't let your parents take you from me." He glances toward the edge of the deck. "Maybe we should just throw ourselves over and hope we can figure something out on the way down."

I stare at the wrinkled parachutes scattered across the roof like used candy wrappers. If they can bring soldiers from the Aeries down here, why can't I go up *there*?

I meet Hunter's eyes—eyes the color of pure water, the most beautiful blue. I take his hand in mine, intertwining our fingers.

I no longer get a jolt of energy when we touch.

But he does. "What—"

"Shh," I say. "Let's not jump off the building. I've got a better idea."

I squeeze his hand and close my eyes. *Up,* I think.

The burning starts in my toes. It shoots up my feet, into my legs, twisting through my entire body and filling me with light. I am dead and alive—someone is poking me with fire and chilling me with ice.

My skin bristles with goose bumps.

My body smolders with heat.

My toes feel like they're resting on a thousand burning coals.

I open my eyes and thrust my free arm into the sky. Jets of electric green energy blast from my fingertips.

Kyle's gun clatters to the ground. "Holy . . ."

The soldiers stare at me. Out of the corner of my eye, I think I see my parents opening the metal door to the observatory deck.

Go, Turk mouths to me. *I'll be fine.*

Hunter's mouth is agape as I take his hand and together we rocket into the sky.

· XXVII ·

Fog twists itself around us like thick curls of smoke.

We fly up, past the Damascus steel beams that support the Aeries, past the crowds of people waving their hands and hollering, lingering along the bridges and outside the light-rail stations, past the shiny glass wrapping around the skyscrapers that shoot toward the heavens like silver beanstalks.

It is not the first time I have soared through the Aeries. Before the battle that led to his mother's death, Hunter and I walked through walls and dropped through ceilings. More recently, I have traveled on webs of light. I have jumped to the Depths and landed in the canals below. I have even been caught midair by a camouflaged motorcycle.

But I have never been the one in charge.

I am leading Hunter through the clouds. *I* am letting out energy like steam heat.

My hand is a burst of green light, shiny rays piercing the sky like laser beams. They are an extension of me; I control them completely.

"This is incredible," I say, glancing back at Hunter. He's holding my hand as we rise into the blue-gray sky. All around us the city sparkles, each building like a cut diamond, reflecting light every which way, showing us the splendor of Manhattan. Even ravaged, the city is awe-inspiring.

I can't tell from Hunter's expression whether he's excited or terrified. He says something in reply, but the wind erases his words.

A few hundred feet away, I spot a sleek, tiered skyscraper that reminds me of my parents' apartment building on the Upper West Side and the rooftop where Hunter and I used to meet. I head toward it and begin to slow down as I reach the top, pulling Hunter with me onto the rocky gravel.

Nearly half of the roof is encased in glass, a greenhouse full of leafy plants and multicolored flowers. The rest of the roof is covered with blue and white pebbles, which crunch beneath our feet as we land. I flex my fingers, and the green rays dissipate as if they were never there to begin with. I stare at my hand, but it looks the same as it always has. The burned skin has healed completely. I rip off my wig and its cap and toss them on the roof, letting my scalp breathe.

"What did you do?" Hunter says. He stares at me curiously. "Aria?"

"I—" How am I supposed to say this? Hunter and Davida were childhood friends. They were engaged, supposed to marry—until he met me. How will he feel about what I've done?

Best to come right out with it. "I ate Davida's heart."

Hunter steps back in shock. "You what?"

"We found her heart," I say. "Turk, Jarek, and I. It was being sold on the black market. Kyle was after it."

"So the smartest thing to do was eat it?" Hunter runs his eyes up and down my body. "All of it? Are you insane? We need to get you to a healer—"

"I'm fine," I say, waving off his concern. "I've never felt better in my entire life. This is what Davida wanted."

Hunter raises an eyebrow. "How could you possibly know that?"

"She left me a note," I say. "In her reliquary. She wanted this to happen. Don't be angry with me."

Hunter stands still for a moment, arms at his side. Then he shakes his head. "I'm not angry with you. I love you, Aria."

He takes my hands in his, pulling them to his waist. I reach up, underneath his shirt, resting my palms on the smooth skin of his back. Hunter tugs me even closer to him so that our chests are pressing together, our two hearts beating as one.

This is the man I love, I think, but then I correct myself. *This is the man I* loved.

Hunter drags his fingertips up my arms, circling his hands behind my head. He kisses my neck, my chin. His breath is hot on my face. Our noses meet, and he rubs his forehead against mine.

Our lips touch.

"No." The word comes out softly, like an afterthought, so quietly I wonder if he even heard me.

But I can tell by the look on his face that he did. "What's wrong?" he asks.

"Everything," I say, pulling away from him.

Hunter sighs. "Why don't you start with one thing?"

"Landon's dead," I say. "It was my fault. Elissa Genevieve killed him, but I was the one who brought him there, to that warehouse—searching for Davida's heart."

"It's not your fault," Hunter says quickly. "You didn't—"

"It doesn't matter who did it," I say. "He went there because of me."

"I don't understand." Hunter looks genuinely bewildered. There's a smudge of dirt on his cheek. I want to wipe it away, but I don't. "You're upset about Landon. So am I. But what does this have to do with us?"

I step away, feeling the pebbles beneath my feet, and stare out at the city. "I don't know who you are anymore, Hunter."

"Don't say that," he says. "I'm me. I just . . . lost my head. I was so pissed about my mom, and frustrated, and upset—all I wanted was to make things right. But I didn't see what was right for the city. I wanted blood, the blood of all the Aeries monsters who stole my mother from me, and who stole so many other mystics from their families, too."

I understand the fury in his voice, but it frightens me.

"I'm sorry that I let my mother's death cloud my sense of what's right and wrong," Hunter goes on. "You didn't know us together. When we met, I was already living underground. But she was still my mom—the woman who took care of me when I was little, my biggest supporter." He starts to choke up. "She was the one person in the world who looked out for me. She wanted a better life for me than she'd had. That's why she was running for office. So I wouldn't have to hide. So I could keep my powers and live my life out in the open." Hunter gulps for air. "She wanted that for me and for every mystic."

I take in his words. There were times when my mother was my protector, but my memories of that part of my life have almost completely faded. The mother I remember is opportunistic and selfish, a woman who would rather live secluded with her riches in the Aeries than open her eyes and see what's going on in the world around her. A woman who lied to me, who stole from me. Who nearly killed me.

Hunter's mother is dead. I don't envy him for that. But in a way, my mother is dead as well. And at least the memories he has are joyous ones.

He strokes the top of my head. "I'm better now, though," he says.

"No one can get better in an instant, Hunter," I say. "You betrayed me. I understand that you weren't yourself, but that doesn't make it all right."

He stares out at the sky, then turns back to me. "So you're just . . . what? What's happening?" Hunter asks, gulping. "Is it over between us?"

This moment is so surreal that I almost laugh. Hunter is the best thing that has ever happened to me. The love of my life. My soul mate—I truly believe that. Only too much has happened. Too much has changed.

So I open my mouth and say the most difficult word I have ever had to say: "Yes."

"I don't believe this," Hunter says, holding his head in his hands. "I just don't. I thought we were forever."

"I thought so, too." I wipe tears from my eyes. "But I can't be with you right now. As much as it breaks my heart."

"This isn't how our story is supposed to go," he says. His voice quavers and I have to hold back my sobs. I don't want to break down in front of him. "You're just going to give up on us? After everything we've been through?"

"Maybe one day—"

"No maybes," Hunter says. "Either you love me and we figure things out, or you never loved me at all and it's over."

I shake my head. "I have always loved you. I *still* love you."

Hunter begins to smile.

"But it's over."

Hunter reaches down, grabs a handful of pebbles, and hurls them into the sky. "No!" he screams, and the sound echoes off buildings.

I blink away more tears. Maybe I wasn't the perfect girlfriend. But Hunter lied to me. He locked me up and refused to listen to me—until the very end. I'm not ready to forgive him, and it wouldn't be fair for me to focus all my time on rebuilding our relationship when so many more important things are going on in the city.

The summit was a failure.

Nothing has been resolved between the Depths and the Aeries.

"I don't know who *we* are anymore," I tell Hunter. "But I know what I have to do. It's clear that the mystics won't rule the city any better than the nonmystics. They need someone to bring everyone together."

Hunter stares at me as though I'm already gone. As though I'm made of nothing but air. He takes a few breaths, trying to calm down. "And that someone is you?"

I nod. "I think so. Yes."

"What are you going to do? How are you going to defeat your family?"

It's a good question—one I don't have the answer to.

Yet.

"I don't know," I say. "But I'm not going to stop until I find out."

He gives me a sad smile. "I know you won't. That's one of the things I love most about you."

For a moment, Hunter seems about to turn away and walk out of my life. But instead, slowly, he reaches one hand into the air and spreads his fingers.

I press the tips of my fingers to his.

A wisp of green light shoots out from our index fingers, looping together into one fine strand that wraps around our hands, binding us for a single moment.

Then Hunter breaks away. The light is gone.

"Goodbye, Aria."

"Goodbye, Hunter."

With a heavy heart, I leap off the roof and soar away.

· EPILOGUE ·

I double back to the Empire State Building. Even though I'm flying, I don't enjoy it. Not after leaving Hunter the way I did, not to mention leaving Turk on the observation deck to defend himself. I have to get back to him, make sure he's all right.

The air has cooled off slightly, and I'm grateful that my long hair is gone—there's nothing for the wind to toss around. Since the bomb threat is over, I expect to see that most of the people who were rallying around the building have gone home.

But if anything, there are *more* people.

So many people I can't believe it. They shout at me from the tops of buildings and from bridges and windows. *"Aria! Aria! Aria!"*

A picture of me soaring against the sky appears on the JumboTrons in the surrounding area. The crowds go wild, tossing hats into the air. I watch the face on the screen—my face, staring back at me. Who is this girl? She looks defiant. Happy. In control.

I don't feel any of those things.

I am too concerned about my friends. Is Turk all right where I left him? Is Ryah doing better? Not to mention Shannon and Jarek, or the fact that Landon's death hasn't truly settled in. I'd barely gotten to know him. How can he be gone forever?

The cries grow louder and louder, until I fear my eardrums will burst. *"Aria! Aria! Aria!"*

The people of Manhattan support me. They see that I am flying, that I have obviously gained some sort of mystic power.

Everyone is rooting for me.

I swoop down toward the Depths, toward the ruin of our city. I will make things right, once and for all—or die trying.

Acknowledgments

Special thanks to the tremendous team at Random House Children's Books, epecially Lauren Donovan, Françoise Bui, Wendy Loggia, Krista Vitola, Colleen Fellingham, and Beverly Horowitz; to the friends and family members who celebrated *Mystic City* with me, especially my parents, Steven and Elizabeth Malawer; my sister, Abby; my grandmother Eileen Honigman; and my uncle, Alan Honigman; to all the readers and booksellers who reached out and urged me to continue; to Ruth Katcher, for her guidance, enthusiasm, and ample number of tracked changes; to Kim Kupperman, Meera Nair, Sharon Wyeth, and my Children's Literature classmates at Fordham for their thoughtful critiques; to the fabulous team of coagents at The Inkhouse who shepherded this trilogy into foreign publication; to Michael Stearns, whose wit and humor always keep me on my toes and who has made this series possible; to Julia Alexander, Kate Berthold, Blair Bodine, Nic Cory, Greta Gerwig, Anna Harb, Jenny Weiner, and Paul Wright for their stalwart support; and to Josh Pultz, for believing in me.